The New Reign
A Lite and Darke Novel
M.L. Ruscsak

M.L.Ruscsak

The New Reign

A Lite and Darke Novel

By: *M.L. Ruscsak*

Cover Design By: *M.L. Ruscsak*

Edited by: *Chyenne Lyons*

M.L.Ruscsak

This book is a work of fiction. Names, characters, places and incidents are products of the author's imagination and are not to be construed as real. Any resemblance to actual events, locales, organizations, or persons living or dead, is entirely coincidental.

COPYRIGHT

The New Reign

Except for the original story material written by the author,
all songs, song titles, and lyrics mentioned in the novel
The New Reign are the exclusive property of the
respective artists, songwriters, and copyright holders

Trient Press

3375 S Rainbow Blvd

#81710, SMB 13135

Las Vegas,NV 89180

Ordering Information:

Quantity sales. Special discounts are available on
quantity purchases by corporations, associations, and
others. For details, contact the publisher at the
address above.

Orders by U.S. trade bookstores and wholesalers.
Please contact Trient Press: Tel: (775) 996-3844;
or visit www.trientpress.com.

Printed in the United States of America

Publisher's Cataloging-in-
Publication data Ruscsak, M.L.

A title of a book :Passions of the Heart

ISBN Hard Cover:9781953975249

Paperback: 9781953975256

E-book: 9781953975263

M.L.Ruscsak

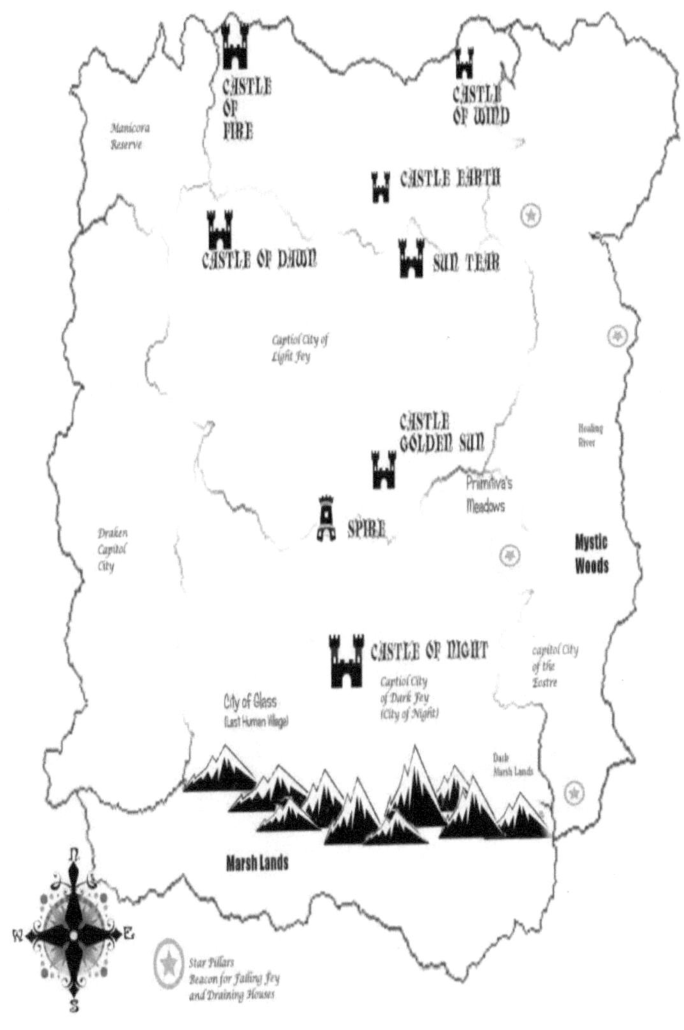
Manicora
Reserve
CASTLE
OF
FIRE
CASTLE
OF WIND
CASTLE EARTH
CASTLE OF DAWN
SUN TEAR
Captiol City of
Light Fey
CASTLE
GOLDEN SUN
Healing
River
Primitiva's
Meadows
Draken
Capitol
City
SPIRE
Mystic
Woods
CASTLE OF NIGHT
capitol City
of the
Eostre
City of Glass
(Last Human Village)
Captiol City
of Dark Fey
(City of Night)
Dark
Marsh Lands
Marsh Lands
N
W
E
S
Star Pillars
Beacon for falling Fey
and Draining Houses

M.L.Ruscsak

For my daughter who has been my editor every step of the way. My mom who has read every word before anyone else. And for Pap who I know is smiling down upon me. And for my family who has given me the wings to fly.

M.L.Ruscsak

Dear Reader,

Thank you for your interest in &The New Reign.& As I hope you enjoy this first book in the series there are some things I wish to point out. Throughout this first book there are several plot holes, spelling errors and misused words.

I understand, as a reader, this can be rather frustrating to read, but I promise these errors are completely intentional. Annoying yes, but there is a reason. Also, for everything written, there is a deeper meaning that will be revealed in later books.

Questions, comments or reviews are always welcome. And I look forward to reading them.

For more information about the series, including a map of the realm please visit me at

TrientPress.com

Happy Reading,
M.L. Ruscsak

The New Reign

M.L.Ruscsak

Prologue

The dark red candles flickered within his study deep below the castle of bones. Like so many nights before he studies studied the on goings of the world of the living. Studied the on goings of the star cities looking for the prophesy to be fulfilled. With the seer's stone resting on the table before him, Karnack sat his quill back into the inkwell. For more than three thousand years he had been doing in death what he had done in life… watching history unfold and keeping a detailed account for his queen.

A queen who even he had not seen since the time of the great war. No, that wasn't completely true. He had seen her but only a handful of times and only to beg for her help. Even then her rage at being disturbed…

He sighed. There was nothing he could do for the queen. Least not yet.

His eyes close for but a moment before he once again gazed into the seer's stone and once again waited for the child to be born that his queen had seen so many years before. A queen who would be able to defeat a threat that was still in the shadows of the Great Stars.

Still, he watched and waited for the child to be born that his queen had seen so many years before. A child who would be born a creator. A queen who would be able to defeat a threat that was still in the shadows of the Great Stars.

The rest of the first Fey, who had settled this land, had already given up on ever finding the child. Nicco had changed his name two or three times in the past three centuries. As had Ean. And Donny… ah the great warrior … he completely sealed himself off from the world shortly after Myrddin had fallen from the stars.

Of the four of them, none had ever been able to find out what had ever happened to their queen's only child. A baby known only as Ari. His father had been the cause of their queen's withdrawal from the realms.

Yet, he held out hope that one day he would find this chosen queen and give her the crown of the dead. A crown that would give her the power to stand and face a threat that only she would be able to defeat.

A token tap on the study door that he ignored. Then a softy breezy female voice,"Karnack? Are still watching the stone?"

He barely glanced over his shoulder to a woman who was just as beautiful today as she was the first he had laid eyes on her. And still just as deadly. Turning slightly, he watched her lean on the door frame. His eye narrowed as he hissed, "I am the scribe to the queen and I will be the one to see the chosen queen long before any other." When she didn't say anything further he turned back to his ledger and began to write another line.

Pulling a knife from her belt, she leaned on the wall watching him write some mindless dribble that none would ever read. A soft smile touched her blood red lips. "When you find her, tell me. I'll make sure no harm ever comes her way."

At that he turned and fought hard to remind himself that the fey that stood before him was a friend. Fought harder to remember that she would never truly harm him. "Freya, darling, if what I know for fact ever comes to pass then even you will need help in protecting her."

She heeled boots clicked on the stone floor as she drew closer. When she reached his working desk her leaned in and whispered, "You let me worry about that."

M.L.Ruscsak

Part 1

280 YEARS AGO

LARNA: PRINCESS OF FEYEN

"A day will come when one will rise to power not by birth but through blood. When that day arises, it will be but the beginning..."

- Ancient scrolls of Feyen

M.L.Ruscsak

Chapter 1:
Larna

Night crept over the castle. The only sounds were those of the water falling over the cliffs. Below her feet Memoks circled her feet waiting to be feed.

Larna glances out of her window at the clouded moon. There would be no light flowing into the castle tonight An evil grin twitched her rose red lips as she snapped her journal shut.

"It's time."

Darting from her room bolts of black mist flowed from her fingers. Guards falling before he had passed them. Their bodies contorting in unnatural positions before death finally took them.

The doors of the royal children… her siblings eased open. Her youngest brother stood there paralyzed looking at her. A heart beat longer and his body was torn apart.

She hadn't needed to kill him. A simple mind spell would have worked. But then again who's to say that someone wouldn't have figured it out? If they did…

No, saving the life of one little brat wasn't worth the trouble.

Larna peered into the bedroom of the crown princess. Her soft breaths from a heavy sleep. Protection shields sounding the bed a soft glow of blue giving way to the darkness.

Her fist clenched. The fool would have tossed Feyen away giving the crown to another. Letting some bile creature rule what was theirs by right.

Rage bubbled inside of her erupting withing the shield that should have protected her dear sister.

Blood not that of a true royal splattered over the bedding and shield. The blankets left in tacked.

A dark laugh that she tried to keep hushed, "Fighter that spell out, dear sister."

Larna looked to her back. So many wasted flesh laid behind her. Guards that never stood a chance. Some could have proven useful in the coming days.

No matter. There were others. Who would care if they came from Feyen or from the city of her dear friend. Would any ever know the difference?

Pulling her cloak around her face he forced the chamber door of the queen's bedroom open.

Yet she paused waiting for the last Feyen warrior to meet her.

Dressed in his night shirt and pants he stood battle ready. A golden sword said to be that of the Great king Magmas gripped tightly within his hands. "Show yourself." he growled.

She stepped into the light her cloack keeping her secret for a moment longer.

"Show your face like a true warrior."

Her hand raised and she lowered her hood. The look of rage and fear crossed her parents face. 'Surprised father? Don't be."

Too quickly a shield fell between them as she raised her black onyx sword.

Alista's eyes widened in fear perhaps for the first time. In a strangled whispered she gasped, "The sword of Obsidian… How?"

Before her father moved fire lit Larna's eyes, "Not all of Obsidian was destroyed"

She stood towering over her mother's body. Her black crystal sword plunged into the heart of the woman who had given her life. Her eyes narrowed into tiny slits as she held her translucent black wings still. Listening to the single sound of her own heart beating against the silence, her head slowly turned to glance over her shoulder, her father's lifeless head on the floor but a few feet away from where his body had fallen. He had been the last Feyen warrior to fall.

The last before her mother. At least there, she had found a worthy adversary to face. Well, at least until she too had faltered and died.

A cruel smile formed on her dark crimson colored lips as she stood there silently watching her mother's blood start to pool around her lifeless body. Not the red lifeblood that most Fey had, oh no window and darkness of the night. Everything so still. So quiet. With the dawn she would be queen.nearly impossible. "Please, you have to help my mother."

His sturdy grip finally failed as that was all he needed to hear. Larna watched only partly amazed as a single bolt of lightning flashed from his fingertips lighting the signal fire. Not a moment later more than a dozen armed guards stood surrounding them. All their eyes battle ready and scanning for the cause for the signal to be lit. Yet none moved for a minute waiting for the captain to join them.

A heart beat then two and the armed guard who was holding her; the sobbing princess, took command. "We'll notify the captain later. The royal family is being attacked. The Queen is the first priority." Glancing down at her he continued, "Princess Larna please come with me. The guard tower will be safe. You have my word."

She had no doubt about that. After all, how would he ever know that it had been she that had killed her family? But even if he somehow did find out, after she was crowned not a soul would ever be able to do anything about it.

She stood towering over her mother's body. Her black crystal sword plunged into the heart of the woman who had given her life. Holding her translucent black wings still, she glanced over her shoulder, her father's lifeless head on the floor but a few feet away from where his body had fallen. He had been the last Feyen warrior to fall.

The last before her mother. At least there, she had found a worthy adversary to face. Well, at least until she too had faltered and died.

A cruel smile formed on her dark crimson colored lips as she stood there silently watching her mother's blood started to pool around her lifeless body. Not the red lifeblood that most Fey had, oh no' her mother's lifeblood was midnight blue. An oddity unto itself. Watching the blood seeping out of her body, Larna could have spat on her mother's face for making her take this drastic measure. But, if she did, it would ruin her plans, and that she wouldn't do no matter what the price. "You should have listened to me, mother. Now look at what has become of you. No longer will you be able to listen to anyone. A justice that serves you right for never hearing the truth that was set before your eyes."

Pulling her black crystal blade free from her mother's heart, she used it to cut the fabric of her golden gown. Methodically she made sure that the cuts on the fabric mirrored the cuts on her own skin. She had to make sure that the cuts were shallow enough not to hinder her movements but deep enough to look like she had escaped the slaughter. Escaping as the last surviving heir... the last of her mother's bloodline. And escaping as the only living Royal Fey in all of Feyen.

After all, anyone who had seen anything was already bound to her. Their memories were whatever she decided that they would be. Right now, in this moment, she chose for all of them to believe that a hooded man had stormed into the castle coming from out of nowhere and slaughtering all that had stood in his way. A cloud, a mist had hidden him until the very moment that he had killed his first victim.

Yes, that would do nicely. And as for the man... Oh well, she had planned for that as well. Myrddin was either going to marry her or every Feyen citizen would believe that he had been behind the massacre. After all, there wasn't a single person alive that didn't know how powerful he truly was nor how dangerous. Nor would any every question his motives. Power, greed, lust? It wouldn't matter what they chose to speculate, his very denials would only further their conviction in his guilt.

A cruel smile formed on her long thin face. But she would offer him another solution. She would offer her hand in marriage, after all, he was exactly what she needed. A Feyen man with more natural ability and dark power then the whole royal family of Feyen. Or she should say the now *dead* royal family.

But tomorrow would be soon enough to work on that... Tonight on the other hand... She had to finish this. Sniffling until tears started to run hot down her face she took a deep breath then took off in a terrified sprint down the bloody castle halls. Her ripped gown collecting blood from the fallen guards as she ran. There wasn't anyone alive in this part of the castle or at least not anyone that would be of any use for her plan to work. So, screaming for help would do her no use at least not until she saw the light coming from the main gate... Then ... and only then did she let out a shrill scream, "HELP! Help Me!"

She saw a single guard at the main gate and knew almost instantly who he was. A member of not just the royal guard but also one that also served as an elite warrior. As there was never more than a dozen in that squad she knew each of them fairly well. However, this one may be a problem for her.

Once she was crowned she might have to see to his death as well. No better yet, to his execution. Not a far leap that he might have something to do with the murders. She would just have to see what played out.

The moment he turned to her she knew two things. First off, he was scanning the area for trouble and secondly, he recognized her as a member of the royal family. In that breath, he partly ran and partly flew to meet her half way inside of the great hall. Just as he made it to her, she collapsed into his arms sobs running down her face as she gasped for air, "Princess... What..." He asked almost puzzled.

Catching her breath, she forced out, "A hooded intruder... My mother, you have to ..." Clawing at his white and gold uniform she tried to push away. Tried to escape his strong grip that even if she had been truly trying she would find nearly impossible. "Please, you have to help my mother."

His sturdy grip finally failed as that was all he needed to hear. Larna watched only partly amazed as a single bolt of lightning flashed from his fingertips lighting the signal fire. Not a moment later more than a dozen armed guards stood surrounding them. All their eyes battle ready and scanning for the cause for the signal to be lit. Yet none moved for a minute waiting for the captain to join them.

A heart beat then two and the armed guard who was holding her; the sobbing princess, took command. "We'll notify the captain later. The royal family is being attacked. The Queen is the first priority." Glancing down at her he continued, "Princess Larna please come with me. The guard tower will be safe. You have my word."

She had no doubt about that. After all, how would he ever know that it had been she that had killed her family? But even if he somehow did find out, after she was crowned not a soul would ever be able to do anything about it.

M.L.Ruscsak

Chapter 2:
Galeron

There was no sign of trouble until they reached the heart of the castle. No sign of struggle except the bloody footprints that the princess had left behind. Then a body. A young guard his name not yet known to all who worked the palace grounds... his body cut nearly in half. In an outcove, not but a few feet away another guard, Gavan, his throat slit from behind. Whoever had done this had to have stepped through the wall behind him. A damn foolish thing to do unless one was trained. Even then, not many had the skill to do so without being trapped in the stone. Of those, none had been near the castle recently.

There was no sign of trouble until they reached the heart of the castle. No sign of struggle except the bloody footprints that the princess had left behind. Then a body. A young guard his name not yet known to all who worked the palace grounds... his body cut nearly in half. In an outcove, not but a few feet away another guard,

Gavan, his throat slit from behind. Whoever had done this had to have stepped through the wall behind him. A damn foolish thing to do unless one was trained. Even then, not many had the skill to do so without being trapped in the stone. Of those, none had been near the castle recently. And that had included the man who was being set up for this atrocity.

Carefully with his golden wings now fluttering at full speed he flew down the corridors. His eyes seeing the bodies of his fallen comrades. Nothing about their deaths made sense. Unless all were asleep... *which was highly unlikely and completely impossible*... one of them should have called for help. One should have signaled for reinforcements or used mind-speech to call for help. Yet none did. And none seemed to have been fighting the unknown attacker. Not a weapon was drawn nor a spell cast. No whatever had happened here was not just a simple attacker. They had a purpose.

Galeron stopped just feet from the royal stronghold and fought not to become sick. Kailen, the youngest prince laid partly in his room and partly in the hall. His purple blood sprayed over his door. Two doors down the heir had been torn apart in her bed. The protective shield around her bed and room still fully intact. The other three royal children killed so thoroughly that there was no reason to send them to the Under Kingdom...

Not even as fodder for those who may still dwell there.

Slowly and carefully, he made his way to the queen's bedchamber. The king's headless body laid in the doorway. His hand still curled around the hilt of his golden sword. The sword itself broken cleanly in half. In impossible feat... yet someone had been able to do so. The amount of strength required to do that? So, few could have done that. And those who possessed that skill were now dead.

Pushing the double door open enough to pass without disturbing the body of the king, his eyes found the queen. Her body lifeless on the floor, her blue blood flowing around her seeping from wounds that were not visible. The blood itself pulling toward the head of the king. The last show of the blood oath they had taken.

For a moment, he swayed at now realizing the royal family had been wiped out. In a span of a breath his mind focused on the only two people in all of the Feyen that could have accomplished this without sounding the alarm... and by the gods, it wasn't Myrddin. Despite the attempt to make it look like it had been... he knew better. The queen's window was open and there would be no time once dawn arrived... No time after his report had been made or when others found the bodies of the royal family. So, he dove from the window and flew over the city of Golden Sun and to the home of his friend.

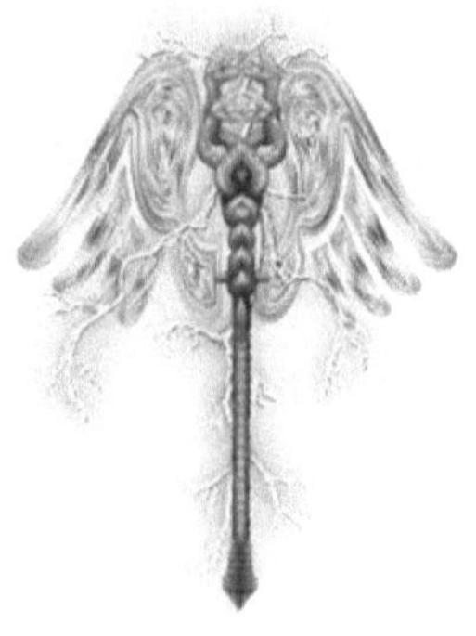

Landing in a back alleyway Galeron hurried down the several twists and turns of the inner city until he came to the door of his friend. Raising his fist, he pounded on the simple wooden door, "Myrddin open the damn door. Or I break it down."

When it finally opened, it wasn't Myrddin but Princess Adrianna standing in front of him. Her long dark hair tussled from sleep. Her eyes not yet open as she sleepily asked, "Galeron, what in the name of Darke is it?"

"We need to talk." Pushing past her, he saw Myrddin just tying the belt to his black robe. "It's started."

For a moment, Myrddin just stood there numb. Finally, he whispered, "Damn it. We should have had more time to prepare."

Closing the door Adrianna looked from her betrothed to her friend confused. Wiping her eyes to fully wake up she asked, "What's started?"

Myrddin shuffled over to his long dark couch and took a deep breath, "Addy you know you hold my heart."

Shuffling over to sit with Myrddin, Adrianna took his hand in hers then said, "Yes, and I know we will be married... So, what..." She looked deep into Galeron's eyes. There was a worry there in his voice but more than that, there was a burning rage in those eyes. "Queen Elista?"

"Murdered. And whoever did it made damn sure it looked like something Myrddin was capable of doing. Or at least, someone who had a strong natural ability in the dark arts."

Addy got up from the couch and turned away. She had only come here last year to learn some from the Feyen Queen how to rule true Fey. And she had. But she had also found scores of friends and the man who held her heart. More than that, she had been working on a treaty that would bind their houses together. A treaty that would fall apart if whoever now ruled didn't see the wisdom in it. "What's going to happen now?"

Myrddin sat back and snorted, "Princess Larna will become Queen. I'm sure all of the Feyen will be torn over it but not enough to do anything about it. At least not with some motivation."

Taking a breath, she spoke as the only person in the room with authority to speak the truth without fear of penalty. "As a Fey, her powers and abilities are yet untested. She will have some years yet before she matures enough to handle the gifts that she currently has let alone be able to handle those of her people without going mad."

A curt laugh then Myrddin growled, "She may be already?"

Addy raised an eyebrow in question, "Myrddin?"

"She's been learning the dark arts." Now both Addy and his friend stared right at him.

"What?" Both said nearly in unison.

"Larna asked if I could teach her. As one of only two people in all of the Feyen that was able, I consulted Queen Elista. After a very detailed conversation about what I was, willing to teach the little brat and listening to what the brat wanted to learn I agreed. As part of the agreement the queen gave her blessing to our union."

For a long time, no one spoke. Slowly Addy shuffled back over to her beloved, "We could leave tonight."

"No." For a moment, he just sat there. His eyes focusing on something far beyond his home. Finally getting up he took the few steps to his window and said, "Adrianna, I need for you to leave. Go to Draken and take my sister with you."

Jumping back with a start she growled, "Like hell I am. I am not letting her get away with this. Nor am I letting you take the fall for the likes of her."

In a deep growl, he snapped. His voice rattling his windows and making both his friend and lover jump. "*Adrianna* this is not up for debate." Slowly he came back to her and took her hand. Taking a deep breath, he needed to reason with her. He just hoped she listened, just this once. "You will be the next queen of Darke. And I swear that I will be married to you well before that ever happens. But, I need you to leave. Larna is in way over her head, and I'm the only one strong enough to put things to right. Or at least, make sure she is limited on options."

"Fine. I'll go and I'll even take Tenanye *and* Faerydae with me. After all, I'm sure Tenanye would love to see her betrothed. But I'll be damned if I leave here without both of you being blood bound to me."

"Now wait one second..."

"Don't you start with me Galeron. I don't know what game the little princess is playing. And frankly, I don't care. But I will not let her use either of you for pawns. Besides The only way that she can't bind you would be to be bound to someone stronger."

"She's right you know."

"Just because *your* future wife is right about something does not mean I have to like it." Galeron hisses as he paced the confines of the sitting room.

Narrowing her dark colored eyes, she spoke, "No, but you're not stupid. So, what's it going to be Galeron... Be the captain of *my* guards and first chair on *my* council or serve her and never live long enough to become a father?"

Chapter 3:
Myrddin

As the first rays of the morning began to light the gold cobbled streets, Myrddin's day started with armed castle guards pounding on his door. If he hadn't been warned last night Adrianna would have been here and naturally accused of the murders. Of course, he had saved her from that... now to do what he could and hope it was enough. Slowly he opened the door and looked deep into the guard's sea green eyes. "I assume there is a reason you are trying to break my door in?"

Fear ran across the man's face. An Elf not a fairy judging by the lack of wings. "Well, or would you like to waste my entire day?"

The guard shook himself from his stupor and forced out, "I... you're wanted at the castle for questioning."

"I see. Then let's get this over with. I'm already late for another important engagement." Not really, but being with Addy had taught him a thing or two. Such as being Feyen and the only dark anything outside Darke... he had the authority to be curt and difficult. More than that... once he married the future queen he could send all those who and offended him to the Under Kingdom... perhaps alive... perhaps not. Either way, it was entertaining to watch the door open and the dead standing far below the opening waiting to greet either their next meal or then newest comrades.

Stepping out if his home Myrddin looked around at the nearly two dozen armed guards. Fairy. Elf. Light bearers. Then his eyes darted to the chosen ride to the Castle. Not a fine carriage but a trolley for trolls. Before he took another step, he used just a bit of simple craft... well simple if you were a master of several kinds of craft... Black smoke then a soft poof before a loud bang and a proper carriage stood before him. "If I'm going to the castle I will go in a style befitting my prestige. But certainly not in an ill-made troll trolley."

"Where is..."

Narrowing his dark soulless eyes, Myrddin slowly turned to the young elf that had once again found his voice. "Where is who?"

"The Princess of Darke. We were told..."

"Hmp. The Lady had appointments else were. I believe she left midday yesterday." That should be enough to keep Addy out of trouble. Then again, with her, he couldn't be too sure. After all, trouble seemed to follow Addy wherever she dared to travel. It was something her twin had been ready to point out several times within the past year.

At least he didn't need to worry about Celeste in all of this. Thankfully, she had left for the Spire some days ago to introduce some poor sap to her mother. Another time he might find Blake's current predicament amusing if it had fallen on the morning after the death of his dear friend.

Looking up from his book where he was trying to find anything useful Lord Eros tapped his book yet again and sighed. So many laws and traditions but none for crowning a child after the loss of her family. But the funeral passages were very clear and needed to be taken care immediately. "Princess we must see to the funerals of ..."

She had to play the distraught daughter who had lost her parents. The problem was that she was bored. Nor did she care what they did with the bodies. Burn them, bury them. Send what was left to the Under Kingdom. It made little difference to her either way. Of course, she couldn't say that. However, she could sniffle once and fight back fake tears. "Oh, can the council please...." She sniffled and turned her head, "I... I just can't."

Handing her his black silk pocket square he patted her back soothingly. "Of course, my dear. I should have considered... Perhaps the council should speak with Lord Devros."

"No..." Larna snapped. Then realizing her mistake, she started again, "No, I would like to see those who could have done this to m-my family."

The large golden doors of the throne room blew open and crashed into the walls behind them. Myrddin strode in his black robe that marked him as a High-born covered most of his natural muscle and actual size. They did nothing to mask the dark power that could be felt from his annoyance. "I assume there is a reason the castle guard has brought me here."

"You will hold your tongue, Lord Devros."

Narrowing his raven colored eyes, Myrddin stared at the first chair of the Feyen council, "As I am the ambassador of Darke and I demand answers Lord Eros. And I will have those answers or you can give them to my queen."

"Gentlemen please, this a somber day." When that did nothing to get either man to back down Larna sniffled. "Please, I would like to speak to Lord Devros privately."

"I should think not--" Lord Eros protested.

"This is my will, Lord Eros. Now, please... I would think that m-my parents would like to be laid to rest."

"As you will princess." Turning back to Myrddin, he whispered, "I will see you sent to the Under Kingdom for your crimes."

Once alone Myrddin circled the dais. "What's the game, Larna?"

Her pale lips curled into a sinister smile. "Oh no game Myrddin. Just a proposition."

"Oh?" Slowly he came to stand before her. "Tell me, what it is you are expecting? Your future told perhaps?"

"Oh, come now. We both know that is not a dark art Myrddin."

He shrugged. "Perhaps not. So, let's get on with it. What was so important for you to murder your family and try to blame me?"

"Figured it out, did you? Should have known you would have a spy in the guards." She sat back on the throne. "No matter, I'll know *who* soon enough."

Putting one foot on the dais he leaned toward her. "Are you going to tell me why I'm here or should I guess?"

"Oh, I guess I will tell you. You are going to marry me."

Like hell I am. It burned in his throat, but he managed to say is a swan song coo, "Am I? Now, why would I marry a child who has little in the way of natural ability?"

If he wasn't towering over her she would have bolted from the throne, but since she couldn't, she crossed her arms. "I'm not a child. I am nearly two hundred years old. And I have plenty natural ability."

Turning away from her he started to the door. "You have not answered my question Larna. And your game is starting to bore me."

"Either marry me or you and Princess Adrianna will be held accountable for the murder of the royal family. And who ever warned you will join you for your death."

Having known how this would play out, he wasn't fazed. "I will marry you on three conditions. As I do like the sound of being married to a queen." Although the only queen he would marry wasn't in this room. Or in this kingdom for that matter.

Larna mumbled, already too preoccupied with the power she would have once they wed, "Ambition suits you. Now, what are your terms?"

"Nothing much. First off, the royal family of Draken should be in attendance. Since my sister will be marrying the crown prince in the next year."

Greed lit her violet eyes. "Done."

"Secondly, you will declare that any child of mine will be your heir unless you have a child with someone else that holds your heart."

"Of course, your child would be my heir. What a silly thing to require."

Uh ha. We'll see about that. "And lastly, as is tradition you will give me your heart."

"Again, Myrddin that would have been said in the vows regardless. Now is there anything else?"

"No." He took a step up onto the dais and towered over her, "We will be married in three days."

"Three..." She gasped already gazing into his eyes.

Smiling as her eyes locked with his, he allowed for them to blaze into a hypnotic blue haze. "You do not want your country without a queen any longer."

Larna's eyes glowed the same color as his. "No… I suppose I don't."

Chapter 4:
Adrianna

"Addy, are you sure you want to be here? I mean my brother..."

Addy turned away from her friend and let herself see beyond the room... beyond what most saw. Looked well beyond the cream-colored flowers and rows of high back chairs. Looked well beyond milk-white walls. Allowed herself a look back over the past three days in this room. Then whispered, "Myrddin knows what he is doing and I plan on being here to find out exactly what... That and I plan on strangling him the very moment that I can for making me witness this to start with."

Tenanye smiled as she watched her betrothed Prince Craykren and her brother discuss something that had both men playfully shoving each other. "I expected this for your wedding day but..."

Signing Addy shook her head, "We should go separate them before this turns into a brawl. Besides, it will give me the excuses to speak to him and possibly finding out something useful."

"Just be careful Addy. There are those here that think you are the one who killed the Queen."

"Aye, I know. I can feel their uneasiness like prickles on my skin. But it helps that my mother and sister are here. They wouldn't dare cross Mum. She is already in a foul mood and I so doubt she will be able to control herself much longer."

Patting her friend's hand Tenanye smiled. "Your mother is always in a mood. But I agree with her if she should decide to destroy this farce. However, none here would dare cross me either now that Craykren has given me a name that sounds more Draken. I doubt anything would be left of Feyen if they did."

Taking Tenanye's arm she smiled. "Oh, you haven't told me, I simply must know what Cray decided on for his bride."

"Alyisope. It was his grandmother's name. I do like it but I think those who have known me my whole life will continue to call me Tenanye." Stepping over to her betrothed she hissed, "Craykren, I do swear if you act like this on our wedding day I will refuse to marry you."

He spun around with the grace of a cat despite his large size. His armored scales looking like he belonged to a reptile race but his horns... those were more bovine. Then again, he didn't bother to place glamor spell on his black talons that he had for fingers or the long tail that held a poison stinger. "It is customary for battle before marrying."

"Yes, and you will do battle the night before our wedding. Not the day of. Do I make myself clear?"

He just turned to Myrddin. "I should eat you."

Myrddin crossed his bare muscled arms giving his friend time to consider the possibility of a real fight rather than the playful shoving. Then gave a twisted smile. "If you eat me, who will continue to teach you to speak properly?"

"I should eat you for introducing me to... to... *sister*."

Pulling on Craykren's arm she hissed, "Come over here before you cause trouble."

Addy smiled as she watched her friend walk away, "Is there something I should know."

"Adrianna my sweet, you already know everything you need to. So, I ask you to please let this play out.

"Because I trust you I will do as you ask. However, do not expect your sister to remain civil to Queen Larna after she marries Craykren."

"This *is* my sister we are talking about... I doubt she would remain civil with anyone I choose to marry." He smiled then touched her mind. *Besides you.*

Returning the smile, she laughed. "I suppose you're right. She is never civil to anyone unless they can best her in fighting. "A soft chime rang softly signaling the ceremony was to begin. Sighing, she asked, "Should I sit with my family or yours?"

"Addy, you are the princess of Darke. You must always sit according to your status. My sister has Cray to keep her from doing anything rash. At least for the moment."

Adrianna sharply nodded once. "Fine. I'll try to keep Celeste from turning your 'bride' into an ornate flower. But I make no promises. Both she and mother are in rare form today."

Adrianna gracefully sat in a white high back chair next to her sister and took her hand. "What have you heard?"

Pulling a strand of golden hair behind her ear she smiled. "Mother is beside herself. Don't expect her to be on her best behavior *if* Myrddin goes through with this farce of a wedding."

Looking slightly behind her, she watched as her mother stood rigidly near the back wall. "Mother is rarely on her best behavior when surrounded by those who wish her family harm. And she is never on her best behavior when Papa isn't around to soothe her."

"True. But she has never had to deal with a loss of a dear friend and children that she has known from birth."

Reaching out to her sister's mind, she decided to have the rest of this conversation privately. *And does mother know what happened that night?*

You know as well as I that she does. But without proof, she is powerless to do anything about it. Then again that had never stopped her before when dealing with troublemakers.

Turning back to the door Adrianna narrowed her eyes and watched the murderer slowly make her way down the aisle. Her dress looking more like something she should wear for the wedding night and not to the wedding itself. *I doubt she will get away with this.*

Celeste wrinkled her nose in distaste of the dress. Or lack of dress. *Does she realize that she looks ridiculous marrying a man who is twice her age and twice her height? Not to mention that thing that should be a dress... I swear her tailor elf forgot more than half of it.*

Addy rolled her eyes. *I doubt she cares about anything but the power that she thinks he can give her.*

Well, it should be interesting watching her learn that she may have bought his hand but she will never have his heart nor his power.

M.L.Ruscsak

Chapter 5: Larna

Larna took the two steps up to the dais never looking at the guests who had shown to watch her become Queen of Feyen... But it was so lovely that the Queen of Lite and Darke had chosen to come but remain furthest from the festivities. Oh well... as long as the old hag didn't cause any trouble then she wouldn't need to have Myrddin dispose of her. Then again, wouldn't it be fun to rule all the countries that held Fey blood?

Tomorrow she would start planning on how to do just that... as for today...

Her voice filled with fake tears as she softly said, "Lord Eros, before we begin I would like to say something."

Bowing accordingly, he smiled. "Of course, your grace."

Now she turned to her guest. "I know this is not what you all imagined for the succession of the Feyen line but I do hope to make my mother proud."

The golden doors of the throne room creaked opened and an older woman slowly made her way to the dais. Even slower she lowered her hood of her crimson cape. "As you have left us no choice, child. Get on with it. I did not come all this way to watch you blabber on."

Her eyes widened in shock. "Grandmother?!?"

The old queen leaned heavily on her crystal cane as she took a single step into the room. "What is it dear? Did you expect me to be long dead?"

"I..." She took a deep breath. Her grandmother hadn't been seen for nearly a century. Not since becoming ill with something that no Fey had ever been able to cure... and yet she was now standing before her. Silver in her hair sure but not looking a bit unwell. Forcing herself to be calm she took a deep breath. "I'm glad you could be here. Thank you."

"Well, get on with it."

She had never met her grandmother and now was thankful for never speaking to the bitter old bat. "As I was saying before the dowager queen arrived, in breaking with the tradition of being wed before being crown I ask my first chair of the Feyen council to add this doctrine to my rein." She called in a signed piece of parchment and handed it to Lord Eros.

Taking the parchment, he began to unroll it. As he read, he stuttered, "Are you sure?"

"I Am."

"Very well, your grace. As this day, any child sired by Lord Devros will be named as heir to Feyen... Unless Queen Larna finds another man who can hold her heart."

Adrianna sat back and tried not to smile. She had known Myrddin for just over a year and he had taught her one thing above all else... always be precise when dealing with the Fey. More so when dealing with a Dark Fey who would use every word to their own advantage.

M.L.Ruscsak

Chapter 6:
Myrddin

Larna stood to her full height now that she wore the silver crown of Feyen. Such a simple circlet but the power that she could now tap into... what a marvelous feeling.

"My Queen, are you ready for the marriage vows?"

"You may proceed, Lord Eros."

"Very well." He took a deep breath and tried to smile. "Do you, Queen Larna, daughter of Elista, freely give this man, Lord Myrddin Devros every part of you. Your hand, your heart and all that you will make together?"

"I, Queen Larna freely give my heart to Lord Devros to have for all time."

Myrddin had been standing there quiet and not really paying attention to anything until this moment.... however, now that she had said what he had expected... He smiled and licked his wine-red lips. "Do you really give me your heart Queen Larna?"

"Yes, I give you my heart." It was then she realized her mistake as his hand reached deep into her chest pulling out her still beating heart.

He looked down at the black blood covering his hand then called in a silver box. "I will keep your cold black heart. Since you have given it to me in trust. And in return, you shall live till someone who can hold your heart is able to give it back to you." Now he turned to the dowager queen. "Queen Alista, as you have ruled Feyen and being the one the one most capable please do so once more. It would seem your grandchild is but a shell of what she had hoped for."

Alista narrowed her old violet eyes. "Very well. My granddaughter will rule in name only and those in this room are forbidden to discuss what had become of her until my death."

"I think I can speak for all here when I say none shall speak a word."

"Did you plan this?"

Helping Adrianna into a black coach he couldn't help but smile. "Sweetheart, must you always ask things that you already know the answer to?"

"Maybe I want to hear you say what I already know."

Settling in next to her he smiled. "If you must know, I asked your mother to dispose of the queen once the vows were complete. But with the arrival of Queen Alista... I improvised. After all, she did just lose her entire family. It would be cruel for her to lose the last link to her daughter. At least, until she decides what to do with her."

"How very kind of you." Looking over to the silver box that sat across from her, "And that..."

"In a century or two, I will return it." Myrddin glanced at the silver box then reconsidered, "Possibly return it. Or any child that we have may choose to. But nothing can destroy the box." *Or the contents within.*

Her eyes looked at the box almost mesmerized. "Enchanting."

"Yes, and if you're a good little apprentice I'll teach you how it works."

Sitting back, she crossed her arms smugly. "You assume I don't already."

Giving her a passionate kiss, he smiled. "Incantation, my dear, not power. And nothing that is close to your current abilities."

Part 2

EIGHTEEN YEARS AGO.

M.L.Ruscsak

"*An unrest is settling in among my people. Why, I cannot say for certain. Whispers are spoken but even I cannot hear all that is being said. I just hope beyond all reason that whatever is wrong will not reveal itself to me until my daughter is born. I pray that I will have at least some time with her before I must be the Queen of Darke.*

Yet somehow I doubt that I will ever get the chance to see my daughter grow into her gifts."

-The private journal of Queen Adrianna. Queen of Darke

M.L.Ruscsak

Chapter 7: Adrianna

Adrianna glanced down at her newborn baby and smiled. Very carefully she picked her up from the smoke black cradle. "I don't know what I'm going to do with you. I can't call you my little sweetie for the rest of your life." She paused and let out a small laugh. "Well, I could, but it's not a good name for a queen who will one day rule all of Darke." A light giggle had her turning to the door.

"Dearest sister, have you given my niece a name yet?"

Looking at the woman who flowed into the room Adrianna could not help but smile. Her twin. Not an identical twin but rather her complete opposite. Where her twin had flowing golden hair her own was the color of the night. Though both were tall and slim and seemed to flutter when they walked but Celeste embodied all things bright and golden. "I just cannot think of one that will do her justice" She pressed her lips together till they were nothing more than a thin line before continuing. "There is not a name I can think of that will embody the next queen that will give her enemies pause."

"Oh dear. Our daughters are not yet three days old and you are already talking enemies. I *do* swear I should have your husband take you to see his homeland. I think all the darkness and gloom of your own kingdom has finally made you a little daft."

Turning away from her sister she lightly scolded her, "Very funny. You know as well as I that I cannot simply visit the Feyen Kingdom. *You* on the other hand... they welcome you."

Celeste rolled her eyes and held out her milky pale arms. "Yes well... Here give me my niece I should have some time with her before I leave for my own Kingdom."

As she placed her precious little daughter in her sister's arms, Adrianna paused. Something in the darkness was being whispered. All those she ruled were speaking of it but what good is a whisper in the dark when she couldn't hear everything that was being said? "I want you to take her with you."

"What?" Celeste spun around to face her sister. She knew that look in her eyes someone... or something was telling her something. What it might be she could never guess but was causing enough distress that her sister looked more like some fairy-tale warrior ready to do battle than a mother who had just given birth. "What is it, sister?"

Black, swirling mist hid her legs and crawled up her back; caressing her long, raven-colored hair. "The whispers are not clear. No matter, I will have whatever it is settled soon enough. Or my dear husband will. In either case, I would like for you to please take our children to Castle Sun-Tear. I will come when it is safe."

Sun-Tear was the furthest of the castles of Lite but the one nearest the Feyen Kingdom. So why of all places did Adrianna want for her daughter to be taken there? Not a question that she could ask. At least not while her sister was still having a conversation that only she could her. But a request phrased as an ultimatum? Not only could she but it would not be the first time that she had done so. "I will but only if you name your daughter. Or I will be sending both of our daughters with our mother and you can explain to her why I am going with you."

Adrianna glanced at her sister through narrowed eyes then down to her baby. "The Fey name their children after things that they can turn to. Or, at least, that is what my dearest husband says." She closed her eyes and let dark tendrils of mist leak from her and to around her daughter. Drawing them back she smiled. "She will be called Nisha, daughter of the night."

Adrianna stood in the street of her great city horrified at she saw. Buildings were crumbling down around her. Fire both natural and that had been magically conjured filled windows trapping her citizens behind walls of smoke.

To many calling for help. Too many that would parish if he did nothing.

Placing her hand over her heart she gasped trying to make sense of what she was seeing,
" ADRIANNA

"What in the name of Darke had happen here? My beloved city is not just on fire but in several places, there are signs of explosions. It doesn't make any sense unless the citizens of marsh had come this far north to started a war. But why now?"

Slowly Myrddin approached her with Galeron and his wife standing just a few steps back.

Silently acknowledging her husband Adrianna shook her head. Right now she needed to be the queen. Right now her people needed her cool head to get them all through this.

 "Dea you and Galeron take the south side of the city, Myrddin and I will take the north.We'll meet up in the castle. Anyone who is making things worse do as you see fit."

Myrddin placed his hand upon her arm his eyes seeing past the fire. "Addy, you sure about this?"

Her eyes narrowed into tiny slits as she hissed "We have two choices. One we do nothing and watch our home burn. Or we take care of this and bring our daughter home."

He winced as took a breath, "Or we ask your sister for help."

Adrianna paused for only a moment and shook her head,"No. Whatever this is… I do not want her here. There is something still elusive to me and until I find out what it is … no one from Lite is stepping foot in my kingdom.

M.L.Ruscsak

Chapter 8: Celeste

It was well past midnight when word had reached then. And at least an hour more before the shock had worn off enough for the tears to fill her eyes. Yet she hadn't been able to remain within her throne room. Instead she had to explain this to her niece. But how would she ever find the words to say to her? How would she ever explain to Nisha that her mother had died? No, not just her mother but also her father and countless number of others who had yet to be named.

Just hours ago, she had ordered a nursery to be put together for her niece. Just hours ago, she had hugged her sister with all of her might trusting that she would see her in a day maybe two at the latest. If she only known it would have been the last time…

…If…

She could not afford to think about "if". There was too much to do before morning. And much, much more to do after day break.

So, with a heavy heart she slipped into her niece's nursery that had been hastily pieced together with a hodgepodge of mix- matched furniture. Leaning over the plain wood cradle, Celeste quivered as she touched her niece's soft milky pale face. Her own tears once again being forced back. "How do I tell you that your mother is gone?"

"Darling, stop."

Pulling herself to her full height, she turned to the man who stole her heart; her husband. "Blake?" His sun-kissed blond hair still neatly in place despite being woken in the middle of the night.

"Come, darling, you need to grieve and I need to make sure the rest of our little family is safe."

Of course, he would, being the captain of her guards; he would need to brace for an attack and find whatever answers that he could find. Then he would allow himself to be her husband and offer her all the hugs and reassurances that he could. But not until he was certain their own kingdom was safe. "You think..."

Blake took a full step into the room and closed his arms around his wife. "I have spoken to your mother. The fire that took your sister and her husband was no accident. For now, I don't think it wise to move Nisha any closer to Darke. Nor do either of think it wise for you, the Queen of Lite, to step foot in the darker kingdom. "

There was more she could almost hear it but she couldn't press him… not tonight… not when her heart ached with grief. Taking some comfort in his embrace she sniffled. "Addy knew. Damn her! She *knew* she wouldn't see her daughter grow."

He held her as she let her tears fall. Held her until he was sure she wouldn't crumble when he spoke. "Ah love, you can't be sure of that."

She pulled away just enough to consider his sea green eyes. "I *know* my sister. We have had our differences but I *know* her. I just can't decide if she wanted me to raise her daughter here, or to ask the Fey for help."

The thought alone of asking the *Fey* for anything sent a quiver down his spine. "The Fey are very difficult people you know this."

"I do. And I know my niece is part Fey. And before you say it, I know her power will eclipse any queen in all the kingdoms combined once she is of age."

For a moment, he didn't breathe. Didn't dare to. Until now, only Celeste and her sister could claim that they were the most powerful and gifted in their own Kingdoms. "Are you sure?"

"I'm sure. I came in here to tell her about her mother. Not that she would understand and... There were... was... my sister called them shadows or whispers. They... It... vanished when I entered. I don't know but I think it tasted her blood. If that is even possible." Then she showed her husband the little pin prick hidden on Nisha's tiny hand. A single drop of blue blood already reforming. Still her niece hadn't made a single sound except those of a very happy baby.

Part 3

PRESENT DAY

M.L.Ruscsak

"One day there will be a queen born of both Lite and Darke. She will be more powerful than any before her. Beware the day when she is crowned queen for all will change. Long forgotten truths will once again be revealed. And out of the shadows will come the end to all that we hold dear."

-The Legend of Darke and the Cursed

M.L.Ruscsak

Chapter 9: Nisha

Pulling the golden wardrobe doors open, Nisha took a deep breath today was her last day in Lite. The last day with her family at all... Well, not really but it would be the last time she came here as a princess. No, the next time she came into Lite she would be a queen of two realms.

For eighteen years, she had lived here. Learning both of her own powers and those of her cousin Lilly. They had both pressed each other to be more ... to be the best. Both knew how to play off one another. Both knew they would be Queens. And both refuse to listen that they were destined to be enemies. After all, how could she ever turn against the one person who understood her even at her worst? Another deep breath and she looked at the wardrobe hanging neatly on the hangers, "What does one wear when seeing their home for the first time?" She asked the question more to herself but it was a tired voice from behind her that answered.

"Colors are muted in Darke. Dark colors are best. Also, your mother use to complain about the cold and lack of natural light."

"My raven feather jacket and red blouse it is." Nisha pulled the jacket off the gold hanger, then she shrugged. "I adored this when I first made it but Lilly and I now agree it makes me look ..."

Finishing her niece's sentence Celeste breathlessly said, "Like the Queen of Darke." Taking the few steps over to her niece and sighed. "You terrified me the first time you wore that. Of course, after seeing several ravens without their feathers and still very much alive did give us all something to laugh about."

Nisha shrugged as she slipped the jacket on. "They all decided I would look lovely as a bird. And it did give me a reason to take up knitting."

Celeste blinked. She should remind her niece that birds don't talk... of course, then they would have a discussion that would be about everything that wasn't important. So, biting back the comment, she entered the room. "You know, now that I'm looking at it I think the shoulders need something a bit more." A single snap of her fingers and a young servant girl with red hair rushed in with a plain white box with a black velvet ribbon. "This was your grandmother's. I think she would be pleased if you had it."

Nisha allowed for a dark mist to reach out toward the box, "May I?"

"My dear, you must learn not to ask for things. You are the queen of Darke, you tell those who serve you what you want."

"Oh, I don't think that they would like that. Shadow responds better when I *ask* rather than *tell* him anything. And the whispers are chattier when I carry on a conversation rather than just ask for information. I can't even describe what the dead do when I give an order. However, they are very pleased when I ask for help."

"The.... Dead!?! When were you...." Taking a few short breaths, she managed to calm herself, "No, don't tell me. The dead have their own place they are not to be roaming the streets of Lite." She padded backward to the bed to sit before she fainted. Hopefully, after her niece was crowned then these little conversations would stop...

...And sheep might grow wings tomorrow.

"Oh, they don't roam... or at least not here. The Under Kingdom is very dull. I give them things to liven it up a bit and they made me their queen. It was unanimous... *I think*. I'm not really sure. The ones that crowned me refused to discuss it while I was there to join in the conversation."

For several long seconds, Celeste forgot to breathe. In truth, if her head hadn't started to buzz she wouldn't have remembered something so mundane. "The... their .... I don't want to hear of this. Actually, I humbly request that you never mention this to anyone who is not family."

Pulling the ribbon from the box Nisha shrugged not really paying attention to her aunt any longer. "Is it wrong?"

"My dear child, No one has ruled the Under Kingdom for nearly a million years. The residents decided that after living under a ruler in life they didn't want one in death." Or, at least, that was what was told in every textbook and classroom in every kingdom. In fact, it was one of the very few things that everyone could agree on.

"Oh. Well, I guess they changed their mind." Nisha paused again. "But I thought you knew that Freya is not of the living? Seeing that she doesn't need sleep nor needs food to survive."

"Freya is also a Fey as well as a trained warrior. I was not going to turn away help in keeping you and your cousin safe." Which at the time sounded like very good advice... however... looking back...? There were half a dozen other things she could have tried first. Should have tried first. After accepting Freya as a guard, it was already too late to try anything including taking Nisha to Queen Alista for help.

"Oh. Well, then you also should know that many of the citizens of the Under Kingdom are also highly trained warriors and will not let anything happen to our family. They swore an oath to that."

For a moment, Celeste's mouth hung open. So many questions she could ask... the possible answers terrified her. "The box. Yes, please open the box."

"Oh *tsk*. What fun is it having a niece if I can't be honest with you?" Sliding the lid open she smiled at the two large feathered claws. "What kind of bird did these come from? They're absolutely perfect."

"I don't recall, from the size of the feathers I would say a rather large bird." Or at least, something that resembled a bird. After all, Darke has animals that no other country has ever heard of, let alone have ever seen. Then again, the animal could have been conjured by her mother just for the claws... it was a possibility. After all her mother had been more than capable of doing just that.

Placing the shoulder pads on her jacket she smiled. "I wonder if I'll see any?"

Oh my, I hope not. "I wouldn't know dear. Now come sit. We need to go over some things before you leave."

Soft tendrils flowed around her lifting her hair into different patterns in a span of a minute her hair was tied up and a small crown of black polished stone was sitting on her head. Three points all honed a sharp edge. "Oh look. I guess I do have a crown to wear to Darke. I was worried that no one would know who I was."

In a firm voice, Celeste said again, "Nisha, please sit." They needed to have this conversation even if she had to drag Lilly in here to do it.

Her lips curled into a smile that was anything but reassuring. "Yes, auntie."

"First, a basket is being prepared for you to take. Do not eat anything there until you have a staff that is blood bound to you."

"Marta is coming as my cook. Her daughter Marigold is to be my personal maid. And I have Emmett, Edgar, and Shadow who are my personal guards." *Plus, Freya and scores of the undead.* Not that she would say that when she had already scared her aunt enough for one day.

"Very well. Please ask Shadow to stay close till the coronation. He ... *it* ... is good at knowing when you're in danger and doesn't much care who is the one putting you in that position." Which they had all almost learned too late when it had nearly killed David because he was trying to teach Nisha how to defend herself and had gotten carried away.

Nisha narrowed her violet eyes and whispered in a tone that was much darker than a girl her age should have. "That and everyone knows that shadows cannot be killed but can kill anything else including Drakens, trolls, and others."

How could I forget? "Yes, everyone knows that. And Darke has others there that are also hard to kill. *DO* you remember the types of citizens that you will rule over?"

"Of course." She began to count on her fingers. "There are the High-born, which consist of Specters who can create dark tendrils out of shadows. They can either be subservient or just mean. Fire dancers, who can look like any other citizen of Darke, but can turn their flesh to embers or create fires wherever they step or touch. And then the Telepaths, I am told they resemble a citizen of Feyen with pointed ears and slanted eyes. But unlike the Fey they cannot use glamour spells to cloak themselves."

Nodding in agreement Celeste asked, "And the other residents?"

"All others have minor abilities. Such as being able to walk through walls. Make items vanish and reappear at will. I'm sure there are many others that I still must learn about." Yet no Fey was said to live within the borders of Darke. None has so much as stepped foot into the country since before the great fire that took so many. And that was something else she would need to investigate since Fey were laws unto themselves and only answered to the Feyen Queen or a queen that they choose to serve willingly.

"Very true. Now once you accept the scepter of Darke all of your abilities will be unlocked." *And May the light protect me when they do.*

"I'll have abilities that I don't already know about? How exciting. Will Lilly be getting new abilities too at her coronation?"

Celeste squeezed the bridge between her nose already feeling the headache that always came from these conversations starting to come on. Knowing by the time her niece left for the Spire, her head would be ready to explode. "Yes, dear."

Nisha clapped her hands in excitement. "We will have to meet every few weeks to practice together. One time here in Lite and the next in Darke. It will be wonderful."

"Nisha, please."

"Sorry, Aunt Celeste."

"Once you are crowned queen, you will be able to tap into every ability of your subject on top of the ones that you already have. And with all that power comes responsibility. There will be those who will press you to use your gifts for their own means. And others who will fear you and will try to harm you."

For a long moment, Nisha sat there quietly. Every time she had thought about how her mother had died the rage burned inside of her. Very coldly she replied, "Don't worry. I'm not my mother. I don't trust the living to protect me. Nor rely only on my abilities."

"Yes, that is what I'm afraid of. Which is why before you were born your mother chose a husband for you. He was bound to you on the day of your birth. Your mother and grandmother oversaw the binding. You can sure it was accurate and precise in the terms."

Nisha jumped up from the bed. "What? You're just telling me about this now? Lilly got to choose her husband. *Sort of.* Well, at least, she got to choose *which* son of Draken that she got to marry. And he has lived here with us for nearly ten years!"

"I know it seems unfair. And I have tried to have him brought here several times. Every time his uncle has refused for reasons that I cannot comprehend. However, he will be meeting you at the Spire. Take some time and talk to him. I was told your father had chosen him from any other male child that had been born within a year of your birth."

There was more to this conversation. Something that was now being whispered deep within the shadows. Murmured conversations and a warning to tread carefully. The shadows didn't trust her aunt with the truth. However, she could use this single moment to ask something else. "My father?" So, little had ever been told to her about him. Now...?

Would she get an honest answer? Or would she need to ask the great fey of old?

Seeing the questions on her niece's face, Celeste continued, "He was from Feyen. And was said to be a seer besides beings able to turn invisible." Giving a long pause, she chose to share a bit more about her sister's husband. "I only met him twice. Once at the wedding to your mother. He took my hand and told me that my daughter would be as beautiful as Lite itself and will be happily married to a son of Draken." There was more that she could tell her but it could wait till after the coronation.

With a sigh Nisha resigned herself to meet this chosen suitor, "Fine, I'll meet him but if he's not as handsome as David I will refuse to marry him. And if he protests I'll turn him into a frog."

"He's blood bound to you. If you tell him you're not to be married he won't protest. His uncle on the other hand very well might. And since he's been ruling as your proxy, because of this union he may make a powerful enemy."

"Fine, I'll turn his uncle into food for David. I do think Drakens love fresh rabbit."

Oh, bless it. "I doubt rabbits are found in Darke."

Squaring her shoulders Nisha sat on the edge of her bed and let her voice take a cold dark tone as she said, "Well, there will be one if this proxy thinks he can give *me* orders."

Chapter 10:
Ethan

Water dropped from the ceiling above.

Plop.

Plop. Plop.

The sound a soothing drone that he had learned to use to relax him despite the pain in his arms and the burning of his back. It was enough to allow for a few moments to rest. A few precious minutes to regain his strength for whatever his uncle had planned for the next day.

"Wake up, dog." A deep voice echoed through the cold damp cellar.

Slowly, Ethan let his eyes adjusted to the darkness and sound of that deep male voice. Lord Edrich. His uncle. If he answered he would be slapped. If he didn't, something much worse. Deciding that he didn't want either he let the chains that bound him to the ceiling rattle and hoped it wasn't enough disobedience to earn him a lashing.

A glow of candlelight came into view as did his uncle and the specter that he employed just as they came down the last few steps. Both were wearing their most elaborate dress clothes. His uncle had on black dress pants and matching jacket with a crushed red shirt and black tie. Gold cuff-links and a dot of gold on the tie to keep it from moving was the only color. The specter? A blood red dress that bled into the swirling gray mist that was her feet. Neither looked like they were here to beat him till he passed out. Then again... with them, he could never be sure. After all, torturing him was their favorite past time. Or at least it seemed to be.

Lord Edrich stopped just out of reach of his prisoner and growled, "It's time for you to earn you keep, you worthless dog."

He didn't see what had happened but burning almost searing pain ran across his back. Choking back a scream, he tried to keep his eyes on his uncle. Tried to listen to the words he was saying as the specter tried to force a scream. Something she had been trying to produce for the last year. And something he would refuse her today.

Reaching out his long boney finger's Edrich grabbed Ethan by his chin and hissed, "Today you get to meet the little *princess*. Don't worry. I'm sure you'll be begging for my kindness long before the wedding." A cruel smile formed on his lips as he leaned closer. "I hear she has a tendency for cruelty more so than her mother had ever dreamed of."

Wedding? Kindness? Ethan couldn't speak. He knew better than to let a single word slip past his dry chapped lips. He wasn't worthy of speech. Not worthy of anything. Or at least, that was what he had been raised to believe. He only lived in his uncle's house because his parents died penniless and owing him a great debt. And he as their only living son, he had been forced to pay that debt. A servant by day and a whipping post by night, or worse, coin for his uncle to pay *his* debts.

"You will go to the Spire and retrieve the little princess. Then return promptly to the palace. Do not linger at the Spire or your flesh will be stripped from your body by morning."

He nodded. His body already trembling from pain.

Edrich told the specter, "Let him down. He'll need to stand to reach the Spire." Then to Ethan, "And if I hear you got one drop of blood on *my* carriage I'll make sure it's the last time you do so.

He knew the threat. His uncle would never turn him out. Some great scandal if he did. Not so much if he killed a lonely servant. Less if he fed him to a troll.

The water was cold, smelled and was turning to gray slime from the maggots that were now living in the bowl. If he washed in this, at best he would offend the princess, at worst his wounds would become infected. If he didn't his clothes would stick to him and would tear the tender skin when they were removed. Closing his eyes, he slipped on a white shirt without trying to wash. From the front, it looked made of fine silk, but the back and arms were of material that scratched and itched. After three years of wearing it, he had learned how to ignore the feeling.

The jacket, however, was a pleasant surprise. It was of excellent quality. Even lined with silk. Black... but then everything was a dark color or white. But mostly black and red.

Passing a lone hall mirror he stole a quick glance. His coal black hair was starting to grow out. Just a fingers width now. His eyes were an unusual color from any other citizen of Darke... so rare that it didn't even have a word that he knew. His skin bleached from any color that it might have. One day he hoped he could see the porcelain cream skin that he could vaguely remember.

Hoped that one day he could see his eyes without the tired look to them. But most of all he hoped he could someday flee his uncle's house. Maybe reach Lite or Draken and beg for asylum. One day when he had the strength to leave this place. When he had some idea of where to turn to for help.

He knew that it was a feeble dream. The princess had returned to Darke and in two weeks he would be dead. A gift for her wedding day. A sacrifice to enrich her powers. Or at least that was what his uncle had told him. And his uncle had no reason to lie to a worthless servant.

Ethan looked up at the Spire. Half in Lite and half in Darke. The side that was of Lite had been made of white stone that glistened in the sun. Where the side that resided in Darke was of black polished stone half hidden in the shadow. This was the border between the two countries. The place when two generations back a single Queen had ruled both. Her daughters then each took control of one or the other. Celeste was said to be made from the sun itself. So, pure that no evil could touch her skin. Whereas Adrianna was pure evil. She abused her power and died because of it. Now her daughter who is rumored to be so powerful that she had been brought up by a shadow and a demon in a tower that was enchanted by the Fey so that she could not do harm outside what she would rule.

And here he was... the one who would take her back to her palace of Night. He would lead her to her wedding and coronation. Then die at her own hand in front of all who wished to attend the ceremony.

Ethan looked across the border into Lite. He could go the few feet across the Spire and into Lite. He could beg to see Queen Celeste... He could...

... No, he couldn't. He was a lot of things but a coward was not one of them. Perhaps he could spend the next two weeks in service of the soon to be queen. If he did, he could make himself invaluable to her then she wouldn't kill him.

Taking a deep breath, he stepped off the back of the carriage.

This would be his only hope. His only chance... and he had to do it without his uncle finding out that he had done this without permission.

Slowly, he made his way up the grand staircase that would take him to the main door. The stones that were the steps looked smooth enough to be slippery and wet but somehow prevented him from slipping. The double door reached up two stories and was made from dark wood. Just standing before them you could feel eyes watching you. Feel breathing on your neck and know that if you turned around no one would be standing there.

Swallowing hard he raised his fist and knocked on the door. He had done so softly but it didn't stop the knock from banging into an echoing roar.

He had just been about to rush down the steps and make his way around the Spire and to the side that resided in Lite when the door creaked open.

For a moment, his eyes locked on the Feyen Warrior who thankfully was unarmed. After his heart once again settled in his chest, he bowed. "I am here to escort the princess." It felt wrong to speak but he had to. Of course, he would be punished later... but right now that didn't matter. Couldn't matter. He had to state why he was there or be dead without ever speaking.

The Feyen warrior smiled as she pulled her smoke gray wings to her sides, "Follow me. The princess will be down shortly."

Chapter 11: Nisha

If they used the carriages to travel to the Spire it could take hours. Still they would be there well before the scheduled time of arrival. However, if she used the gate of the dead it would only take a few heart beats. And that meant…

"Freya!" Nisha let out an excited squeal.

"Your grace?" That cautious tone coming from this steeled warrior was enough to know that at least one of her subjects knew when she was about to do something terrifying and breathtaking.

"Please tell those who are joining me in Darke that they should not delay. I have another appointment that is taking priority. I shall meet you all at the Spire at the appointed time."

Freya dipped her head slightly. After all she was one of the few people who understood who would require a meeting with the Queen. "Please convey my regrets at not joining you."

A wicked smile bloomed on Nisha's young face. "I'll try not to rumple Uncle Magmas up too much in your absence."

Deep within the City of the Dead, Nisha sat in a small dwelling of her own making. A large round table with several high back raven colored chairs. One for each of the men who made up the counsel of the fey. One for her grandmother and Alista. And two that remained empty at the counsel's request.

Magmas had taught her all of the gifts belonging to the royal fey of the star cities. Donavan had been her trainer in all things considered to be either dark abilities or training to fight. Both Flint and Karnack had spent countless hours going over laws of both the star cities and of Darke. And both her Grandmother and Alista had given her lessons on how to be a good queen and true leader.

Yet none of them had told her anything about her father. Nor had she asked, until now.

She was calmly seated and smiled as Magmas entered escorting his daughter to her seat. Flint and Donnavan trailing behind them with her grandmother entering last. Yet it was Appollo who stayed in the doorway holding his wings perfectly still as he measured her temperament.

"Uncle Appollo, won't you be joining us at the table?"

His eyes narrowed into tiny slits. "I have known you for only a few light cycles but when you smile like that…" He shook his head and gave her a very insincere smile. "There is nothing that can get me to move from this spot."

"Oh, tsk. What fun is it having an honorary niece if I can't scare the shit of you on occasion?"

Magmas let a cough that sounded close to a laugh slip past his lips. "Very well. Appollo can guard the doorway. However, you asked for all of us to come and we're here. So why is it when you should be on your way to embrace your destiny that you needed to have a moment with a bunch of old cranky fey."

Her smile faded. "I have questions and I am not leaving this room until they are answered."

Flint nodded once. "Understood? Now what questions do you needed answered?"

"I need to know about my father. My betrothed. And the powers both are known to have."

Returning to the Spire, Nisha took a deep breath and changed from her long black skirt and crushed red blouse. Vanished her raven fathered jacket and allowed for a dress of her own making form to her thin body. White and black mirroring the woods of the dead. It was perfect for the setting of the spire. Perfect to lift her mood.

She had needed to find out the truth of not only her family but that of her betrothed. And she had but now questions swarmed in her mind.

Taking a deep breath, she pushed her thoughts aside and decided to take in the rare beauty of the Spire. Take in all that she had never seen before. Now this was her one opportunity to see the place where her mother had been raised. The place where her grandmother had ruled over not just lite but also Darke.

This was her chance to explore the greatest trove of power and secrets in all of the known lands.

Humming as she walked the halls of the Spire. Finding it mesmerizing. The halls that paired the two halves were pieced together like a grand puzzle. A wisp of black and gray stone swirling into white and cream stone. Joining together working in harmony but able to stand on their own.

"Princess?"

The woman who stood before her she knew for years. Tall and slim. Blue-green eyes that looked like little rivers around a little round misty black marble. Cocoa brown hair that ended just below the shoulders. Her delicate pointed ears that looked more of an elf than of a Fey poked out from hair that she was currently wearing down. A crystal sword was now hanging loosely at her side. The sword didn't make her a warrior but it was the speed and skill of what she could do with nothing more than her hands that did. "Freya."

Giving a nod that was the most that Freya would allow for herself to do in the way of showing respect, she softly spoke, "Your betrothed is has arrived."

Squeezing the bridge of her nose and preparing for the worse Nisha whispered, "Is he truly hideous? Tell me he is not an ugly hairy troll slug"

Freya smiled softly. "I think you shall be pleasantly surprised."

That she was not expecting, or maybe she had. "Oh, good. Then you must send for Lilly. I cannot get married without my dear cousin and David too I suppose."

"Of course, your majesty. I will ask them to arrive on the morrow. And if I may?"

They have had this discussion several times so it was really a habit when she rolled her eyes and said, "Freya, you don't need to ask. You are my dear friend. Please speak freely."

"You should try to call the prince by his real name. It may give him pause. At least for a moment. He is, after all, chatty for a Draken."

"Oh yes. Let's see his full name. Prince Davkren son of King Craykren and Queen

Alyisope of Feyen. Third in line to the crown of Draken. Or second if his sister gets her way."

"Yes, I see your point. *David* is so much simpler."

A little laugh slipped passed her lips. "I know. I am so glad Lilly came up with it."

Stopping mid-step Nisha watched the tall young man that stood nervously looking out the window that faced Lite. Something about him reminded her of a fox that she and Lilly had happened to cross paths with some time ago. At the time, the fox had been slinking around the edge of the meadow yet watching them as if ready for attack. The fox had been hurt and in need of help. She had known that within a moment of spotting the poor creature... But it had been Lilly who had been able to heal its paw. As for the young man? She didn't think it was a hurt paw that was troubling him… no. If she was reading him correctly, he was trying not to show that he was in pain yet expecting far worse.

Staying in the doorway, she removed her stone crown and let the dark mist take it to wherever they took things to store. Right now, she wanted to be Nisha a young healer in training. Not Nisha the crown Princess of Darke and the Queen of the Under Kingdom. "Um... Excuse me?" Her voice quivered just a bit... more from nerves but the sound should be enough for the young man not to think of her as a threat.

At the sound of her voice, he turned on his heels. High cheekbones and a chiseled jaw. Thin, pale, chapped lips... but it was his eyes that held her. The rest of him said he was fine yet waiting for instruction.... but his eyes screamed of the pain that he was hiding.

A small breath and he tried to smile yet didn't dare speak.

"Are you waiting for someone?"

His eyes watched her take a step into the room. Finally, he whispered, "I'm to escort Princess Nisha to the Castle of Night. Lord Edrich is awaiting her arrival."

"I see." She took another step toward him and watched the fear register in his eyes. Even *if* she was only an apprentice here at the Spire her clothes would scream high-born. His however screamed servant and definitely not of those that her betrothed should be wearing. Perhaps Freya had been wrong about who had come to the Spire.

No, Freya would have been certain before coming to find her. Allowing herself to feel she too felt the binding that her mother had used. Still, she could tell that he there was something off about him. Not wrong... just off. Almost as if he didn't know he belonged to her. Or possibly if he did, he didn't understand what it was that he was now feeling. Only one way to find out and playing that of a healer would never get her that answer. "I thought we wouldn't be required at the castle till midday tomorrow at best."

Very quickly he dropped to one knee. "Princess, I'm ...."

Black tendrils circled around him, softly caressing his skin. By the time they rescinded she knew every wound that he had and every mark that was already showing signs of healing. Today she would be a passive visitor. Tomorrow she would have a better idea on how the laws in Darke worked. And by then she would have Lilly here to help her deal with whoever had caused those wounds. "Perhaps we should go. I would like to speak to Lord... ed... Edrich."

The fear was gone for the moment but sadness now took hold. "The carriage is on its way."

She turned then paused at the door. "A moment, please. I need to advise my personal staff that we are leaving. You wouldn't believe how ruffled they get if they are not told things beforehand." And it would give her a moment before she decided on how to handle her betrothed.

He wasn't what she had thought he would be. If what she was picking up from the tendrils could be trusted he had, at least, some Feyen blood in him. Not half as much as she did but enough to recognize that he has some. That was a puzzle for another day since there was no record of any living Fey in all of Darke. In fact, the dead didn't know of any that were even part Fey within the borders… at least not since the fire.

A deep breath and she made a mental note of yet another thing she would need to ponder. That she would have to wait on…

…and add to the ever-growing list of things she would need to find answers to and fix.

For today, she would have to find out why her betrothed was dressed as a servant when he belonged to a high-born house. Not only that, his mother had been a lady in waiting to her own mother but she had also owned several businesses in both Darke and Lite. Not to mention his father had been the first chair on the royal council. A man who at one time had been the captain of her mother's guards before stepping aside for another.

All of which she had learned herself once coming to the Spire and asking the Seneschal for information about her betrothed and his family.

The only piece of information that she didn't much care for was Lord Edrich. He had been the only living adult from the fire that had taken so many eighteen years ago. The only high-born adult that had survived a blaze that had wiped out nearly half of the population of the city and castle of Darke.

An oddity. But more than that just reading it... something didn't sound right and prickled her skin in warning. Something else had been off with what she had read... Her mother had been able to create and manipulate fire among other things. So, if she had truly perished in the flames...

... Then why did Ethan feel of power that only a Feyen queen could possibly possess? He felt of a power that should have vanished with her death.

So many confusing things... and so much more that she would have to figure out before she could marry Ethan and take her place as Queen. And so many more questions that needed to be answered after she had been crowned.

Nisha hurried down the dark stone steps and stopped short just paces away from the carriage that would take her to the castle. The carriage was small, gloomy and smelled of rot. Before thinking about what she should say, she blurted out, "I am not stepping foot in that rotted piece filth."

Ethan stammered to respond, "This is the best..."

She didn't care if she sounded like a whiny child or a pampered princess... she was not sitting in filth. "If this is the best that *my* palace has then I will be making changes as of this very moment."

Gasping to form words, any words so to be helpful and not look like a babbling idiot, Ethan tried to say, "Not the palace. My uncle... He... This is his."

Well, at least, *she* didn't own such a disgusting, rotten piece of filth that wouldn't even suit as a trolley for the destitute. "I see. Then Lord Edrich is a poor excuse for a proxy." She turned sharply back to face the Spire. "Freya?"

Already standing by her queen's side she smiled. "Your grace?"

A deep breath and she squared her shoulders as she had watched her aunt do countless times before when addressing someone for an important task. A posture that never wished to use when addressing Freya. "Please send word to my aunt. I will be in need of her assistance after all. Tomorrow will be soon enough for her arrival. Please extend the invitation to my Uncle Blake as well." Not that he wouldn't tag along invited or not but she might as well make it look like she was requesting him as well. Besides if Lord Edrich was as much of an ass that she was suspecting she would need her uncle to deal with him. Or at least deal with him while she dealt with the state of her kingdom.

"Very well. I will have a page seek her out." Freya stopped and looked back at the Spire, "A *proper* carriage and Pegasi are being brought around. Both belonged to your grandmother. They are of the finest quality."

"Thank you, Freya. Will it be large enough for the staff as well?"

"Your staff will follow in a second carriage. It is not proper for them to sit with you. Your Grace."

Shit, if she was using her title... not once, but twice... then she had already caused enough of a scene for the moment. "Oh, alright. I'll *try* not to have a great scandal started over what carriage my personal staff is seated in. At least not today. I make no promises about tomorrow." Her only answer was Ethan's face losing all color and

Freya rolling her eyes as she hurried back into the Spire.

The coach was large enough to hold at least ten people and still have plenty of room to stretch out in. The dark blue velvet seats with gold trim had her grandmother's grand touch of posh yet still looked average among other coaches for high-born citizens. Well, that was until you got close enough to see the seal of Darke engraved into the doors. Then and only then would there be no mistake who would be riding in this carriage.

…And it was now hers.

For a long time, Ethan didn't speak. If she hadn't been looking right at him she wouldn't have known that he was even sitting there. "So, are you going to tell me about what we are passing or am I going to be giving the sites new names and require everyone to remember them for me?" Not that she would but the thought alone made her smile. Then again, she had always wanted to name a city. Perhaps she could create one just for the experience? Later she could ponder it in more detail.

A look of absolute horror fell on Ethan's face as he stammered, "My apologies, but I was instructed not to speak."

"Well, that is the most absurd thing I have ever heard. And I'm telling you I have heard several things that are simply preposterous. More so after the words had been said out loud for me to hear them."

The fear came back to his eyes but he had managed to appear calm otherwise. A short breath and he leaned so he could really see where they were. "We are south of the Spire, Near the bottomless lake. The town of Manticora is to the west. Despite the name the town populous has a good mixture of low-born and not many Manticores. Although they did find the village and, therefore, named it after their home country."

She couldn't see the village from here but she could feel it. Locking her eyes on a faraway point she allowed herself to see what her eyes could not... The village looked run down, houses falling in on themselves too far gone to save... others how anyone lived in them was far beyond her grasp... A deep breath that was slowly let out... Not someplace she would like to visit but someplace she would *need* to see sometime very soon. "Do you know which low-born reside there?"

"Uh..." He rubbed his head slightly at a loss for words. "Being this close to the lake, I think you would find some Sirens, Charons maybe. The Charybdis reside in the lake itself. Nasty beast. They have been overrunning most of the waterways for some time now." *Unless someone found a way to remove them.* Which was highly unlikely. "Hippocampi tend to stay close to the water if not in it." He paused. "In the City of Night, I could tell you about the high-born that reside there. I know of many of them."

Giving a nod, she smiled as she said, "Please. I wasn't sure if the city had been rebuilt or not. My aunt had not been able to find out before sending me here."

"It's not as grand as it was before the fire. But it has been mostly rebuilt. The High-born all have homes near the Castle. They tend to fight over who gets to have their home closest. It's quite ridiculous if you think about it. Since their status is kept by staying well in your good graces and not having anything to do with how much money they have or what powers they possess."

In a mumbled more to herself than to him, she let out, "I haven't thought about that."

Taking anything that was said as something needing response Ethan continued, "As a servant, I'm able to see things that most would pretend not to notice."

Odd choice for words seeing we're betrothed. "You're a *servant* yet your uncle is my *proxy*? How is that even possible?" Her voice shook not with astonishment but with barely controlled anger.

"My parents died penniless according to my uncle. I pay their debt since they can't."

She took a deep breath to keep from yelling at him. It wasn't his fault that he had been lied to. But she would be *damned* if she let the lie continue after today. "I see."

Sensing that he had somehow offended her he very quickly said, "I apologize, you wanted to know about who resided in the city." With her nod, he closed his eyes, "There is an Empousa that runs the matchmaking service for the High-born. Of course, if you can't pay her she may try to make you her dinner."

"Empousa?" She knew of them. However, what she had been told made them sound like low-borne. Not someone who run a shop. Unless paid by the owner to do so.

"A vampire hybrid. Their hair is usually red like fire. Legs look like a bronze statue and they all have donkey feet. Of course, they all have mean tempers to go with them."

"Good to know. So, no real ability then?"

"No, they just like fresh meat and blood."

Rolling her eyes Nisha slowly said as she sat back in her seat, "Great."

"There is a family of Manticores. You must watch them. They shoot spikes from their tails at those that they pass. I think it's their idea of entertainment. Not much in the way of brains, though. Of course, neither are the Minotaur. The Telkhines run the metal shops. Two Typhons sit on the council now. No one dares to cross them. Although I don't know why they are here rather than in the Swamp Marsh.

"Then you have the Specters. Most are just mean instead of subservient. The Fire Dancers stay in stone houses and don't care who they burn when they are out. The Telepaths own most of the stores. Then you have my uncle. As far as I know, he is the only living Wendigo hybrid. But I don't know what he is a hybrid with."

Wow. She blinked at just learning more in a few minutes from Ethan, then what she had been able to learn in all of her years of living with her aunt. "With so many who live on fresh blood, I'm surprised they can live in the same city." And only a few who would consider high-born. Another oddity that didn't really make sense. Add that to the Typhons who had been banned from Darke more than one hundred years ago... Another thing to add to the list of questions was the sheer number of low-born citizens posing as high-born... Oh, she would need to speak to Lilly sooner than later. Hell, at this point she could open a door to the Under Kingdom and speak to the long dead queens and maybe find out some answers. Then again, she could wait to see what her aunt had to say. A day wouldn't make much of a difference. At least not to her.

"Yes, well I didn't say they get along. But I'm sure they will figure it out now that you have come home." There was an odd blend of hope in his voice mixed with just a hint of sorrow.

Chapter 12:
Magmas

Leaning back in the high back chair, Magmas swirled a glass of honeyed nectar more for something to do than to watch the violence of the fluid crashing against the glass.

He could have left after his chosen queen had departed for the Spire. He could have slipped back to the Star Cities and reported to the Great Magnar to the reason Nisha was summoning the counsel but instead he sat in the now empty meeting room hidden in such a simple dwelling that the child queen preferred.

"Something troubling you, Mags?"

He knew the voice. How could he not? Raising his eyes from his glass he saw his younger brother leaning within the doorway. Not in the room but not waiting outside either.

Tall with a sinewy build, Flint was built for the daunting task of being a clerk or stuffed away spending countless hours reading. Yet there were still those who still remembered that looks could greatly deceiving. As this was a Fey who could be as ruthless and as deadly as any steeled warrior. This was a Fey who had the speed and power to destroy anything that he wished or build anything that he could dream. No, Flint was not a Fey to be taken lightly.

So, for him to be standing in the doorway could mean more than simple curiosity.

For along moment he just sat there before fixing his lava red eyes on Flint's crystal dagger that hung loose at his side. Nothing wrong with a warrior wearing his weapon openly. Nothing that screamed agitation. Yet…

Yes. there in Flint's eyes. Worry. He too understood their queen and the questions that she was now asking.

"We prepared Nisha the best that we could. She's strong, gifted, talented, and does not trust the words that come from those around her. Yet, I wonder if we should have fought harder to bring the boy here. If he should have been raised in our care. Or at the very least in the care of someone we trusted."

Slowly Flint pushed off of the door frame and took a steady step into the round room. He ignored the walls carved from clay to resemble bone. Just as he ignored the lava that flowed within the cracks of the floor that gave this room heat.

Today wasn't a day to ponder Nisha's choice in décor. It wasn't a day to waste words or mix feelings in decisions that had already been made years past. But today was a good day to voice truths that even Magmas hadn't been privy to. "The night of the fire, Vasilissa was asked about the boy. Whatever she saw. Whatever she knows… she has her reasons for keeping the boy with his uncle and tucked away in Darke. And, that night Magnar agreed."

There was more to that story he could almost hear it in Flint's steady voice. Yet he couldn't question that decision. But he would voice his concern. "Did either of them take in account that the boy would be thrust into powers and abilities that he wouldn't be trained in? That he wouldn't have any knowledge that the powers that he possesses … that he can wield even exists?"

Pouring himself a glass of nectar Flint took a generous sip before answering. "He will have Nisha. She's a good queen and had the makings of a great leader."

"Good queen or not she may not be ready for what the bastard of Pallas has in store."

Flint flashed a bone chilling smile and pulled out his dagger testing the sharpness of the blade against his skin. "No, but we are. And he won't be meeting an untrained child on the battlefield, he'll be meeting a skilled army." He paused and leaned forward. "And he'll be meeting the great dragon queen herself."

Magmas sat the chair back down on all of it legs. His eyes narrowing just a bit, 'And I finally get the revenge owed to me."

Chapter 13: Ethan

His heart slammed into his chest. *She couldn't really be serious about renaming everything... could she?* He had to think and do so fast. If he spoke he could win her trust and maybe she would keep him in her service...

... then again if his uncle found out... No, not if... When...

... No, he would not dare think about that. Keeping his voice low... just barely a above a whisper he replied, "My apologies but I was instructed not to speak."

She had a pretty face. Almost kind and she looked almost amused when she spoke. Perhaps she didn't believe him, didn't believe that he a was a servant. Then again, maybe he did amuse her.

Hope swelled inside him.

He was so lost in thought he almost didn't notice that she was still waiting for an answer.

Very quickly he peered out the window. *They couldn't be here already yet somehow, they had traveled two hours' worth of distance in just a few minutes*? "We are south of the Spire, near the bottomless lake. The town of Manticora is to the west. Despite the name the town populous has a good mixture of low-born and not many Manticora." Taking a breath, he relaxed and hoped that would be the end of the conversation. In a heartbeat, he knew that it wouldn't be.

"Do you know which low-born reside there?"

"Uh..." *Oh shit. Who lives here? I don't know. But I can't say that.* Another quick breath and he closed his eyes and rubbed his head. "Being this close to the lake, I think you would find some Sirens, Charons maybe. The Charybdis resides in the lake itself. Nasty beast. They have been overrunning most of the waterways for some time now." *Unless someone found a way to remove them. Which was entirely possible,* "Hippocampi tend to stay close to the water if not in it." He paused, "In the city of Night I could tell you about the high-born that reside there. I know of many of them." *Please let me prove I'm an asset. Please.*

She looked like she was thinking. Weighing her options, then ... "Please. I wasn't sure if the city had been rebuilt or not. My Aunt had not been able to find out before sending me here. "

Thank you, "It's not as grand as it was before the fire." *Or at least according to those who remember it, it wasn't.* "But it had been mostly rebuilt. The High-Born all have homes near the Castle. They tend to fight over who gets to have their home closer. It's quite ridiculous if you think about it. Since their status is kept by staying in well your good graces and not having anything to do with how much money they have or what powers they have." *Oh, sweet darkness I'm rambling.*

"I haven't thought about that."

"As a servant, I'm able to see things that most would pretend not to notice." *Why did I just say that? Servants see everything and know nothing. Everyone knows that and to admit otherwise... Shit... I want to save my own hide not find a more elaborate way to die.*

"You're a servant yet your uncle is my proxy? How is that even possible?"

She sounded suspicious about something. No worse, she sounded pissed. I must fix this... My parents' maybe ..."My parents died penniless according to my uncle. I pay their debt since they can't."

"I see."

Shit. "I apologize, you wanted to know about who resided in the city." With her nod, he closed his eyes once more. "There is an Empousa that runs the matchmaking service for the High-born. Of course, if you can't pay her she may try to make you her dinner."

"Empousa?"

"A vampire hybrid. Their hair is usually red like fire. Legs look like a bronze statue and they all have donkey feet. Of course, they all have mean tempers to boot."

"Good to know. So, no real ability then?"

"No, they just like fresh meat and blood."

"Great." Her tone did not sound pleased. Yet she didn't sound mad either. Almost like she was thinking about what she was going to do with all those who needed fresh blood to survive.

"There is a family of Manticores. You must watch them. They shoot spikes from their tails at those that they pass. I think it's their idea of entertainment. Not much in the way of brains, though. Of course, neither are the Minotaur. The Telkhines run the metal shops. Two Typhon sit on the council now. No one dares to cross them. Although I don't know why they are here rather than in the Swamp Marsh.

"Then you have the Specters. Most are just mean instead of subservient. The Fire Dancers stay in stone houses and don't care who they burn when they are out. The telepaths own most of the stores. Then you have my uncle. As far as I know, he is the only living Wendigo hybrid. But I don't know what he is a hybrid with."

"So many live on fresh blood I'm surprised they can live in the same city." *Yes, he had been right. She was just trying to figure things out. So maybe he was useful to her after all.*

"Yes, well I didn't say they get along. But I'm sure they will figure it out now that you have come home."

Watching her turn her attention out the window and away from him, he relaxed. Or at least, relaxed enough for his heart to settle a bit. He had told her everything he knew. Everything that a princess should know. However, he couldn't tell her how the shops ran. How there was a class of citizens that outnumbered the low-born but didn't really exist. He couldn't tell her that he wasn't just a servant ... but a less than a slave. He had no social standing. Nothing he could call his own. Not a shirt, nor bed. Everything he used belonged to someone else. By tonight, she would know and he would be punished far worse than anything he had ever experienced before, because for a dog to speak or even think of speaking before a high-born was punished by torture until the high-born was satisfied that the offense was rectified.

She could do anything to him... or have anything done to him while she watched... and he wouldn't be able to so much as scream. Not so much as think of screaming or the punishment would be worse. Far worse than what she had already come up with.

Chapter 14: Nisha

The gray stone walls of the city came into view much too quickly. She should have told the carriage to go slower until her temper had simmered down enough where she wouldn't say everything that she wanted to. Oh, but how she wanted to take Lord Edrich aside and strip the flesh from his bones then save the whole bloody mess for David. Not that her cousin would ever eat anything that he hadn't killed himself but he would do something with it just to show the contempt of the offending ass.

Possibly David would use the carcass to draw out a troll for his father. Yes, that was definitely something David would do. On second thought, it was something that she could do herself.

No, she couldn't. At least not, till after the coronation. After all, she had to at least pretend to be a well-mannered princess even it was for only a day or two. And at this rate it would only be a day or two.

Another deep breath and she watched the shops pass by. Nothing out the ordinary. Not really caught her attention. Unless you considered dirty sidewalks and muck covered windows out of the ordinary. Then in almost every window was little hand-written signs. Later she would need to find out what the little signs that said "*dogs around back*" meant but for right now, she had enough to think about. She had more than enough to keep her occupied until Lilly arrived.

Looking back to Ethan, he looked more scared and worried than he had at the Spire. Then there was a feeling in the pit of her stomach that felt like and ominous warning that whatever was going to happen... She would need to act swiftly and carefully. Of course, she could order her warriors to occupy the city... it would buy her time for her family to arrive.

Nisha sighed to herself. There had to be another way. One that didn't involve the undead coming to this city. One that bought her time that she needed to handle all that she was seeing. And one that wouldn't make her show the depth of her true power...

... all that she had to do was make it through today.

Pulling up in front of a massive black stone castle her heart leaped to her throat. Not only was the castle three times the size of Castle Sun-Tear, the Spire, and the Draken winter castle combined... there were large stone creatures looking down at her. Glowing red eyes. And despite being made completely of polished stone she would bet her life the things were alive... and not one bit friendly...

.... That was fine. She was safe...

... Shadow was with her. Nothing could touch her without being killed first by him. Nothing including a Draken. Not even the king of the Drakens.

As the carriage door opened, Nisha allowed her eyes to float up to the grand staircase and to the huge stone double door until finally settling on a slim tall man in a black suit glaring down at her from the top of the staircase. When his glare had finally fell on Ethan his eyes narrowed but still showed the barely controlled rage.

"Princess." His voice sounded as it had been said with a mouth full of rocks.

Pompous ass. Do you not know who I am? Not that she would say that, at least not yet. A curt greeting, however... "Lord Edrich, I presume."

He didn't nod, just ignored her and spoke to Ethan instead. "I was expecting *my* carriage over an hour ago." When he noticed that she had taken offense he added while placing his bony hand over his heart. "I was worried."

Like hell you were. I know better, you worthless piece of troll fat. Your filth ridden carriage would not have made any better time than what my grandmother's had. In fact, I doubt it would have made it here at all. Not that she would say that to him, but the words burned in her throat. Making her way up the stairs and ignoring that no one had offered to escort her she continued in a tone that would have made her aunt shudder, "Your carriage was inadequate. However, my grandmother's was not. Now, are we to go inside *my* castle or would you like to debate my decision on which carriage I prefer to be seated in?"

For a moment, he glared at her. He had paid a hefty price to ensure the princess would become incapacitated during the ride. Had paid more to get a sample of her blood for the snake prince. And now… he was sure the flea ridden *dog* had something to do with this. "My apologies *princess*. Please allow me to give you a quick tour."

"That won't be necessary. As this is my home, I will explore it at my leisure. Now I do believe you have prepared a banquette for tonight." When he didn't answer she slipped passed him into the main foyer. Another grand staircase was before her with a set of huge red double doors at the top. Arched doorways led off to the left and right reviling several other doors and hallways. *A labyrinth. How wonderful.* If she wasn't already pissed off, the discovery of her own maze would have thrilled her. Tomorrow would be soon enough to explore… As for today…

"The dinner is a tradition for a royal's eighteenth birthday."

Not turning toward Edrich just yet, she narrowed her eyes and trying not to show the rage that was building inside her. *If you spoke to me in that tone in front of my family, you would be dinner for a Draken by now.* She thought it but managed to say, "And it is being held in the room at the top of the stairs. Yes, Lord Edrich… *I know.*" Taking a breath, she continued, "Ethan, will escort me into the room. Please find him something due to his stature."

"Ethan? Oh, but princess... wouldn't you much rather...?"

Now she turned sharply to face him her eyes blazing in true anger and simmering rage. "This is not up for debate, monsieur. This is *my* will. And as it is my eighteenth birthday you are no longer my Proxy." Turning away yet again she gritted her teeth and hissed, "Freya?"

"Your Grace?"

"Please come with me. I would like to see some of my home before I have my first public appearance in *my* kingdom."

Freya very calmly made sure she had enough room to maneuver if Nisha were to let her temper slip. Then very politely replied, "Of course. Shall I tell your ladies where to take your belongings?"

"No need. I will call for them when I am ready."

"Overbearing, pompous ass. How could he ever be my proxy? And look at this?" She ran her black gloved finger over the edge of a tapestry, "It's nearly ruined. Dust, mites and who knows what else has begun to eat at it."

Still walking a step behind her queen Freya tried to reason with her, "He was placed in the position because of his nephew, not because he was qualified."

In a huff, Nisha spun toward her friend and spat out, "He's not qualified to be a court *jester* let alone my proxy."

Freya nodded once and tried not to smile at the honesty of that assessment. "Very true, however, it would behoove you to point that out before the morrow when your family arrives."

That gave her pause. In the morning, her aunt would be here and she could ask her as one queen to another on how to handle the ass. "I suppose you're right." Turning a corner and nearly stepped through a house spirit. "My apologies... "For a moment, she paused and narrowed her eyes. Something was off about this house spirit.

"You should be more careful where you step." The spirit of an old Elf hissed.

It wasn't the sneer in the voice but the voice itself that told she was right about this house spirit not being what she appeared to be. "You know it is very unwise to hide behind a glamor spell when speaking to the crown princess?"

The spirit didn't seem fazed by the warning. "I doubt you will ever be more than a crown princess."

And that was enough of that. A small gesture with her finger and white smoke filled the hall engulfing the spirit with it. Once it rescinded it was no elf but a fire walker standing before her. Gray skin that looked like ash with hints of glowing embers. Eyes that were flames rather than eyes. And her hair was merely tendrils of smoke flowing down just past her shoulders. *Interesting, A fire walker should not be able to turn into a spirit. A solid citizen sure but not that of a spirit. Unless there were citizens of the Under Kingdom that were still citizens of Darke. And that was* something that was banned after the first Fey settled this land. Narrowing her eyes into tiny slits she very calmly asked, "Now would you like to tell me why I won't be crowned."

"You broke my glamor!"

Letting out a bored yawn Nisha replied, "Obviously."

She lunged at Nisha and screamed, "You bitch! I'll..."

Another small gesture and this time not white smoke but red. As it clogged the hall, Nisha closed her eyes and whispered, "Rabbit." When the smoke cleared, she didn't know what it was but she knew it was not a *rabbit*.

For a moment, no one spoke. A moment longer and Freya snatched the creature up by the long ears the belonged to a form of rabbit that lived in Feyen. "My I ask what you were trying to create?"

"Oh well, David loves fresh rabbit." She shrugged. "I guess rabbits don't look the same here."

Glaring at the creature in her hand, Freya examined it. "Well it does have the face and ears of a rabbit. As well as the size ... however... the teeth are those of a vampire? The horns look closer to those of a satyr. And I'm not even sure where the talon for the toes came from."

"Yes, she does look a bit confused. Hopefully, it tastes like a rabbit... maybe?"

"You are really going to..." Freya looked at the thing in the eyes. "... As long as you don't tell the prince what he is eating I'm sure he will give you an accurate description of his meal."

"Oh, don't be ridiculous, you know as well as I that David will never actually eat that. Even he has some rules for food. Such as he will not eat anything he cannot identify. And since that thing has no name it is saved from the dinner table." Taking a deep breath, she allowed herself to feel around her. "Grandmother told me once that she once had a menagerie. I do believe there should be a cage small enough for this one. Will you please see if you can find it? I need some time to think before dinner."

"Of course, your Grace. Shadow will stay with you?" Not so much a question but confirmation.

Continuing down the hall Nisha called over her shoulder, "Oh, I almost forgot. Shadow isn't really a shadow. He's a shade. He was limited on what he could do while in Lite. I do look forward to learning more about him now he is not restricted."

Freya stumbled back a step. A shade? And actual shade? They were untamable. Her breathing hitched. Shades didn't take orders from anyone… in fact, they didn't help the living nor the dead. If this was her dear friend then and only then would Nisha be safe…

However, *if* this was another. If this was one that hadn't been bound to him long before the Great War…

Wary she backed down the hall keeping watch for a shadow that shouldn't be there. A flutter in the air. Anything that would say a Shade was close. Her eyes never leaving Nisha's back until she had disappeared down yet another hall.

Only one race ever became a Shade after death. They had been fierce hunters as well as warriors. She could remember them clearly from before her own death. She could clearly remember how they had only ever been controlled by one queen in life. The first queen.

There was so much danger now that one had chosen to befriend her queen. Assuming it had been only one that had befriended her. If not… it would be more than trouble. It could mean war.

No, it could mean the war that her queen had long ago foreseen was now coming into being.

Chapter 15:
Ethan

Nearly falling out of the carriage Ethan froze. Lord Edrich was glaring at him. The glare alone didn't bother him... the rage in those dark eyes... oh yes ... he was in trouble... no... more than trouble. *Please don't leave me alone with him. Please.* It was useless to wish that Nisha could hear him... useless to think that she would understand the danger that Lord Edrich truly posed. How could she? After all, she had just arrived.

Lost in his own thought he barely heard the princess say, "Your carriage was inadequate. However, my grandmother's was not."

Shit. *You shouldn't say that to him. He'll destroy you.* Panic set in. He should grab her hand and run. He should tell her guard. He should... do nothing. If he touched the princess, she would kill him. If he betrayed his uncle, he would do much worse.

Forcing himself to take steady breaths, he slowly came up the steps. Surprised that his uncle didn't smack him when he walked past almost made him pause mid-step. If he would have, he would be smacked for sure. Or worse, he could be pushed down the steep stairs breaking something that would not mend before the wedding preventing him from being useful to the princess.

Of course, he didn't have time to truly look around the great all before hearing the princess say, "Ethan, will escort me into the room. Please find him something due to his stature."

Ethan? The name meant little to him although it clearly meant something to his un...cle ... A snippet of a memory. A beautiful woman with radiant golden fire-kissed hair and delicately pointed ears... holding ... it had to be him... had to be... he could just see his small hands reaching for the woman's face. *"Oh Ethan, my silly, silly boy."*

"You... What did you do?!?!" Edrich was on him the second the princess had disappeared down one of the corridors.

"I..." He didn't his uncle move before his back slammed against the course stone wall that had been behind him.

"You're going to ruin everything." His uncle paced before him. Leaning close enough to nearly touch noses Edrich hissed, "I would kill you if not for the inconvenience of telling her highness of your departure... However..." He now stood before him once more. "...don't think for one moment that you'll be enjoying the party. Or for that matter don't even think about enjoying a single breath that you be forced to take."

His mother must have been part, Fey. Feyen... Elf? ... Fairy?... Another citizen of Feyen? ... But that made little sense. All High-born Fey had been banished decades ago. Hadn't they? It was no use trying to find the answers. Not now... but soon. He had to know the truth even if it killed him.

Ethan looked around at his surroundings and tried to find a way not to move another step. He hadn't realized that he had been deep in thought and not paying attention to what had been going on around him. Now... it was too late.

He was deep beneath his uncle's home. Not in the cellar but lower. In a small room, that was covered in his dried blood. His screams still vibrated in the muck and bedrock. Edrich had done vile things to him when he had been down here last. That had been nearly five years ago. Five years and until today it had been the last time he had spoken. Five years and it had been the last time he remembered seeing the true color of his skin or his hair.

A shove from behind had him falling to his knees. The sound of fire sizzled in the air but it was the cold that more was unnerving.

"His hands and above the shoulders should be left alone. Be creative my dear the dog almost ruined my plans." He hadn't seen his uncle but it didn't matter he understood the words well enough. He understood the cold anger in the man's deep growl.

He didn't allow himself to look up to see the grin of the specter. Didn't dare show signs of being scared but that didn't stop the shiver when she asked, "Will his highness be needing any of his blood before dinner?"

His Highness. The third in line to the Serpent Throne. The creature that was to marry the princess. The man who had feasted on his blood every few nights for the past three years. Sometimes right from the vein the other times from a golden goblet filled to the brim. They had tried to bleed him dry over those years. Tried to starve him... drown him. Burn him alive. They had done vile things that he wished he could forget... But tonight, would be the cruelest.

Tonight, he would be beaten, burned, whipped... it didn't matter... but being dressed up and made to play escort to the princess then sit through the dinner with tables filled with food and not being allowed to so much as touch it. Not allowed to drink a single sip of wine that he was sure would taste more than wonderful... That beyond everything would be the cruelest...

...or so he thought.

Trying not to breathe Ethan closed his eyes and tried to calm himself. The soles of his feet had been lashed and burned so just the feeling of someone's breath made him want to scream. So, standing here, and walking... it was taking every drop of energy he had not to collapse... not to scream... and more than that not to shed the tears that he had to blink back.

Telling anyone that he was unwell or in pain was unacceptable. Not escorting the Princess... far worse. She had ordered his attendance so there was no acceptable excuse not to escort her.

Tiny breaths. Slow deliberate steps on the tips of his toes... resisting the urge to peel off the layers of binding that was hiding the blood from seeping through to the shirt was all he could think about...

... All he would allow himself to think about until he was relieved from this nightmare and he could be alone in his tiny cinder-block cell that he called his room.

Opening his eyes, he glanced down the steps and saw her...

... Saw a vision that had to be a dream for he had never seen anything lovelier nor more powerful.

When she looked up at him the pain no longer mattered. The people in the room that were behind him could have been a million miles away. No, right now the only thing... the only person that mattered was this vision coming up the steps. All that mattered now was finding a way to be in her service for as long as she would allow him to.

All that mattered was the rage building in her eyes. The cold brutal rage that he could see burning in those unrelenting eyes.

Chapter 16:
Nisha

Storming into the first room that looked close to a bedroom Nisha slammed the door behind her. Her abilities didn't work here.

No, that wasn't true. They worked but not as they did in Lite. The results here were more terrifying compared to the refined version that she had grown accustomed to while growing up with her cousin.

A hesitant voice came from the door. "Miss?"

Turning sharply to the now open door she saw the short thin elf that she had known for years. A slow smile twitched her lips. "Marigold?"

"You should start getting ready for the party. You would not want to be late."

Late? They couldn't start without her and right now she could care less about anyone who might be in attendance. Then again, it would give her time to speak to Ethan. Maybe even find out more about the ongoings of the city from his point of view.

And that was the only reason that she had for going to any function that Edrich had planned.

Looking at her friend who had yet to actually enter the room, she took in her dress. Her smile genuine now. Of course, her friend and housekeeper would find the one lightly colored dress that looked high-born and still be considered a servant garb. Although if she was really a servant she should do away with the gold trim on the bottom of the dress. "Oh fine, I guess I can be the gracious guest for *one* night."

Taking a full step into the room Marigold called in several onyx trunks with gold inlay. "I have some ladies that need my attention but I will be back in a few moments to help you get ready. And Nisha, I may be just a house elf but that does not mean I enjoy picking every article of clothing off the floor. Please try to keep at least some of them in the trunks until we find the proper place for them." She could ask her to leave the trunks alone but it would do little use. Her only hope was asking Nisha to not make a mess.

When Marigold was nearly at the door Nisha called after her, "Hmm, and I thought you were going to be my personal maid." She was only teasing. They had grown up together. Or mostly together since Marigold was, at least, a decade older but didn't look a day over sixteen.

"Tomorrow I will be your personal house elf. Today I am asking my dear friend not to take your frustration out on your wardrobe."

"Oh fine. I will find another ass to turn into a new creature."

Startled by the thought Marigold began to speak, "You'll ... No, no, don't tell me. I am quite sure I do not want to know." Almost out the door, she turned back, "I *will* be but a few minutes."

"Go, I'll be fine till you return."

Throwing open the lid on the nearest trunk she began to pull out blouses and skirts. "Now what do I wear to my party?" Holding up a blouse that fit tight at the top and flared out at the bottom she scrunched up her nose, "Too plain." Coming across a wine-red dress she hacked, "Oh yuck, why did aunt Celeste pack this?"

"Nisha?!?!"

"Oh, Mari..."

Snatching a crumbled blouse from Nisha's hand, Marigold scolded in a way that only she would dare, "I was not gone two minutes. Two..."

Nisha shrugged. "I thought I would find something to wear... After all, it is *my* party."

"Which is why I made you something special." Surveying the mess before her, she shook her head. "At least I have some idea on what will be going to the fireplace and what will need to be hung."

"See, I'm good at helping."

"You're good at making messes out of fabric. I should ask David if he can find you a personal whatever that can choose your clothes for you so you never need to touch a wardrobe closet. Actually, I insist that you never touch one again for as long as I oversee your house staff."

Rolling her eyes, Nisha smiled. "You know you're not supposed to scold me I am a queen."

"You're right as a maid I'm not. However, you are my friend so I very well will scold you whenever you make a mess for no reason. More so when I have to be the one to clean it up."

Plopping down on the bed she pretended to be subdued for a brief moment before tartly asking, "Oh fine... so *friend* what did you make for me to wear?"

Narrowing her lilac colored eyes, Marigold hissed, "I don't think you deserve it." For a long moment, the two stared at each other till warm laughter filled both their eyes. "But I'll give it to you anyways." A whiff of white smoke and...

Jumping back to her feet Nisha took the dress and swirled around with it in joy. "It's perfect. How did you know?"

"Yes well, while we were at the Spire I asked the Seneschal what your mother wore to her party. As it turns out she had written, a journal of what she thought you would wear to your coming of age party and had list upon list of whom she wanted there. What *they* should wear. And then there was this drawing..." She handed it over to her.

"My mother drew this?" Disbelief filled her voice. *Did Aunt Celeste know about this?*

"It's not the best rendition of a dress so I took some liberties with it. I do hope you don't mind."

Now she really looked at the drawing and the dress. The same flowing black mesh on the bottom that would appear to be a fine black mist around her feet and legs. The same velvet red belt to break up the different shades of black material. Gold trim around the collar instead of the white that was pictured. A traditional black silk sash to hold the pins of her accomplishments. Tears clogged her throat, "You gave me a gift that means so much. Thank you."

Throwing her arms around her friend, Mari whispered, "Your welcome. I only met your mother once that I can remember but I think she would be happy that you chose to wear something that she suggested."

Wiping her eyes, she could only nod. "Did you find out how many p-pins I should have?"

"Both your mother and Aunt wore six. Every Queen before them only four. So, we are left with, do we announce how powerful you really are or just choose a handful?"

Lightly fingering the sash, she let the tendrils of darkness seep out around her. For a moment, she just listened to the whispers. When she opened her eyes, and turned to her friend, she squared her shoulders, "My mother made a mistake letting those around her know her powers at her party. There is no reason for me to follow that example."

"So, we choose."

"No, I'll choose."

Calling a small box Marigold sat it on the small table next to a large bed. Slowly she opened the lid. Several small pins. Some gold, others made of silver or gemstones lined the bottom. Each was made to represent a different ability and power that had been mastered. Even the most skilled usually only had a handful by their eighteenth year. Very rarely would they even master more than three or four more in the years after. Nisha had already mastered twenty and was close to mastering seven more. "My Queen."

"I need to look powerful but still uncertain of any major ability."

"Then may I suggest not wearing any that only can be mastered by those in the Under Kingdom."

"Yes. There is no reason for the citizens of Darke to know about my other kingdom. At least not until after the coronation." *Or until I discuss it with Lilly.*

Pointing at one of the crystal pins Marigold whispered, "Both your mother and father were seers; however, I don't think it wise to boast that."

"Very true." She paused, "You know I never thought of it before, but... As a seer, either my mother or father would have known about the attack. Mum, could control any fire both natural and unnatural... so how did she perish in a fire?" Another pin not to wear. The pins representing fire both natural and unnatural.

Weighing her words Marigold finally answered, "Sometimes things have two meanings. Now to me... and this just me talking for I have no proof... but... everyone said the fire *took* the queen and so many others. I have never heard anyone say that the queen was dead. Nor that any bodies were ever found."

A jolt went through her as she inhaled sharply. "Mari, you're a genius. Why didn't I think of it?" She turned then paced a few steps. "Tomorrow once Lilly arrives, we will explore the castle. I'm sure there is some clue that has been overlooked."

"In that case, I would start with the royal apartments. From what I hear, that is where the fire started. Also, it is the only room that has yet to be touch by anyone since that night."

Standing in front of a large mirror Nisha smiled as she marveled at how stunning she was looking in the dress that her mother had designed. Still, she could not hide the melancholy from her voice as she asked, "I should have an escort till I get to the main foyer." *My father should be here to escort me.*

A soft breezy cough from the door made her turn. She hadn't seen him in the mirror... but... Oh... how she had wished that she had.

He was the most handsome man that she had ever seen. Well if you got past the fact that he was completely made up of a fine mist. "My Queen." he gave a low bow and waited till she recognized him.

"Shade?"

His voice a deep timber yet a soft as the wind, "Mmm. Shade is my... what you call *race*. It is hardly my name, my dear."

Oh, my. She had been looking forward to knowing what would be different between a shade and a shadow but nothing had prepared her for this. She could see his suit was a mirror of superior quality. Could just make out the place where an embroidery would be. Then he smiled, revealing teeth so white that they appeared to be polished stones. A moment longer till she noticed the finely pointed tops that looked like razors. When he spoke, she saw more... she saw three rows of those finely sharp teeth. "You really could have had David for a snack if you wanted to."

"In my opinion, Drakens, even part Drakens, are much too bony to make a decent meal. But they do have a pleasant taste." He took what appeared to be a step into the room. "If you prefer I can remain as a shadow."

"Like Hell you are. Just look at you. Just the sight of a Shade should be enough warning.... well after tomorrow. If you don't mind." For a moment, she watched him take a few steps toward her. To an untrained eye, he was taking a full step but she saw the truth. When he stepped, the mist vanished from the leg that would be behind him and reshaped before him almost so seamlessly that she almost hadn't noticed. "That's amazing."

Shade paused, "What is?"

His voice washed over her. If he hadn't been blood bound to her she knew she would fall into a trance... knew those who did would become his next meal. Smiling brightly, she answered, "The way you move. It's truly memorizing."

"I should hope so. It makes finding my next meal that much easier."

"I have your word you will not make a meal out of any citizen unless I say otherwise."

"I have never made a meal out of house guests. However, you have my word I will not eat any offending ass unless you so wish it."

Clearly, they were both thinking of Lord Edrich. It was enough for her to smile.

Walking with Shade, she was able to see things that she hadn't noticed with Freya. Not that anything mattered right now, but things she would like to come back to and take in their rare beauty. "So, what would you like to be called? Or does Shade work?"

For a long moment, he didn't answer, "It's been too long since I have used a name."

"Do you mind me asking how long?"

"Nearly two thousand years give or take a century."

She was expecting a decade or two, not two millennia. "Oh, wow."

"Hmmm. In truth, this is not my real form. Except for the teeth."

"Will you show me?"

"Later my dear. You have much to take in tonight to be distracted by my vanity."

"You're teeth. They look like the pictures of the Serpent... man... a ...tore?"

"We have similar teeth but are hardly the same. Perhaps we should start with my name. I was once called Gwydion. My people were once called Eostre."

"Fascinating."

For a moment, Gwydion paused then very carefully asked, "Is it?"

"Oh yes. Lilly and I once debated once on the existence of the Eostre. She said they were fairy tales. I said that there had to be some truth in the tales for they were too detailed to be just made up."

"Yes, I too have heard the stories. Many leave a great deal out. Some day we will talk about the past. Not today."

Again, she looked at what he chose to wear. Very faintly she could see a ring or a shadow of a ring on his right hand. "You were a High-born."

Again, he paused. "You see more than most."

"Yes, I suppose I do."

After being bound to her nearly since birth he had already learned either answer or she would find something much more uncomfortable to talk about. Thankfully until now he had never been the one having one of those conversations. "I was once the king. The last king of my people."

True concern and sorrow filled her voice as she asked, "Oh. May I ask what happen to your people?"

"I was betrayed by someone that I trusted. Don't worry my dear that person didn't survive his betrayal. I only regret the innocent lives that were lost that day."

"Is there anything I can do? I have a really good friendship with many in the Under Kingdom."

"No, my dear. We have everything that we need." Pausing once more he turned to her. "I was here the night of the fire. I did nothing to help then. Perhaps, I could have. Though I do not know what."

"You came to me that night." She knew that a shadow had come to her that night. Her aunt only mentioned once a few years ago.

"Yes."

"You chose to bind yourself to me and to protect me. You did so with anyone asking nor for asking anything in return. So, don't blame yourself for what happen in the past. "

"You are a rare gift, my queen." He patted her hand. "There is one thing you should know. As a king, I still have many that are blood bound to me. Even in death, that binding does not fade...

not completely. They may not take orders from me or even consider me their king... but they are bound to you... completely. If you are ever in danger you have several scores of Eostre ready to protect and destroy anything or *anyone* that may threaten you. The blood lust that they now possess makes them very dangerous to those who would oppose you." He took a single step back and blended into a shadow that crept along the wall.

Nisha waited till he vanished from her sight then whispered, "Thank you Gwydion. I will remember."

For several long moments, Nisha cursed herself for choosing a room so far away from the main Foyer. At the time, it had seemed like an innovative idea…At the time she needed to be far away from the ballroom and Lord Edrich. But now…being this far away… it was beyond frustrating. For a few moments longer, she growled at herself and vowed to spell a chair to float her from one side of the castle to the other. Finally, she saw the arched doorway that would lead her to her party. If she could even call this farce or a gathering a party. After all, a party was where you would mingle with friends not sit and be glared at by people who really didn't care who you were… regardless if you are their queen or not. People who would see her dead before they allowed her to put the kingdom back to rights.

Pausing at yet another arched doorway she glanced up the grand staircase to where Ethan was standing and looking down at her... waiting. A second glance and she didn't like what she saw. She had told Lord Edrich to find Ethan proper clothing. At first, glance he had. But that had been at first glance.

Keeping her steps careful and deliberate she carefully went up the stairs. Half way up she could see the edges of another illusion spell. Taking a few more steps she froze allowing herself to really see past the spell and see the truth. Allowing herself to see the tattered jacket, the filth ridden dress shirt, and the muck covered shoes that she knew almost instantly that were, at least, a size too small. Then she looked deep into his midnight blue eyes and saw the pain that he was trying to hide. Panicked and enraged she raced up the few remaining stairs. Gasping she asked "Are you alright? What happened?" *And so, help me if Lord Edrich had anything to do with it.*

"I..." Taking a jagged breath Ethan stopped. A lie would be so easy. He had said it a thousand times though never to anyone who might help. But to lie to her? He could not stop himself from breathing, let alone tell her a lie. He just knew he could not. "I'll be fine in few days."

This has happened before and he doesn't want me to know. "Edrich did this." Not so much a question then confirmation.

He shook his head then softly whispered, "He only gave the order. His mistress took extraordinary pride in carrying out what he had told her to do."

Turning sharply, she had every intent on storming into the ballroom bringing every ounce of terrifying powers with her. Calling out to the undead and allowing them free rein in all of Darke. Hell, she could call on the lightning in the sky, or the fire raging in the hearths and take every person in that room before they ever had a thought about what was going to happen. A warm, trembling hand on her elbow was the only thing stopping her from doing so. Very calmly she spoke in deathly calm voice. A voice that would terrify anyone within her family and with good reason. "Ethan, let go."

In truth, he almost did but something deep inside himself kept him from doing so. "I thank you for your concern, Princess. But it is unnecessary."

Unnecessary? Like hell it was. And Edrich, as well as the rest of Darke, would learn that fast. But perhaps not tonight. Perhaps tonight she would just yield to Ethan's request then once he was tucked in somewhere safe… then… and only then she would take care of those who had dared harm him. "Fine. I won't cause a scene over your appearance. At least not tonight." Now she faced him. She could see the fear in his eyes. Not afraid of her, she decided, but of what she would do. The two were completely different. "However, you are no longer under your uncle's control. You are a member of my house. If he or anyone else has a problem with that I will be more than happy to discuss it with them."

"But.... but..."

Making sure her voice had all the authority that a queen should have, she very calmly said, "This is not up to debate, Ethan. This is mine to do. And it is something that I should have done before we left the Spire."

With nothing else to say, he bowed his head. Relief written on his face as clear as day. "Thank you."

She had come dressed so not to boast her abilities. Hadn't really decided on sharing anything with Ethan until after the wedding... but... slowly she touched his mind with hers. It was dangerous if one didn't know what they were doing. Even then... very few choose to use it. Even less used it to communicate rather than control the person that they had linked with. Knowing this she allowed herself a moment to acknowledge his fear of what she was doing. Knew he was expecting a fate much worse than the beating he had already received. *Ethan*

It only took him a breath to respond. This was something that should have taken him much longer unless he too processed this rare ability. *Pr-princess?*

You have no reason to fear me.

Not really understand what was happening or how to control it Ethan's mind went back to everything that he had been told. Back to every bit of torture that he had lived through. His mind retraced every ounce of pain that he had been forced to endure. His mind raced with images, memories of being set on fire... nearly drowned... times when his uncle and others had tried to bleed him dry. With every image, her rage sharpened until she was ready to burst.

Now she understood the fear. Later she would deal with those who had harmed him. And much... much later she would allow her betrothed to truly understand this link that she was creating for him. But not today... Very softly, she placed her long narrow finger under his chin, "Ethan?"

All he did was swallow once.

Barely above a whisper she softly spoke, "Will you be alright for a few moments in that room?" Indicating the double door that they were standing in front of. If he said no she wouldn't hesitate to take him somewhere safe then destroy every person in that room.

Hell, even if he said yes, she still might.

Swallowing hard he forced out, "Yes."

His fear was eating at her but she had to make sure whatever she did, that she didn't make that fear worse. Some way, somehow, she had to make sure that he knew that he was safe with her. "You have my word we will only stay long enough to make some small disturbance then we will see what needs mending tonight and what can wait till my cousin arrives."

Once again, he grabbed her arm. This time in earnest, "Don't eat anything. You can't trust the food. *Never* trust what you haven't seen made yourself. I know for a fact some of the dishes are poisoned and others... poison would be too kind."

Now she let a smile start to curl her lips. "My darling I didn't have any intention to eat anything that my personal cook hasn't made with her own two hands. But I thank you for your concern." No use telling him that poison wouldn't do her harm at least not since she became the Queen of the Under Kingdom. Nor was there any use telling him that other additives would have very little to no effect on her... and that had been since birth. No, it would be no use... not when he wouldn't be able to understand.

"And..." Ethan took a deep breath then slowly let it out, "The serpent prince is here. He has already killed at least three of his siblings. He is currently third in line to the throne. Please be careful he is very dangerous. More so than any other from his kingdom. That is unless you count his father."

Well, she would just have to see about that. A moment to ponder what she would do with the offending prince. Then a thought that eased her temper... she wondered if her uncle liked the taste of serpent.

When the doors open to the ballroom Nisha held her breath. The room was much larger than she had assumed. Three stories high. Each floor open in the center to the room below. And each floor having huge stone pillars to hold the floor above it and some kind of spell so the people could appear to be dancing in the air yet still allowing a view of the main floor. Later she would explore each of the other floors but tonight...

She took Ethan's arm. It wasn't until he took a sharp breath from pain she touched his mind, *Sorry.*

He didn't respond only fixed his eyes on the long table that sat on the long platform that sat more than three steps higher than the main floor. Chaining his fear, Ethan forced himself to remain completely passive.

Being linked, she could see where he was looking but she still allowed herself to follow his gaze even though she really didn't need to. Lord Edrich was speaking to a tall thin man who even from this distance she could see the scales on the back of his neck despite the illusion spell. "Does anyone not wear a glamor spell?" Every citizen that had been standing on the steps must have heard her question since they took one look at her and scurried away before Ethan could answer.

"No." He paused and lowered his voice as he said, "Everyone is convinced that no one can see past them. Of course, anyone who says anything about them is punished."

`"I see. Well, it looks like my little disturbance will be a bit more entertaining once I break them."

"Break? Oh, please be careful, Princess there are very dangerous people in this room and every one of them is a killer."

Slowly so not to make Ethan move faster than he was comfortable with, they made their way through a sea of people. None of the crowd bowed their heads or showed a single bit of the respect that they should have. That too could wait until morning. After all, she had already figured out what she needed help with. Of course, her ruse of only wearing five of her pins did seem to be working since she could hear several people whispering on how weak she was or that her mother was twice as gifted. Although the comments of how easily it would be to kill her did not go unnoticed.

Let them think what they will. Nisha stopped just out of arms reach from the man who would be her first part of the little disturbance, "Lord Edrich." Her voice both bored and annoyed.

Nothing that hinted to her true feelings were revealed in those two simple words.

It wasn't Lord Edrich she greeted her but the prince turned, "Ah, Princessss it issss good to meet you."

A good glamor could hide a lot but even the best couldn't hide a forked tongue. "Prince Ciron I presume."

His smile was anything but charming. "I wasss not aware that you knew that I wass in attendance."

Moving past him, Nisha replied, "How foolish of you to think that I had not been informed. However," She turned back to him after stepping onto the platform. "I do believe that my mother forbade all of your kinsmen from Darke, so I am curious on how you are here?"

The crowd was drawing around to listen and watch this little drama. None seemed to think that she, the princess, would be the victor. Seeing this she felt Ethan call out to her and heard the warning in his voice. *Princess.*

Trust me.

Ciron waved off her question with great gusto. "Oh, the counssel resscinded that ssome time ago."

"I see. In that case, I would like a copy of the treaty presented to me by morning. In the meantime, we can sit and enjoy the festivities." She paused. It was customary for the head of the royal family to sit in the center. His or her spouse to the right and the heir to the left. Since her mother and father were gone... She took her mother's place and patted the seat to her right, "Ethan please join me."

"Princess, your seat..."

Very calmly she sat straighter. "Lord Edrich, As I have already explained to you, as I am eighteen you are no longer the proxy and have no function in this room or at my table. You, sir, are excused."

Edrich snapped, "You are not crowned yet my dear."

"Very true, however, my aunt will be here on the morrow and will oversee anything that needs to be taken care of until the coronation."

Prince Ciron leaned across the table and looked deep into her eyes. "I think that would be unwisse."

Anyone else would have fallen prey to that deadly stare, she, however, let out a bored yawn. A feather light touch wrapped around her ankle. Her dear shadow friend or possibly one that was still bound to him, way she was more than safe. "Shadow my friend please ask Freya escort Prince Ciron to the dungeon until I can properly deal with him." Then to the prince, who looked confused that she was unaffected by his trance. "I do not take lightly to people trying to use force to force me into doing something that I otherwise would not."

A fine mist climbed the chair to her left and a dark shape began to form. Not her dear friend but another shade. This one female. Long feathery hair and sharp claws for fingers, "Your guard is on her way. Is there any assistance that I can offer?" She sat back and steepled her fingers making sure her eyes now locked with the serpent. No doubt sizing up her next meal.

The room filled with a collective gasp. Neither Shades nor Shadows come this far north. In fact, most stayed in the ruins of bones. If not in the Mystic Woods themselves. But never near the castle. The sight of one warranted caution. The fact that it... she... was offering assistance to the princess... was a cause of great concern. More so if the little princess could actually control it.

"You... you sshould be..." Ciron stuttered as he tried to back away from the platform.

"I am not easily fooled Ciron." Standing up she raised her voice so everyone on all the floors was sure to hear. "All those who are citizens of the

Marshlands are to be out of Darke by morning. Anyone who does not heed my warning will be dead by tomorrow night. Those of you with illusion spells of any kind, I tell you this, they do not work on those of the royal house of Devros. Hiding behind them will no longer suit you and therefore they are now banned at the castle doors. Any who dare cross the thresh-hold wearing one will be given to the Shades that now stalk these halls. You are now all dismissed." When no one moved she added, "My dear friend Shade, please do as you wish to those in this room. Ethan, with me." A door that had been hidden behind her opened with Freya in its doorway looking anything but pleased.

Once in another hall, the door shut behind them and Ethan gasped, "A shade?"

"Oh, well I'm not sure what her name but I am friends with a great deal of them. They are truly interesting people." *Well, at least, the king was anyhow.* In time, she may be able to learn more about the shades. No, she would learn more about them. Survival demanded that she did.

Chapter 17: Adrianna

Adrianna paced the confines of her prison. Not that it looked like a prison, but some fine suite for a divine guess... well, if you got past the glass dome that had been hexed so none of her spells or abilities worked. And the fact that the dome was inside of a stone room with no windows to see even a hint of daylight just made the time spent here maddening. She took a deep breath and made another circle around the sitting area, another circle around the pastel blue couch with gold trim. Then another around the oblong room. A path that she had done sometimes for days on end. And other times just to move. But today her pacing was from nervous energy. Dae had found a way out a few days ago. A way to escape. Of course, she had to turn into a mouse to find the small hole... but she had found it. Even it had taken her eighteen years... She had finally found it. So, for now, all she had to do was wait and hope that Dae had found help... or at the very least had not been caught.

The again there was no guarantee that Dae could change back into a useful form once she had cleared the dome or the room where they were held in. Her heart stopped when the stone door that led beyond the spelled dome opened and her captor peered in. As always, he was draped in a dark green robe that hid most of his scales and his legs that seemed to belong to a chicken rather than a reptile. Just the sight of him had words burning her throat but only allowed herself to say, "Apep."

"My dear, where isssss your maid?"

A thousand things ran through her mind... then from the bedroom, she heard, "Tell the bastard snake he just interrupted a wonderful dream." Turning slightly, she watched as her friend shuffled out of the room her dull golden red hair in such a mess it was hard not to know that it hadn't been caused by sleep.

Taking her cue from her friend she snapped, "Well you see her with your own eyes. Now *why* are you here? Come to gloat once more? Oh, *I* know, you've come to see if I decided to marry you." She turned away from him and spat, "Like I would ever, *ever* be with someone who just looking at makes me sick." Not to mention she was already married. It didn't matter if her husband were alive or not... she was bound to him... her heart was his. As it would always be even in death. Just as his belonged to her.

His yellow eyes narrowed in a fit of anger. "I come to sssshare newssss. Sssssoon my sssssson will be wed to your girl. Sssso naive, that one. Ssssso ripe for the taking."

Taking a deep breath, she turned back toward him. It would do no use to argue with him. No use to curse nor swear things that she no longer had the power to do. At least not until she was free of this damned forsaken prison. "You forget *Apep*. My mother and sister raised *my* girl." Then she turned from him no longer able to hide all of the emotions that she was feeling. Her heart longed to see her daughter. More so now that she acknowledged who had raised her darling little girl, then all the years that she had to spend trapped in this prison.

"I know. My sssspyss have watched for many yearsssss. No, my dear, I know all that I need to."

Damn irritating snake, he didn't have to sound so smug. In a distance, she could hear the stone door slam behind him. Once more she was alone... or mostly alone. Adrianna snapped at the only person that she left to yell at. "Dae, I told you to leave."

Stepping completely out of the bedroom Dae stepped but a few feet from her queen and friend. "Addy really. I have not left in all these years I will not leave you now." Going over to the mirror that was hung above the hearth, she shook her head. "I will be so glad when we are free of this place. This place is horrible for my skin. And not to mention my hair."

"Free? Did you..." Hope warmed her voice in a way that few things rarely did anymore.

"I know where we are. But right now, that is not important."

"Faerydae?" Both a question and a command to tell her everything.

"Several things I must tell you, but first. Some good news. First off Apep is a liar and should not be trusted."

She knew that. Hell, she knew that before being held captive. Which was why she had banned all of his kind from Darke. Not that she had told anyone about her suspicions; oh no she had used some other information that she had found... or more to the point that her dear husband had found. But that wasn't important today. No, what was important was whatever Dae had found out. Padding over to the couch she patted the seat next to her. Asking her friend anything never yielded answers. But she was a Fey. Their news was told in their own time and in their own way. Never directly, and never when asked outright. So, she instead opted to ask, "Are you certain the bastard cannot hear us?"

Faerydae brought herself to her full height and hissed in annoyance, "Am I or am I not a third generation Feyen?"

She knew her friend and she was not asking about where she was born but her bloodlines. There were several kinds of Fey. Fairies and Elves being the most common of Feyen. But, true Feyen were those who were those with one parent a Fairy and the other an Elf. And not just a Fey of minor abilities but ones that were stronger than most. In Faerydae's case, her grandparents on both sides had been Feyen. Both her parents were senior members of the Feyen council and very difficult people. Over the years, she had long thought about the reasons that they hadn't paid ransom to have their daughter return... the reason they thought her as dead. "I'm sorry. I may be the queen here but right now you are the one with the power."

"Very true. Even if it has taken years for me to adjust to this cursed place. But happy news first. Our dear husbands are not dead, as the bastard has suggested. However, I do not think that have access to their abilities at this time."

"If they are alive, being cut off from their powers would be the only way one or both haven't found us." It also meant they were in greater trouble and unable to defend themselves.

"Yes, well... I can safely say that if they get access we are going to have two very pissed off Feyen Men who are..."

"Hard to control even when not pissed off about something?" Remembering the last person to piss her husband off gave her a shiver. Luckily, she had never truly known the current Feyen queen nor did she wish to after seeing what had happened.

"Yes well. Your husband is known to be lethal on a good day whereas mine is better known for being a pain in my ass... even *if* he was always right."

After a moment of remembering their lives before the uprising, Adrianna finally asked, "May I ask how you found out?"

Now Dae smiled. Such a demented smile for a Fey to have it was almost scary. Then she held out her hand. Two simple gold rings. "Do you remember the spell I cast before your wedding?"

Slowly she nodded, "I do."

"For as long as both draw breath both are bound in life and death. Set in stone wearer be known." When Adrianna didn't take the ring, she grabbed her hand and shoved it on her finger. "Really, Addy you should pay more attention to my words. You have to wear the ring to understand."

Closing her eyes, she let herself feel. For a minute, she didn't feel anything then a light hum. A soft pulse. A heartbeat beating in time with her own but not her own. "Myrddin." Her eyes opened in shock "*Myrddin?*"

"As I said... alive. But something is wrong. I felt it when I found my Galeron. I do not know what it means... yet. But they are alive."

Happy tears clogged her throat. "Then there is hope."

Dae sat up straighter and smiled a real genuine smile of the purest joy. "Oh, my dear friend we have more than hope for I know one more thing for certain."

"Are you going to tell me, or should I guess?"

"You are a terrible guesser without your whispers, so I shall tell you. The princess has found my Ethan."

Excitement overpowered her better judgment as she flung her arms around her friend. "Then we do have more than hope."

Then her smile faded. "Yes, but our children will be needed to free us."

That didn't sound like hope. That sounded like giving up. That sounded like they would be here forever. "What are you not telling me?"

"We are in the Mystic Woods. Learned powers do not work here only natural ones. But worse, we are caged in the once home of Eostre. I fear that the only thing keeping us alive now is our captors. And worse yet, I think this was one of the landing sites for the first Fey. A place to drain their powers into the land."

Shit. The Mystic Woods have been forbidden for nearly a Millennia. No more than that...Nearly two. It had been that way since the great war and those who claimed the woods threatened to destroy any who dared to enter. So how or why did the snakes have permission to be here? Were they now somehow working together? Or had the serpents became so powerful that those who lived here now lived in fear of them. "You can't escape, can you?"

Giving Addy an annoyed glance, Dae hissed, "I will not leave you behind, my dear friend."

Desperation filled her voice. One of them had to be free of this place. One of them had to warn the children. "Dae that is not what I asked you. If I ordered you..."

She placed a finger on her queen's lips. "Our escape will happen when it happens not when you decide."

Of course. Why would she ever think Dae would listen to reason? "Then for tonight, we speak no more about our blight only on the hope that our husbands are alive."

"Yes, and the hope that your girl has more natural ability than her mother."

M.L.Ruscsak

Chapter 18:
Ethan

The moment that the gray stone wall sealed Ethan grabbed for the wall to keep from falling. He could feel the warm sticky liquid that was filling his shoes and knew that there was no way he would be walking much further. Actually, if the buzzing in his head didn't stop he wouldn't be conscious long enough to try. This had been his uncle's plan. Not only make him look weak but make sure he couldn't do anything to earn his keep. Couldn't do anything that the princess would find useful.

If it didn't hurt so much then he would laugh to himself. Laugh because useful or not he was already a part of the princess' house. There was nothing Edrich could do to him now to change that. However, just because he was a part of her house didn't mean he could go without earning his keep. She didn't seem as cruel as other high-born so maybe just maybe she would let him start earning his keep after the bleeding stopped. One way to find out. "Princess."

He saw her spin toward him but didn't see her take the handful of steps that brought her back to his side. "Damn it, Ethan, why didn't you tell me you couldn't walk? We would have never went into that farce of a party."

"I..." He tried to take a normal breath and was barely able to do so without crying from the way his ribs moved beneath the skin. Giving himself a moment to steady himself then he softly spoke. "...I thought I could."

"Fine, I won't scold you for lying to me; however, you will not do so again."

What? Scold... Yell? If he would have grabbed a wall within his uncle's view he would be beaten till he passed out. Then kicked for passing out. Yelling didn't sound like punishment but then again, he didn't want to press the subject either. "You have my word."

"Good." Nisha paused for a moment then sighed. "If I help you to the ground will you be alright for a moment?"

"I... I think so."

Black mist flowed around him as he was gently helped to the ground. "Now I'm going to find a chair, I will try not to go and take too long but I have not been to this side of the castle yet."

"Thank you, but..."

Kneeling down in front of him she placed her finger under chin once more, "Ethan, you're injured and are in no condition to be moving around. Now I can sit here and debate me going to find a chair that I can use to get you to where I want you to be for the night. Or you can just debate it with yourself since that will no doubt save time on both our parts."

He thought about protesting but decided against it. After all, when had he ever successfully argued for anything and won more than the punishment that followed? "Thank you, princess."

"Oh, that was another thing. My name is Nisha. You may call me by that. Formal titles are so boring. I do so detest those in my house using them just for causal conversation."

For a moment, he watched as she got to her feet then closed his eyes, "There should be a parlor not far from here. The furniture isn't the best but it should suit for whatever you have in mind." Maybe he should tell her he used to sneak into the palace to hide from his uncle. Maybe he should tell her where the most interesting rooms were. Maybe... no, he would tell her just as soon as he could take a normal breath.

"See now, wasn't that easier than arguing?"

Chapter 19:

Nisha

Nisha waited until she was out of Ethan's sight before saying, "Gwydion?" The mist swirled around her almost playfully before forming into her friend.

"My Queen?"

Looking straight ahead , Nisha narrowed her eyes. "Please walk with me, I do not trust those who lurk in the halls."

"Very well. Two of my people will keep watch over the boy... Ethan."

She paused. "You have been watching?"

He didn't turn to her but locked his eyes on something far away. "As a shade, I can watch several things at once. Such as the parlor that is just up ahead. And the snake prince that is in the palace."

"One day I would like to know more about your abilities of both before the Great War and now. Somehow, I think most of what is known is nothing more than speculation or of little truth."

"As you wish but I do suggest waiting till after the coronation. You will have much more time to talk then. For there is much that has never been told outside of the woods. More that has not been whispered since the Great War."

She nodded once in agreement. Pausing at the entrance of the door she asked, "Is the snake prince placed somewhere where he cannot escape?"

"The serpent prince values his life too much to try. I have requested a garrison of your best fighters to defend this palace. Freya has agreed that there is more danger her then she had anticipated."

Nisha stumbled a step gaping at her friend. Freya rarely agreed to anything that wasn't her own idea first. Hearing this she couldn't believe it. "The two of you...spoke and she actually agreed?"

Gwydion looked puzzled at her tone but answered in a tone that was more matter-of-fact than casual, "You are much too busy at the moment to consider all of those who wish to harm you. However, both Freya and I are free to indulge in their game." He paused and decided to share a bit more about not only himself but about Freya as well. "Besides I have known the Lady Freya since well before her death. And that was many years before the war."

Choosing not to say anything about the admission about how long both of her trusted friends knew one another she allowed herself to think about more constructive thoughts. Ones about how she might set up her own court. I wonder if I could make a shade my captain of the guards? Or have him on my council? Then again it is my council and I choose who serves on it. But that was a thought for another day. Today however they did have something to discuss. "I see. Then thank you, but please in the future consult me before bringing several scores of citizens here that are not ... how to say this politely... fully alive back into Night. I have yet to decide on how I will serve both of kingdoms, but I doubt allowing those of the Under Kingdom to roam freely would sit well with the citizens of Darke."

"Of course, however, you did declare that those who belong to the snake kingdom leave this Darke by morning or be dead by tomorrow at nightfall. Did you not?"

She was being baited… she could feel it, "Yes..."

"Who do you expect to carry out that order? Those are among the living and are waiting for you to fail. Or those who belong to the Under Kingdom and know you will not?"

She closed her eyes, "Damn, you really have been paying far more attention to this place than I have."

"Being what I am for as long as I have does have its advantages, my dear."

Rolling her eyes, she took a single step into the parlor and stopped short. Ethan had said the furniture wasn't the best but she had hoped it would look half way decent. However, the overstuffed chair with the high back looked like it wouldn't fall apart if she placed a float spell on it.

A few steps closer to inspect it and two yellow eyes stared back at her. "Oh wow. I didn't know that there were those that could turn into furniture." She said in complete awe.

Staying in the doorway Gwydion arched his back seeing the creature that had caught the attention of his little queen. "I doubt the creature did so on its own."

"You mean..."

Slowly Gwydion stepped into the room. "Some years ago, several creatures, do forgive me it has been too long to remember what they had been." It was a lie, but it wasn't his place to reveal the truth.

"Just tell me what you know... There has to be a book or something around her that can tell me the rest."

He gave a nod of understanding then continued, "They were turned into what is commonly called a Fury. The creatures are placed in communal areas where unimportant or troublesome guess can wait. One will approach the Fury seeing that it is the only seat that looks inviting... and will be its next meal. However, most can live years, even a handful of decades without needing a meal."

"How fascinating." Coming closer to the chair... Fury... she knelt down in front of it. Her fingers caressing its arm. "You will not eat those who sit on you. In exchange, I will try to reverse the spell as soon as I find the correct one that was used on you."

The two yellow eyes blinked with understanding. Or at least, she thought it was understanding. "See, that was simple. Now for my float spell..." A whiff of black smoke and the chair was lifted just a breath off the ground. "Splendid. Now to get Ethan and find.... somewhere..."

Gwydion looked over his shoulder nodding to a gray mist hovering near the door. "Your house elf has found a suitable room on this side of the castle. No doubt quicker to reach than the other."

Chapter 20: Ethan

Ethan closed his eyes as Nisha disappeared down the hall. It hurt to breathe but not doing so was not an option. Trying to concentrate on something... anything he let his mind wonder to the fragment of a memory that he had remembered this morning. He wasn't sure how but he knew Nisha had triggered it... he only hoped he could remember it enough now.

Slowly the woman's face came into view. High cheek bones. Thin nose. blood red lips. Was that the natural color or had she done something to make them appear that way? Not something he would ever truly be able to find out. Not with her dead...

Taking a slow jagged breath, he focused in on her fire red hair and delicately pointed ears. His had been like that once... until his uncle decided that mutilating them would better suit his purpose. He could, even now, still feel the dull knife carving into his flesh. Could hear the screams that had escaped his lips on that day, and the tears that had ran hot down his face while he was bound and forced to endure the pain. Forced to watch through the mirror that had been stood before him. Ethan tried to shake off the memory. Best not to think about that now. No... he just wanted to think of her... his mother and his only memory of her.

A small smile twitched on his lips as he saw her eyes. The same color as his... well almost... hers had what looked like glitter sparkling in them where his were a solid color. Or at least, he thought they were.

"Ethan?"

That breezy voice he knew. Soft like the summer wind.

A soft touch on his face. "Ethan." The feel of pure velvet upon his skin.

Slowly he opened his eyes to the female voice... to the princess. "I'm sorry... I..." Her finger pressed against his lips to keep him from speaking.

"I found a chair. And my friend found a suitable room not far from here."

Chair? Room? His mind was to muddled to really comprehend what she was telling him. Yes, that must be the answer since he was sure that the man who was now helping him into the chair had not been there a moment before. Or why the chair seemed to be purring. Yes, that had to be the reason.

Then again, the man disappeared into mist. A shade? A shade had just helped him into a chair that purred? Yes, he had to be dying since nothing was making any sense. Or perhaps this was how those worthy of the Under Kingdom had been taken… in a chair that purred escorted by a shade. Too bad he couldn't keep his eyes open long enough to find out.

M.L.Ruscsak

Chapter 21:
Lilly and David

Lilly sat on her overly soft bed intensely reading over the laws of Darke. Laws that she was sure her dear cousin had never laid eyes on. Books upon books that she knew Nisha would never look at unless someone made her read them. With a deep sigh, she resigned herself to being the one who got her cousin to read these books.

Flipping yet another page she let her fingers danced through David's soft stone-gray fur. Of course, if he wasn't in cat form she would be debating the laws of her cousin's kingdom with him instead of lazily petting him. Which she would prefer to making mental notes of what laws needed to be tossed out the window and which ones needed to be adjusted to make better sense. Not that she found many that should be kept but she was keeping track of them anyhow.

A soft knock on the pale colored door made her look up from her current volume, "You may enter."

The door opened just enough for a footman from the Spire to peer into the room. His dark blue suit was enough to know which side of the Spire that he had come from. The ember skin ... well, she would worry as to why a fire-walker had chosen to become a footman later.

When he didn't speak, she did, "You have a message for me?" It came out more snappish than she normally would have spoken but something about his posture mixed with all that she had been reading .... had her on edge... now if she could only find a reason. One that wouldn't end with the messenger being killed.

"Princess Nisha requests your immediate presence."

The way his voice sounded like fire crackling in the hearth bothered her... but it was the way that he looked like he was ready for an attack that made her arch her back. A movement that made her betrothed stretch out his cat paws and change back into his true form. Fear resonated in the footman's eyes as he watched her David. It was enough to be no longer fearful of this person so she regained her composure. "And did my dear cousin say why she needed me to come before her coronation?"

His eyes never left the Draken that was now sizing up his next meal. "I-I was not told."

David yawned allowing his long scaly tail to flick in warning, "Since you have no other instructions you may leave."

"I..."

Leaning forward David smiled revealing his razor-sharp teeth. "Leave or be dinner. Let me assure you fire-walkers do have a delightful taste." He turned to Lilly and continued, "Do you think Nisha will have one on the menu for the banquet?"

Smiling oh so sweetly she answered, "If you ask I'm sure she would be delighted to find one that Darke could do without... after all your father has already requested several different delicacies for himself." If it were true or not didn't matter. Making the footman believe she was telling the truth ... well... that was an entirely different story.

Neither paid much attention to the fire-walker as he fled from their room and down the long hallway. Still, Lilly made sure to wait a few moments to make sure that he had truly left before getting up and closing the door. "Do you think something is wrong... I mean with Nisha... I know something was wrong with the footman."

Laying back on the large soft bed David stared up at the pale pink canopy, "If something was truly wrong, Freya would have come herself... or sent one of our dear cousin's other *friends*. That said I do not think it wise to leave her alone too long. Father would hate to have to find another... um... *person?*... that would be willing to clip his toenails."

Pulling her long golden hair back into a loose ponytail, she asked, "Why is it that your mother refuses to... she said once but I didn't speak the Feyen language then."

"Apparently she doesn't care to find out *who or what* is left in his nails since father tends to boast after hunting. It is also why he no longer hunts as often as he wishes." For a moment, he closed his lava red eyes, "I was just thinking..."

"Oh, don't do that... every time you do mama doesn't know rather to laugh, cry or send you back to your family. And frankly neither do I."

"Funny, very funny." He waited until she was close enough then wrapped his tail around her pinning her to the bed. A breath later, he was using his body to hold her against her own bed. "I think I still need to work on your defensive skills."

"You really think that I can't get away from you if I really wanted to?" Her smile was not comforting.

"You wouldn't dare.... not if you wish to ever become a mother."

Softly she brought her hand up and caressed his long-curved horns knowing he would move rather than indulge in what the caress would lead to if they were already married. The moment he was standing and growling she smiled. "See, I don't need any more defensive training. Now, what were you thinking that would indubitably get both of us in trouble?"

"Just so you know that won't work once we marry."

She shrugged, "I'll think of something when that time comes... besides you are only half Draken."

For a minute, he paced around her room. One day he would sleep in a room that wasn't all bright and golden. One day he would have a bed that he didn't sink into... somehow, he didn't think he would be alive when that day came. "Are you ready to hear what I was thinking or should I turn back into a cat and continue being petted?"

Already rummaging through her wardrobe closet Lilly smiled, "Oh go on. You can talk while I pack."

"If you pack your ladies will glare at you."

"If we're not here, then they can't," Lilly retorted.

It was no use to argue with her... not when he couldn't win anyway... not when he really didn't care what they were arguing about to start with. "Do you know the story of how my mother and father met?"

"Mum said Uncle Myrddin had something to do with it but since even mentioning his name made her think of her sister I never asked for all of the details. And you know I would never ask your mother."

Slowly he made his way over to the window and looked over her garden. Even from three stories up, he could see the tiniest of the fairies tending to the flowers. He knew most saw them as bees or butterflies... only someone who understood garden fairies would be able to see their true form... only someone who was of Feyen blood would be able to speak to them... right now that didn't matter. "Myrddin is... *was* my mother's brother."

"What?!?" Lilly jumped back from her wardrobe closet. "And you're just now telling me!"

"Mother didn't want you to know before Nisha was ready to rule."

He hadn't turned to her and his refusal to meet her face on... oh yes, he was hiding something, "Davkren look at me."

If she was using his real name then he was in trouble. He sighed to himself. At least she wasn't using his full name or he would need to be a cat just to keep out of sight. "I need to tell you something and I do not want you to overreact."

Shit. This could not be good. Not good at all. "Should you wait till Nisha is close by to hear it as well?"

Now he did turn to her. In ten years, he had never felt so nervous, "No. I think... I want you to know first then if you think it's okay then we will tell her. Who knows what she will do with the information."

Placing her hand on her hip Lilly snorted, "You know what she will do... She will get that look in her eyes... you know the one that says we're going to be in trouble. Then she'll smile. Not her friendly smile but that terrifying one that says you're going to be yelled at... then she'll say I have a wonderful idea. Then we will be the ones in trouble I just don't know with who."

"Yes, that's what I'm afraid of." That and what Nisha would do after she was alone with the information... alone with no one to stop her from doing something so unbelievable that it would take years to understand the full consequence of that decision.

"So why don't you tell me on the way to see her. Then if she must know we can tell her in her castle and away from both of our parents."

David paused long enough to take in the time before hesitantly adding, "If we leave now we will be there before morning."

Taking his face between her hands, she smiled, "Darling, if we leave now we will be there well before dawn."

Carefully seated in her private coach Lilly sweetly asked, "Ok, since it will be a few hours before we reach the Spire, what is it that I need to hear and decide if our cousin must know it?"

David took a deep breath. "Alright. Please let me finish before you interrupt." When she nodded, he started again, "Some hundred years ago, maybe longer since mum is very close-lipped on her actual age. My mother was known by a different name… I think it was Tenanye. Anyways, she served as an apprentice in the Feyen queen's court. The queen's name I think was Elista. Around that time, her brother came back from the Mystic Woods. Mum never said why he was there but he came back knowing the dark arts among other things. He told her that he had arranged her marriage. Being the oldest and both their parents I *assume* no longer alive, it was his right although she was not very happy with him since she was so young."

Lilly raised her hand slightly to interrupt even though she has promised not to, "Older than eighteen but younger than two centuries?"

Rolling his lava red eyes David continued, "Something like that. According to mother, her brute of a brother dragged her to the border for Darken and plopped her down on a rotted tree stump. I'm sure she exaggerated a bit but I have no one else to ask. And father only says he should have eaten Myrddin many times for introducing him to my mother."

"Your father tells everyone he should eat them. It's high praise I think."

"Of course, it is. After all, Father never tells his meals *if* he should eat them... he just does."

A playful slap on his arm and Lilly hissed, "I do not really want to know your families eating habits. It's bad enough your brother devoured that troll in front of me."

David narrowed his eyes and shrugged. "It attacked you. What else would you have my brother do? Let it kill a visiting princess?"

"Well no. But he didn't have to eat it in front of me. I'm sure killing it would have done the same thing."

"Lilly my sweet. One must never waste food. Especially trolls. They so seldom cross into Draken."

Lilly blinked not really caring when trolls crossed into Draken as long as she didn't have to deal with the nasty beasts. "We will discuss trolls later. Please continue your story."

"Fine. Myrddin was to marry princess Larna. Something happened to her family. Mother won't give any detail on whatever it was that had happened. But the day of the wedding Larna declared as her first act as the queen that she was declaring any child that Myrddin sired be named the heir to the Feyen crown."

She reached her hand to David's arm. "Any? She was Fey... she wouldn't have..."

"She was barely two hundred years old. Still a child and not trained in word play. Mother trained all of her children to in wordplay since birth because of it."

Lilly's mint green eyes widened, "That means..."

"Nisha is crown princess of Feyen. But that is not the worst of it."

With a groan, Lilly asked, "What can be worst then ..."

"The wedding vows that Larna took said as in tradition that she gives her heart to Myrddin. He literately took her beating heart from her chest and locked it away in a spelled box. Only he or his children can hold the heart to give back to Larna. Unless she found someone else that could hold it. Or at least that is the assumption that mum is choosing to live by."

"I don't want to hear this."

Exactly the response that he had thought that Lilly would have. And the reason that he wanted her to know before saying anything to Nisha. "Larna's grandmother has ruled unofficially since then. Twenty years ago, a man came to

Feyen. He took an interest in Larna. Now mind you she was... is ... mostly a shell. She eats, gets dressed, acts accordingly for a puppet, but has no emotions. From what I learned, she hasn't spoken a word since that day."

That figured since every spell that she knew of that involved a person's heart left the person either dead or near dead. Somehow, she didn't think Nisha's father used any of those spells. Lilly didn't want to ask but she did anyhow. "What does that have to do with Nisha?"

"Two years later he was expelled from Feyen and ordered never to return. He fled to Darke. Mother thinks it was Faerydae's relative. Or at least, he said he was. But a few *days* after fleeing to Darke... the fire happened. Now it could be just a coincidence but..." He shrugged, "I was thinking..."

Lilly leaned back in her seat and moaned, "I really wish you hadn't... but what are you thinking?"

"What if he ... assuming it's the same guy... he found out who was betrothed to the crown princess and wanted to use her to rule both Darke and Feyen."

"Then he's twice the fool. Damn it, David, did you forget what Nisha did the first time we visited your home? We were barely five when those trolls attacked. Your brother, who was already twenty, ate the first one but Nisha shredded the other four into pieces with nothing more than a look. *A look*. I remember how terrifying she was after that. She turned her head and her eyes... I didn't recognize anything that resembled my cousin in her face."

"Lilly..."

"No, you came after. Your brother took the credit for defending us because he was protecting her. The next time when we came... and your people tried to attack Nisha...."

"Lilly, I was there then. I know. And it was the reason I have not left your side." For a heartbeat, he paused then told her the truth that he had been keeping for more years than not. "They were not there to attack Nisha they were there to kill you."

"Me? But... why? I have no problems with your people. In fact, I find most very interesting."

"You are your mother's only child. Some think if you were not alive then Nisha could rule all the Feyen lands. "

With eyes wide, Lilly gasped, "We have to tell her."

David took her hands making sure he had her full attention before saying, "I know."

"David, you don't understand. Nisha is the queen of the Under Kingdom. If someone tries to use her to rule ..."

With a gasp, David was barely able to whisper, "They will unleash..."

"Those who no longer can die... that includes races that no longer exists that are far deadlier than Drakens. Nisha has already hinted that they are very protective of her."

Sitting back in his seat, David closed his eyes. "Then I pray we are not too late."

Chapter 22: Nisha

With the chair following her Nisha stopped just a few feet from where she had left Ethan. His eyes were tightly closed now... and his breathing...She had heard trolls with infections of the lungs that sounded better than he did. For a Fey... or even part Fey to sound like that... her heart leaped into her throat. "Damn it."

"Such language for a young queen."

"Not now, Gwydion, I have to get his bleeding to stop. Or at least enough that Lilly will think I have some skill in healing."

Taking the two steps over to Ethan, Gwydion smiled. "My dear there is nothing you can do to make him worse."

She turned her head sharply to face him. "You know what is keeping him alive?"

"Aye, I do. Though there are very few who are alive that know this incantation. Even fewer that could complete it without leaving a fingerprint as it were to their identity."

Too worried to care what she was saying or to whom, Nisha snapped, "Oh good. We can discuss the possible people after I get him settled for the night."

"As you wish my queen, However..."

"However nothing. I want him comfortable *before* Lilly arrives." Turning her attention back to Ethan she called out to him softly, "Ethan?"

When he only gave a slight moan, she let a soft tendril of mist caress his face. "Ethan."

Slowly he opened his eyes to her soft voice... "I'm sorry... I..." Her finger pressed against his lips to keep him from speaking.

"We'll have you settled for the night fairly soon. You have my word."

After passing three arched corridors and a dozen rooms, Nisha let out a frustrated growl. "Isn't there any bedroom close to the main hall?"

Holding back a laugh, Gwydion softly said as he turned yet another corner, "This way my queen."

Two hallways later she used a gust of wind to blow open the bedroom door. "Mari."

Marigold rushed out of the adjoining room. "I have a bath ready. What else do you need?"

"My bag. The blue one that Lilly gave me to hold healing tonics."

Holding it up Mari smiled. "Just tell me what needs to be done. Miss Lilly will be here in the morning for the rest."

Of course, Mari would know who was the better healer. "The blue vial. Put three caps full in the tub."

Making sure that Nisha knew about the all the variables that she would need to consider in order to begin the healing while in water, Marigold countered, "The tub it big enough for a Hippocampus."

"That's fine. Three caps would be enough to treat six Hippocampi and a walrus in the same pool."

Mari stammered, "A.... walrus... never mind, I humbly ask not to be told."

Nisha rolled her eyes and continued, "And three drops of the green." Nisha looked at Ethan still unconscious "Better make that six drops. I want him blissfully numb until Lilly can decide on what else needs to be done. Oh, Mari..."

"Yes?"

"I need my suit. The one Queen Sedna had commissioned for me so I may visit her underwater kingdom. I wouldn't want to fall asleep while tending to him."

"Of course. May I suggest Edgar help get the young man into the tub while you change?"

"Thank you, Mari." She turned to see Edgar standing in the doorway waiting to be noticed. *I wonder why I hadn't seen him standing there before. It wasn't like he is hard to miss.* Then again, he did blend in well as a wall. Looking at him now hunched over, he still took up the entire doorway and could have mistaken for a door if he was dressed in anything other than his uniform. "Edgar, will you please help Ethan into the tub? I'll deal with his clothing once he is in it."

"Of course, your grace." His deep soft voice filled the room as he took a step inside. Standing at his full height his deep voice filled with the up most respect as he asked, "The chair, will not try to eat me if I help the boy?"

Looking over her shoulder Nisha shrugged. "Ari will not eat anyone who is bound to me if he wishes to return to whatever form he should be." Not waiting for any question that could be asked she hurried into the anti-chamber to change and allow her trusted guard time to settle Ethan into the tub.

M.L.Ruscsak

Chapter 23:
Ethan

He had been lost in what he assumed had be a dream. And a lovely dream at that.

A woman- his mother- sitting near a stream singing. He could almost hear the soft melody slipping from her lips. Flowers sprouted from the ground as her words faded into the wind. A Feyen man lightly landing some yards away. A dark blue uniform of some kind. Tied at his waist was a large golden sword and pure white gloves covering his hands. The man's golden wings held loosely at his back. His mother slowly stood up smiling. Golden sun turning her fire red hair to a river of red gold flowing down her back covering her red translucent wings.

She turned back toward him and started to speak just before a wave pulled him down and into the river.

Something warm and wet wrapped around his legs pulling him down. Frantically he tried to claw away from whatever was holding him... *Please... Not water... Anything but water....*

"Ethan?"

Panicked now he opened his eyes to the voice. Even after recognizing the voice it took his eyes a while longer to really see who was speaking. A breath more to understand who was sitting with him dressed in some kind of black rubber suit. Ethan gasped as he tried to form words. "Pri- Nisha?"

Slowly she took his hand in hers, her eyes softening as she gazed into his. "You're safe, Ethan. I swear that you are."

He wasn't sure about that. He was in a pool of water up to his neck. The thought of not speaking no longer dominating his better senses as he tried to calm himself, "I- I..." He took as deep of breath as he could before his ribs ached,

"Where are we?" A stone pool of some kind. Smooth black walls. Nothing he could recognize beyond that.

Pulling her long hair back and making it into a knot on top of her head Nisha smiled, "Well if I had to guess, I would say we are in a guest room that would be given to a water dwelling citizen. But it was the nearest room with a suitable tub and bed. At least for the night."

Guest room? Tub? Bed? He knew that he should end this charade but he may never have another day... another night to... No... Waiting until morning or even for another hour would only earn him a worse fate. "There's something I need to tell you."

Slipping dark tendrils of black mist under the tattered shirt Nisha paused for a span of a breath. "I need you to be very still. I've only done this once before and do not wish to do more damage than what I expect is already there."

"I-" He just nodded expecting pain. Instead, he watched as black mist that was translucent cut through the cloth of his pants, undergarments, and shirt. Watched as the torn cloth peeled away from his skin and floated in the water. Darker mist covered his middle as the garments were taken away.

"There, now I can have a proper look-"

She was sitting behind him but he could feel the anger rising off her. "I can explain."

Chapter 24: Karnack

Deep within the Castle of Bones. Deeply hidden side of his private study Karnack gripped the Seer's stone tightly in his feeble hands. Over the years since the boy's birth he had looked in on him from time to time. Carefully he had kept his notes on the boy's life and upbringing. Each time he had voiced his concerns to the counsel when they could be bothered to listen to him.

Each of those times he had warned them about the abuse the boy was enduring. And now....

Despite not being in the same realm with the Queen of the Under Kingdom, despite not having a true emotional link with her... he could feel her dark fury swirling... spiraling within the depths of the stone that he now held within his hands. He could feel her rage at seeing such abuse to one that belonged to her. Could see her rage taking shape in the dragon wings that were now pressed tightly to her sides.

Pushing back from his desk he gave himself a moment to let himself acknowledge the tremor of fear that he was now feeling. Gave himself only a moment to decide how to best handle this foreseen problem.

And by the light, Magmas was going to deal with it. Or at the very least use whatever power he held over the others to convince Magnar that he had been wrong. And that was after the former King of Feyen explained this to Appollo. And then …

And only then…

Could the great Fey of the forgotten war begin to prepare for the rage of their queen once she found out that not only had they all known about this abuse but had done nothing to end it.

Tucking the stone into his tattered robes, he allowed for his heavy boots to thunder from the study.

He didn't use his temper much. But he was not shouldering the responsibility for this alone. And he was *NOT* dealing with the queen when her abilities were terrifying enough without being provoked.

It had been a century or better since he had held on to this fury enough to have the citizens of the Under Kingdom scurry out of his way. Longer than that since the bones of the dead had rattled as he passed. But it wasn't true rage that was keeping him moving.

Oh No. It was fear. Cold and deadly. It was the rage that he could still feel pulsating from the stone that was held with in pocket. It was the way that those who were completely bound to the Queen were sharpening their blades and preparing for battle.

They felt it to. They understood her rage and they would be the ones who would be unleashed just as soon as their queen commanded.

Hurrying down the wide street of Dabria, Karnack stormed into the domed villa that Nisha had created just a few years ago. Pushed the double doors open to the great meeting room where the counsel gathered at her command.

Locking eyes on the Great King of Feyen, he hissed, "I warned you. Now you will damn well fix it."

Chapter 25:

Nisha

Peeling the layers of cloth away from Ethan's flesh, she knew it was going to be bad. She knew there had been layers of wounds that had been in various stages of healing... but that had been this morning...

Nothing she had felt then compared to this. Black splotches that were deep bruises. Cuts that were going nearly to the bone. Over that deep burns, infected boils and scores of other wounds that already smelled of rot despite just being made.

She didn't hear Ethan stammer trying to explain... Whatever it was that he was trying to say. Only her anger mattered right now... only the cold, deadly rage that coursed through her body... Only...

Taking a deep breath, she slowly let it out. Lilly would be here in the morning... more importantly, David would be here... He could find the pieces of filth and find something so creative to do with those who had dared do this to a member of their family that the Draken people would write a song about it. But that would be tomorrow... right now...

Nisha turned her head to face the door to the bedroom and called, "Mari."

Coming as far as the doorway she started to say "Nis-" then Marigold gasped seeing the condition of Ethan's back. "By the light..." She rushed over to the side of the tub. "What can I do to help?"

"Did Lilly send any of that soap that she uses?"

A small dish floated on the water not a moment later. Liquid gel sitting within its crystal bowl. A small bit of clean soft cloth was pressed into Nisha's hand. "Anything else?"

"Please see that there are plenty of dry bandages laid out. And I will need any ointments that were made before we left Lite."

"I'll have them ready for you for when you need them." Marigold paused. "Should I ask Mother to make some tea? I bet she has one to calm nerves?" *That one not for Ethan but Nisha... She had already decided that Ethan needed a healing tea and something to help him relax while being healed.*

"Yes, please." Nisha waited until she was once again alone with her betrothed. "Ethan?"

"Princess?"

She rolled her eyes, "I'm going to try to gentle but even with what was put in the water cleaning these wounds may hurt."

"I understand."

"No, I don't think you do but that more to do with the ass that raised you than anything else. But that is a discussion for another day." Before touching him, she let the soft black tendrils wrap around him cradling him freeing both of her hands while she worked.

The water was warm and almost made him forget about the pain in his ribs... almost numbed his skin enough so that he didn't think about the water or being in it. Something cold touched his tender skin... Nisha said it may hurt... hurt was not the word he would choose to describe the burning, blistering pain and whatever she was doing that was causing it. Even so, this was nothing that he hadn't been through before. Pulling his knees to his chest, he wrapped his arms around his knees and decided to talk to keep his mind off whatever she decided that she was going to do... and hope by talking he didn't make things worse. "You don't know much about the way Darke is run... would you like me to tell you some?"

She peered around his shoulder to see his face tight with pain. "If talking will help you keep your mind off of what I'm doing... then please enlighten me."

She sounded mad, bordering pissed yet he didn't think she was mad at him... which was more than confusing... "Do you know about how the citizen are divided?"

Her hand paused over his shoulder as she spoke, "Do you mean why some are high-born and others low-born?"

"Y-yes..." he hissed when she touched his side.

"Sorry. I'm not as good with this as my cousin Lilly is. She is much more skilled with kind of thing. "

Ethan nodded in understanding regardless if he did or not. "In Darke, there are four types of ... um... citizens."

Now she paused. "Please explain. I know about high-born and low-born but not others."

"High-Born are the employers. Low-Born work for High-Born. " He paused he wanted her to understand ... maybe if he told her this way instead of her finding out by someone else she would forgive him for all the laws he broke since her arrival...

... probably not. But it was worth the risk.

"Slaves outnumber the low-born two to one."

"Slaves?" It is sounding like she was testing the word.

"Hmm. They are given a room by their owner. Uniform and enough food to sustain them. Most have little to no natural abilities or have never been given the right to develop them. There is no way to know for sure what those abilities may be. Or at least, I don't know of any way to tell."

"I see. Then I will find out more once my cousin arrives. She tends to read laws before visiting any country. It can be annoying but she is very knowledgeable on laws. "

Shit. Maybe I'll have to deal with her instead of the princess. Would she understand I tried to follow the laws? Would she care?

"Now, what is the fourth group?"

She wasn't touching him any longer. The fact that she was still behind him... was not comforting. The prospect of dealing with someone else about everything was much more terrifying, "Dogs."

"Dogs? What do dogs have to..." she paused, "Ohhh... I was wondering what the signs meant?"

"Dogs are a form of a slave. Most work in jobs that are too dangerous such as in the deeper parts of mines or in troll caves. Most but not all."

"Go on."

Those to words made him think that telling her now had been a misjudgment so he said hurriedly, "Any of the upper three groups can own a dog. Slaves use them as coin for things that they want or need."

"They trade..." Anger resonated within those two words.

"A pint of blood can buy a day's worth of rations. Thin slivers of flesh... a new uniform."

"I see."

He heard her stand up. Then didn't hear anything after that. Nor feel the pain he thought he deserved.

Chapter 26: Magmas

The double doors to the Queen's counsel chamber blew open and for one fleeting moment he thought Nisha had brought all of her dark fury into the Under Kingdom. Of a single heartbeat he worried that he wouldn't be strong enough to deal with that temper. Then Karnack entered and the rage and fear bubbling up from him was more of a warning than anything else.

He didn't have a chance to ask anything before Karnack hissed, "I warned you. Now You will damn well fix it."

That didn't explain anything. "Fix what?"

Reaching into his pocket Karnack tossed the precious stone to him. "What do you feel Magmas? Tell me?"

Closing his fingers around the stone, he wanted to drop it. To move away from the object that screamed threat. But it wasn't the stone that was causing the feeling... it was... "Nisha?"

He understood now. Karnack had been warning him… had been warning all of them to handle her with care. And now… "What happened?"

Carefully Karnack stepped up to the round table and leaned forward. "Our queen has found Ethan. She has witnessed the abuse that I have been warning you all about. This is the reaction that I feared." Pulling away from the table he pointed a single narrow finger at Magmas, "You deal with her. Or have Magnar explain why this abuse is acceptable. But I tell you this right now. I am not dealing with her rage. And I am not smoothing this over with the dead."

No Karnack would never face an enraged queen. Magnar on the other hand usually found it entertaining. "I'll tell you what the council decided when I inform them. In the meantime. I will remind you that it was Vasilissa who decided where the boy would be raised. And it has always been Magnar who sided with Vasilissa on this matter despite the remaining council members repeated objections. However, this may be the reaction to get Magnar to admit that he may have been wrong on the matter."

"This abuse has been long outlawed within the Star Cities ruled by Magnar or the other council members."

Magmas nodded once. "It has…" He paused and got to his feet. A breath more and swayed before he collapsed back into his chair "By the gods this is why they needed the boy …"

Karnack very slowly turned to face him. Not liking what he saw in the Great king's face he too carefully spoke, "Magmas?"

"She wouldn't understand the abuse that is condoned by Pallas unless someone who belongs to her…" He collapsed in his seat not sure if he should be terrified or laugh like a fool. "She's going to kill them when she finds out. I have no doubt about that. But they will both understand why she must be the one to stand up for those most greatly affected by the rule of Pallas."

The counsel gathered around once more, only this time the chosen queen had not summoned them. This time it had been the First King of Feyen. His dragon crested breastplate shinning under his long royal blue robe.

"Gentlemen, ladies." He nodded to both Vasilissa and Alista as they took their places at the great table. "We have a situation and we all need to reach an agreement of what will be or won't be done according to the laws that were established by Primitiva."

Hushed mummers and hint of fear. None had spoken her name since she went into hiding. None dared to say it for what may happen should she over hear it. None until now.

Magnar leaned back in his seat his boots dripping in muck propped up on the table. Spitting out a piece of bone he smiled. "And what do we need to agree on, boy?"

"The queen has seen the abuse that her betrothed as undergone." He leaned forward, his eyes never leaving Magnar's face. "And the Lady is not please."

"Of course she's not pleased," Vasilissa snapped. "That was the point."

Tossing the stone to Vasilissa, Magmas smiled. "So glad you think so. So, tell me, how do we deal with a Fey when they are seeping with that much cold rage? Because for the life of me, I have never felt anything like it. Not even during the Great War."

Snatching the stone from Vasilissa, Magnar glared. "This is impossible."

It was satisfying to see Magnar tossed off his stride. "And yet… you hold the proof in your hands."

M.L.Ruscsak

Chapter 27:
Ethan

Ethan moved ever so slightly. He didn't remember falling asleep... nor finding something soft to lay on... but he did remember being in the pool of water with the princess. He remembered feeling her stand and the water dripping off her and back into the pool. Then nothing. Not a sound nor a flash of pain and right now he didn't know whether to be thankful or terrified. Something brushed against his foot. Not skin. No, he would expect skin, but that something that was touching him was also moving a silky fabric that was wrapped around his foot. The simple touch hadn't been what woke him... no that had come after ...

So, what...

Laying perfectly still, he tried to identify where he was, who was in the room and anything else he could use to decide how much trouble he would be in once he was found awake. Occasional crackle of a fire. No smoke that he could smell, so the fire had to be in a hearth close by but not too close. It was then he felt... heard what was wrong with whatever his head was resting on... it moved ever so slightly and had a heartbeat. Something caressed his head. Not threatening, but a touch that calmed in a way that he had never experienced. A touch that made him want to float in this moment for all time. But he knew he couldn't... Trying to sit up, he found it nearly impossible with his bones throbbing, not to mention the burning in his chest. "You should be sleeping."

Nisha? Hard to tell with how heavy her voice sounded. "I-"

"Mari will be in shortly with some nice tea. It will take some of the congestion out of your chest. Help you breathe a bit easier." Still keeping his eyes shut, he nuzzled back down into the softness that was surrounding him. "I'm in a bed?"

Slowly she moved, carefully helping him position off of her chest that he had been using as a pillow replacing it with cloud-soft cotton under his head.

For a long moment, she only sat next to him, her fingers tracing the curves of his ear and the coarse stubble he had for hair. Finally, she let out a sigh, "If I gave you an order would you, obey it?"

He knew a trap when he heard one, but there was only one answer for this type of question, wasn't there? "Yes."

"I thought so."

She didn't sound very happy with his answer so he forced his eyes open to the softly lit room. Slowly took in what he was seeing. The bed was large enough to be its own room. The hearth where the fire was slowly burning was tall enough to stand in or sleep in. And the room itself. Gray walls, he couldn't be sure if they had been painted or if it was some kind of polished stone... at least not with the light that scarcely lit the room. Ever so slowly he moved just enough to see her sitting near him... watching him without comment. Unsure what he could say or should, he chose to ask, "Is there a reason I shouldn't?"

"Several actually but I think it would be better if I let David discuss that with you. He has a far better understand what to do with people than I do. More so when the person has yet to find their footing around me."

David? Footing? "I don't understand." And he didn't. He was a servant, a slave. No, less than a slave; he was a worthless dog. If she told him to do something he would do it without question for fear of the punishment. Yet the more he was around her the less he was beginning to think she would truly harm him. "While you were sleeping, I found out everything about all the citizens of Darke. After my aunt arrives, I'll deal with what I can before the coronation and then everything else sometime after."

Again, he went still, "I- I can explain."

Her finger pressed to his lips, something that he was being to understand that meant he wasn't to speak for a moment, "I am going to give you an order I need this one to be obeyed."

Ethan nodded once.

"Lilly is a better healer than myself so once she takes a good look at your injuries I need you to listen to her instructions. Until then I need you are to remain in this bed. Regardless of what you hear out of this room, you are not to leave this bed."

That was it? "So, all I have to do is stay in this bed until Lilly says otherwise?" It had to be a trick.

"Yes. My guards have confirmed the castle isn't as safe as it should be. Nor have I've been able to locate Mr. Edrich, which considering who is looking for him it is very distressing."

Edrich? Lord Edrich? "You searched under his house?"

Nisha paused before she started to climb out of bed. "Your house, Ethan, not his. And yes, it has been searched."

"My... house?" Ethan squawked out.

She pulled on her black house robe over her midnight blue sleep suit before answering, "I was going to wait until morning to explain everything to you, but I can start now if you prefer?"

The bedroom door eased open as the woman he vaguely remembered seeing earlier padded into the room. A long nightshirt that covered her to her feet and a stocking cap...

"Oh yuck, I didn't realize anyone still wore sleep hats."

The woman paused, clearly stunned that the princess had spoken on something so mundane. "If I want bountiful curls in the morning I very well will wear my cap tonight. And if you make another comment I will attach one to you for your wedding night."

"If you do, I'll reverse the spell."

"My dear you may be able to manipulate many of my abilities, but my spells that I created are still far beyond your reach."

He watched Nisha glare at the woman. "Oh fine. I'll be nice for my own sake."

Sliding the rest of the way out of the bed, Nisha shuffled over to the hearth. "Aunt Celeste wasn't joking when she said the nights get frigid here."

The tall woman just glared, then snapped, "You so much as touch a log I will refuse to get the soot off anything you touch."

"Oh fine." Nisha paused and turned toward the window. "Lilly is just outside the city walls. Will you please see that Ethan is comfortable and don't ask him too much. He hasn't found his footing yet."

"Fine, I will behave myself. Since he is unwell." Waiting until Nisha was out of the room Ethan asked, "You're allowed to speak to her like that?"

"Of course, I am." The woman placed her thin bony hand over heart. "Nisha is my dear friend and we have an agreement."

"Oh?"

"I am a Fey. Therefore, I do not have to be nice just because someone is from a high house. They have to earn my respect just like everyone else. Besides, would you like me to tell you about when I first met Nisha?"

"Please?"

Taking a seat on the edge of the bed, she held out her hand. "We haven't been properly introduced; I'm Marigold, by the way, Nisha's personal house elf."

Taking her hand, he tried to smile, "Pleasure to meet you?"

"I doubt it, but we'll see." Her smile was anything but friendly. "Anyways, I was about twenty at the time. Nish swears I was younger, but who am I to argue. I heard my mother, who was a cook at Castle Sun Tear-- that's the castle that is nearest to the Feyen border-- that the poor little orphan princess had been so grumpy lately, and how she would never have a single friend. Of course, me being, well me, I had to see who the little orphan was."

"You yelled at her the first time you met." How the name of Darke do I know that?

Marigold made a face "Yes?" Then she perked up, "Oh Nish connected with you. She must have made a permanent connection so you can share things with each other."

"I- I don't understand."

"Really, I don't either, but what I do know is if she did make a permanent connection you would be able to know things about her... like a memory and she with you. So, should I continue with the story?"

"I... Um... yes?" *So, does that mean she knows everything about my life? Was that how she had found out about the slaves?* The possibility was enough to force a shiver.

"Well, I found her knee high in dresses and blankets and other forms of fabric and I yelled. Make no mistake, I had every right to yell at her. She had made such a mess it took me a whole hour to figure out what to do with it all. And that was with using my abilities."

Ethan smiled, but looked down at his lap.

"Anyways, I told her flat out just because she was a princess didn't give her right to make a mess and make everyone around her miserable. There's more, but that was said in confidence and I refuse to break that trust. Anyways, she promised to earn my trust. When she is the Princess or Queen or whatever I am her silent house elf who sees everything and knows nothing. I also am in charge of the entire cleaning staff."

"And when she is... alone in her apartment?"

Ethan nodded once.

"Then she is Nisha my dear friend who I scold because no one else would dare to. I tell her what I overhear that she otherwise would never know about. And we are always honest with each other. No sugar coating the facts just to the point conversation. It's better that way."

She looked over at the tray now floating in the middle of the room. "Oh good, your tea has arrived. It should help you relax until Lilly can take a look at you."

"Lilly? Nisha told me her cousin was coming but didn't say much else about her."

"Ah, yes. Let me see… the Princess Lilly Aileen Kairavi, the Crown Princess of Lite. And a cousin of our Nisha. Betrothed to a son of Draken. And you should also know that Lilly has a knack of getting into trouble and pulling her pet Draken into the fire with her."

Pet Draken? How could she… was she so powerful that she enslaved a Draken? "She's coming here?! To see me?!"

"Well I wouldn't say just to see you but there is no better person Fey or otherwise that is a gifted healer. Besides I suspect you would like to find your feet before Nisha comes up any hair brain scheme that will make most of the citizens of Darke either sit down and weep or drink themselves into a stupor. Providing they just don't hide to avoid hearing the idea, to begin with."

"She would really do that? Do something to scare every citizen in Darke?"

"Darling, you have no idea. You saw her jacket at the Spire?"

"Y-Yes. It was made of feathers."

"Yes. She took the feathers from a dozen blackbirds, then made each of them sweaters until their feathers grew back. Of course, she swears to this day that the birds came up with the idea and explained how to safely remove their feathers. Then you have that black suit she was wearing in the tub."

Shit. He hadn't paid any attention to it other than it fit her form. "I don't recall."

"Uh huh. It was made for her by Queen Sedna and she lives in the Endless Sea. Think about that for a moment. Nisha would have had to meet her and the Queen never leaves her palace... ever."

"That's impossible... no one has ever... seen..." No wait, there were stories of people going into the sea... the question has always been if they ever returned. Then again, she had seemed interested in the water dwelling citizens when they spoke.

"Exactly. So, would you like to know your job as part of Nisha's house?"

Ethan moaned, "No. But I think I should anyways."

"You get to keep her from doing something before she thinks it through."

Chapter 28:

Lilly

Lilly peered out the carriage window and her heart ached. It was well past midnight but still hours away from dawn, yet there were people scurrying around in the shadows. Whether or not if they were male or female she couldn't tell but she could see they were scarcely dressed in little more than rags. More than that, she could feel the distinct feel of Fey blood. The power contained in that blood making the air heavy with worry and fear. "David?"

He was leafing through one of the books of laws that she had been reading but he too was trying to find the source of what he was feeling. "You feel it too." The book snapped shut in his hands as he tried to pinpoint the cause of the smell. Or the reason for the fear.

Focusing her eyes on the street, she gasped, "Fey. Lots of Fey... but..."

"According to everything that the council has provided, there is no Fey or even part Fey anywhere in Darke." David paused. "Do you think Nisha knows?"

At that Lilly snorted. "If she doesn't right now, she will by dawn."

Too quickly, he grabbed her arm. "There might be another problem."

"David."

His nostrils flared as he sniffed the air. "I can smell blood. Fresh, hot Fey blood. Not just the remnants of it."

She looked worried now. "Are you sure?"

"I'm Darken. I know the difference in the smell. I *will* be contacting my father once we arrive."

"B-but." *He would show up ready for battle with dozens of his best fighters. Nisha would not be happy.*

"Lilly listen to me. Fey regardless of where they live are protected by Feyen. If one of them is being harmed here, it could mean war. If scores of them are here undocumented and being harmed it will tear the whole continent apart or worse."

Looking back out of the window Lilly paled. "Your father could ..." *Kill everything that is harming a Fey? It was a good possibility. Keep war from breaking out? Now that was a good question.* For the last thousand years, they had been the undisputed police force of all of the lands. They had been tasked with keeping war from breaking out between the Fey and the Serpent Marsh. Now that the threat was much closer…

"Between my father and *your* mother, I think we can convince Nisha into launching a formal investigation. Not that I doubt that she hasn't already begun to figure out what needs to be done. Once she got used to being here she would know something was terribly wrong. Or at the very least Freya or her shadow would figure it out for her. "

Very calmly, Lilly took a deep breath before saying, "Alright. So, we bully our cousin into doing something reasonable instead of something rash?"

"No, we stand out of her way if she has already decided on something rash and hope we can convince her into doing something reasonable."

Lilly took a deep breath and watched the castle come into view. "Alright, I think we can do that. However, I don't think we shouldn't let the citizens of Darke should see who or more to the point what you are right now."

David rolled his eyes. "So is the princess traveling with her vicious guard dog or her trusted kitty."

"I think... a pampered princess should have an equally pampered kitty."

Of course. "So, you want something fluffy and that looks lazy." *And nothing that looks like a threat.*

She gave a playful smile. "Just think if you have long golden fur it would be easier to pet you."

"Fine. I will change into a damn fat cat."

"Oh, you know you love being petted." She smiled as he leaped onto her lap, already content to play his part.

Stepping out of the coach she had never been more nervous. She couldn't see the top of the castle but could feel eyes - feral eyes - watching her. There was not a single lamp post lit, nor light coming from any window. Not so much as a flicker of a fire from any room that she could see. *"The staff won't arrive until morning. Mother is bringing several from Lite."* She told herself as she petted David who was nestled in her arms. A deep breath. She was safe. David was with her. He wouldn't let anything harm her.

For that matter, neither would Nisha or her legions of shadow people.

Slowly she made her way up the dark stone steps and waited for the door to open. When it didn't she raised the gold knocker and let it fall. The clang of metal echoed through both the castle and the air around her.

The door snapped open. "What in the name of Darke do you want?" A large man in a guard's uniform growled. Shrouded by darkness nothing other than his size and ember colored eyes was shown.

Lilly jumped at the crackle in the guard's voice half-expecting fire to follow his words. "I am Princess Lilly of Lite. I am here at the request of Crown Princess Nisha."

The guard glared at her for a long moment his ember eyes flickering warning, "No one enters without approval. And no... *cats* ... allowed. *Ever.*"

Nish, I need you.

"What do you mean my kitty cannot enter?" Lilly stomped her foot in front of the guard. Her grandfather had loved turning into a cat... She knew that after all her grandmother had told her the stories several times.

"No cats allowed in the palace. No exceptions."

Clearly, he hadn't heard the stories of the royal family. "I was told to come as fast as I can and you are delaying my audience with my cousin. Now stand aside." She stomped her foot with frustration. Or to appear that she was getting frustrated now that she saw her cousin coming into view.

"Come back in the morning and leave the... the *thing* at home."

Chapter 29:

Nisha

Nisha paused making sure she had Lilly's attention. After listing for a moment longer to the dribble that the guard was spewing she growled, "It's the middle of the night. What is the problem here?"

The guard turned to see Nisha standing just feet away from him. Black tendrils freely flowing from all around her. Black and gray swirling mist creating a breathtakingly yet deadly pair of wings. He swallowed hard seeing something that he could not name flickering deep within her eyes. "Troublemaker your majesty."

"Yes, I can see *you* are. Now let my cousin pass before I feed you to a Draken."

The guard stumbled back a few steps. "B-but..."

Nisha's eyes narrowed with annoyance. "Did I stutter? And do not think for a minute I wouldn't contact my uncle and tell him I have a fire-walker for him to dine on."

The guard took another step back. "No ma'am, but the cat--"

"Is welcome in my house. Come on Lilly, the main hall is much too chilly to keep the poor kitty in the doorway."

It wasn't until they were out of sight of the guard that David jumped down and turned into his full form. "So, do I get to have dinner now or should I be the polite guest? Providing you really don't want that ass for my father."

Nisha gave him an annoyed glare. "Tonight you're an honored guest. Tomorrow I might have several things for you to choose from for your dinner."

David grabbed her arm and swung her into the first nook he could find. "What happened?"

"Not now. This hall has ears that don't belong to me."

"I have an answer for that."

Holding her ground Nisha sharply hissed, "Not now, Prince Davkren."

After turning several corners Nisha took a deep breath and smiled. "We can talk now."

"Are you sure?"

"Lil, honestly do you think I would say we could if there was as much as a mouse that wasn't bound to me in this area."

"Well, no... but..."

"Gwydion has people in this wing on all floors. Neither he nor Freya has been able to go through the entire castle to see who can be trusted and who can't. I figure Aunt Celeste can help me with that when she arrives."

Who is Gwydion? No better not to ask that. Lilly thought. Instead, she asked, "Have you read the laws yet? David and I started to and..."

Nisha snorted. "If you mean the laws that the council made, I heard about them and after tomorrow most will be overturned."

"And the Fey?"

Now Nisha froze. *"I thought I was wrong,"* she whispered to herself. "Damn it. Come on I want your opinion then I need you to be the gifted healer that you are and please don't tell me that I made a mess of things."

Linking her arm with Nisha's Lilly tried to smile. "Well darling you always make a mess of things if you try to heal it. However, you are very proficient in bringing those who should be dead back to full life." And that was something that outside the three of them would never be told to another person... including her mother. Well except Edgar, who had been the one that Nisha had brought back to life after an encounter with a troll.

Opening the polished black door Nisha froze, seeing Ethan alone and trying to shuffle over to a chair. He was still wearing the silk nightshirt and matching bottoms that she had helped him into while he slept... Was still wearing his miles of bandaged that were under the night shirt... and still looked in pain. Which he was. One look at his face told her that. "I thought I said to stay in bed."

He looked over at her and sighed, "The maid... *Marigold...* said she wouldn't give me the tea until I was in a chair."

She would talk to Mari later. And without question, they would have one of their very restrained arguments that would have one of them remembering who the queen was and who needed to yield to direct orders. "Fine. I'll deal with her tomorrow." She took a full step into the room. "Ethan, this is my cousin Lilly. Lilly if you wouldn't mind..." She didn't finish the sentence when her cousin pushed past her.

Lilly skidded to a stop just before the bed. Her eyes already fixated on what was hidden beneath the layers of fabric. With a gasp she asked, "By the gods... what happened?"

"I-" Ethan started at the same time Nisha huffed out, "My proxy decided to take some liberties."

David closed the door behind him. Sometime between Nisha opening the door and Lilly passing the threshold he had hidden his curled horns and pointed ears. Right now, he looked more serpent in the eyes then either Draken or Feyen. "Nish, perhaps while Lilly works we can go into another room and you can explain some things."

"Lilly?"

"It will take me some time to get a good look at everything. It would help if you were..." She paused looking at the tip of Ethan's ear. "...not here while I get a good look at everything."

Leaning on the door that led into the sitting room David growled, "Now, would you like to tell me what is going on, and who that boy is?"

Her eyes narrowed. For anyone who was sensible it would be warning not to push. Darkens were excluded. However, David would understand her deep growl and would take care not to provoke her. "The *boy* is Ethan, is my betrothed. He's allowed to be in my room unless you would like to debate you being in Lilly's bed for the past few years. And that was before Aunt Celeste knew *you* were even in the castle. "

David noted the dark undertones to Nisha's voice. Noted the narrowing of her eyes and knew his cousin was one breath away from terrify them all. Giving a smile that he hoped would look friendly, he conceded, "Fine, I won't eat him."

Of course, you won't. Fluffing her hair, Nisha moved away from David and closer to one of the long couches. "Now from I know for a fact is that sometime after the fire a large group of people... *People who I'm assuming were blood bound to my mother and were very confused at suddenly being unbound...* were somehow rounded up and locked up until they submitted into slavery. Those who were children, like Ethan; were told very early on they were dogs. Their flesh is coin for anyone who owns them and their blood is for those who rely on it. I was hoping I was wrong that they were the *missing* Fey."

Missing? What did she mean missing and why hadn't the Draken people been told? The answer was either Celeste or Alista didn't think they were missing as much as living somewhere else. And either one or both were very quietly looking for them. "*Shit.*"

"I have a plan to deal with that once Aunt Celeste arrives. Though to be fair I don't think she will be at all pleased with it. Which is why I don't plan on telling her everything until after the fact."

David rolled his now golden eyes and shook his head. "She'll be less pleased if the Feyen kingdom declares war because of it."

Shuffling over to the other long couch that had overstuffed arms, Nisha leaned on the arm of it and crossed her arms. "Very true. Which is why I sent Freya to Feyen to speak not to Larna but her grandmother Alista. It's best if she knows it's already being handled since I was just made aware of the situation. With luck, it should give me a week or more to deal with everything before she demands retribution."

"Sounds reasonable." David pushed off the door and stood towering over her. "So, what are you not telling me that will no doubt lead to me wishing I truly was a cat?"

Tapping her finger to her lips, Nisha sat quietly for a matter of a heartbeat before smiling. "Well I don't know about being a cat... but I could use a Draken right now."

That David wasn't expecting. Or maybe after smelling the blood of Fey he had. Either way, he asked, "Well you have one standing before you so how may I be of service?"

Pausing for another heartbeat, Nisha confirmed what she had already heard at least once from the shades before making an attempt to explain to the only Draken that was currently in all of Darke. "The proxy that was to raise Ethan has caused great harm to him... I need him…" *the slippery troll slug* "…found. So far, he has been able to hide himself from Freya and a legion of shades. Not to mention the others that are now hunting him."

Stumbling back a step David squeaked out, "Shades? Here?" *How? Why?* No best not to ask that or he might actually get an answer.

Patting David's back reassuringly, Nisha smiled as she said, "Oh, they are the most delightful people who are also blood bound to me. So, don't worry they cannot harm those who are my blood. Believe me you are safe however please ask Uncle Craykren not to look menacing toward me. I doubt they will be as forgiving as shadow was with you."

Catching his breath David tried to smile. Almost succeeded. "Alright I will do what I can for father but you know he loves a good fight."

"Yes, but it wouldn't be a fair fight since he couldn't harm a shade... them being made of mist and all." Nisha let her hand hang loosely at her side then made a swirling motion with her fingers. A dark mist teased the tips of her fingers making appear like she was petting whatever or whoever it was.

Forcing a smile, David said nothing about the mist. "Good point. Now, what do I need to know about my prey?"

"He's part Wendigo and part Fey." Then Nisha locked eyes with David and in low growl said, "I want him alive."

M.L.Ruscsak

Chapter 30:

Lilly

Helping Ethan back into bed, Lilly floated the cup of tea over to him. "Here you go. It's a numbing tonic mixed with something to help you rest."

Not yet taking a sip, Ethan asked, "Why would the maid tell me to move if she knew it would piss the princess off?"

Sitting by Ethan's foot, Lilly looked like she was considering the answer for a long while before shrugging. "Well, if I had to guess she was wanting *you* to tell her no. But that's Mari you will get to know her eventually. Maybe. Of course, the only person Mari is nice too is Nisha but just barely. Then again, most house elves are rarely pleasant to be around. So, it is rather possible she was trying to be annoying."

Ethan took a sip of the tea and changed the subject. "This is really good."

"Of course, it is, Marta is a magnificent cook and is also trained as an assistant healer so she knows a thing or two about how to make proper healing teas." Then she patted his leg reassuringly. "Never ask Nisha to make one herself. She tries but making teas or tonics is not something she is good at. Don't tell her, but her last batch killed the plants at the Spire. Zilla who is the… um… Head healer of the Spire… was not happy."

"Ok."

Since he was starting to sound sleepy she Lilly asked, "Are you alright with me removing your shirt?"

"I can..."

"No Ethan, I don't want you moving more than you have to."

He only nodded.

Slowly she unbuttoned the top and let it slide off his bandaged shoulders and fall to the bed. Carefully she starting to unwrap the pale outer layer of cloth to reveal a layer of gauze that was starting to seep through with not red blood that one would expect … or even green that some of the lowborn citizens had but a deep blue blood that was so rare that very few high-born Fey had it… and none outside of Feyen had ever seen. A whiff of silver smoke and a gold box with silver inlay sat next to her.

"Does the princess have a box like that?" It was the only acceptable question he could think of. Or at least the only question he could ask that might get an answer.

Checking several of the little bottles for the one she was looking for, Lilly answered him as nonchalantly as she could so not to worry him. "Oh, this? Nisha has one but it's not as well stocked as mine. Besides this is just for emergencies. I left my bigger one at the Spire."

"Oh but..."

Peering around his shoulder she smiled. "Ethan, darling, you're bleeding; I call that an emergency."

"Most of the bleeding has stopped."

"Well that's all well and good, but the flesh is going to be healed. Now... "She reached into her box and pulled out two tubes both with little medicine droppers attached. "Stick out your tongue, please. I think you will be much happier if you slept through this."

"I-" Seeing a look in her eyes that dared him to argue he wisely opened his mouth and held out his tongue as requested. Three drops from each vial were placed on his tongue. Before he could close his mouth, his vision swayed. "Should I feel woozy?"

"Just sleep, Ethan. You will feel much better in the morning."

Lilly slammed the heavy bedroom door behind her letting the deep rumble echo into the room. Soft white mist swirled around her legs and up her back creating a spectacular pair of wings that could belong to a fancy butterfly. "We need to talk. ***Now***."

Nisha crossed her arms unfazed by the small show of temper. After all, this was Lilly and she rarely showed temper, and when she did it would fizzle out as suddenly as it came. However, her dear cousin did seem more pissed off than she had ever seen her before. "Shouldn't you be taking care of Ethan?"

"Lord Ethan is blissfully asleep and will remain that way till sometime after dawn. Providing there is a dawn here. And providing that he does not fight the sleep that his body needs."

David edged closer to his betrothed. "There is a dawn darling, it just looks like you're looking at it from a spot beneath a shade tree."

"Don't you start, *David*. Don't you dare. I have every right to my anger. And I do not need you telling me otherwise."

Nisha smiled as she tried not to laugh. Yes, her cousin was definitely more pissed off then she had ever been before. "David, will you please keep Ethan company while Lilly and I talk?"

David nodded once. Any other time he would kiss Lilly's cheek as he left the room or at the very least softly touched her arm. Right now, he didn't think she would welcome either movement so he transformed into a thin tabby cat with brown and gray stripes and slinked out of the room.

"Alright, what do you have to be mad about that I have not yet considered?"

Looking at her cousin, she didn't see a woman who was mad not even a little pissed but looking deeper into her eyes and seeing flames flickering behind the rivers of ice. And worse still she could just make out souls of the dead screaming to be released... oh yes, she had better be very careful. "Ethan is Fey."

"Yes. I know this. However, it wasn't until I had him in a pool of water and was looking at every inch of his skin that I was able to tell. In any account, I have already tasked David with bringing me the sack of rotting flesh that decided that they were worth more than a member of my house. And as for the other Fey... I already have a plan for them but I will not tell you because I want people to know why I should be feared."

The mist that had been flowing around her settled too fast to the ground. She knew her cousin and Nisha never wanted anyone to fear her... never... "Nisha...?" Worry filled her soft voice.

"I know what I'm doing Lilly." Nisha's voice hitched not yet wanting to admit what she needed to do. "I have always taken great care in making sure people did not fear me. Not letting anyone know how powerful I truly am and that was before I became the Queen of the Under Kingdom. But that is done now. I know the legend of the Fey far better than any who are alive. So, I know who and what will revenge those who are of true Feyen blood."

Lilly's anger drained, as did the color in her face. "Are you sure?"

"You and I are family. Friends. As well as blood sisters. I never want you to fear me but... If that's the price I need to pay in order to keep our family safe... Then that is the price I will gladly pay." Nisha sat down on an arm of a short couch and closed her eyes. "Did you know my father was feared by most of the high-born but none of the low-born? And my mother despite it being a far greater feat than she was capable at the time, she was suspect in killing the royal family of Feyen?"

"Oh, Nisha ..." Lilly wrapped her armed around her cousin giving as much comfort as she could. "Now don't do that..."

Wiping a single tear from her face Nisha sniffled. "Do what? I didn't get to know my parents because someone else didn't understand them. I lost them both because neither realized that people needed to fear them to keep what they built safe. And damn it, they both were seers... they should have known about the attack... they should have..." She wiped her nose on the sleeve of her house robe. "I'm sorry. Being here... knowing how many have suffered since my mother was taken... it hurts. I didn't expect it to hurt this much."

"Would you like me to cheer you up?"

"I don't think turning into butterflies and listening to conversations that we shouldn't hear is a great idea right now."

"Oh fine. How about we decide on if I should repair Ethan's wings and ears or leave them cropped." Not that the wings had been cropped but rather had been ripped from his back… both from the skin and the muscle where they had been attached.

"I think... " Nisha paused wiping the remaining tears from her eyes, " I need him able to stand to for the coronation ... after we leave for the Spire, then if you feel inclined you can give him back what was taken from him." She pulled back just enough to look at her cousin, "I would like to see his wings if possible, but it may be good to wait till he is settled into his new station a bit before you do."

"Agreed." Taking a deep breath and moving away from her cousin Lilly asked, "So what will be David be doing while you scare everyone?"

"Oh well, Ethan will need something to wear. So, I thought since he so loves to tinker with bits of cloth..."

Patting Nisha's raven colored hair back down, Lilly softly said, "If you don't mind me saying."

"Lil, I always appreciate your insight."

"I think telling a tailor to make something for your betrothed will send a better message to your people."

A rueful smile twitched her lips as she sniffled. "Yes, I think I will ask them. Or else will just be assumed."

Rolling her eyes, Lilly forced a laugh. "Of course. However, I think that adding that Draken will have their hide if you are not completely satisfied with the work, would make a wonderful addition."

"Oh dear. I simply must ask David to inquire if his brothers will be attending as well."

Was this Nisha's way of changing subjects? Somehow, she didn't think so. Closing her eyes, Lilly almost hated to ask, "W-Why?"

"Well at this point both David and his father will have more potential dinner selections then they would need for two years."

Closing her eyes Lilly muttered, "Why did I ever ask?"

M.L.Ruscsak

Chapter 31:
Ethan

Ethan tried not to moan from the dull pain in his joints… tried and failed. At least, he was alone… at least…

Something moved on the edge of the bed… something… "Easy now, Lilly will have my hide if I let you move around too much."

Shit. Too quickly he opened his eyes to see a breathtakingly handsome Feyen boy… man… sitting near his feet and watching him with too much interest. "I didn't realize I wasn't alone."

"It's fine." The man reached over to the nightstand and poured a glass of red liquid into a transparent glass. "Here this will help with the stiffness."

"Th-thank you?" The liquid was sweet. Fruity… And better than anything he had ever tasted. "Who are you, if you don't mind me asking?" The last was said a bit too fast after thinking he had offended this stranger.

"You may call me David. Most of the royal family of Lite does. And Nisha too I suppose."

David? That was not a Feyen name. Or at least, he didn't think it was. "That's an... um... uncommon name."

Pouring himself some of the drink David casually said, "Yes, well my real name is much too long for casual conversation so Lilly decided on David. After ten years it has grown on me."

For a long time, Ethan stared into his glass swirling the red liquid around before very softly asking, "It is alright that we talk?"

David tilted his head in question before answering, "Why would it not be? This time tomorrow you will be married to my dear cousin."

"M-married? Tomorrow?" No that couldn't be right. The coronation was in two weeks, not tomorrow. And he was not the chosen suitor... not even close to the chosen suitor. In fact, he couldn't be. He was a *dog* not some royal Fey or some other kind of royal.

"Of course. Oh, but you were told that she would marry the snake prince. Is that correct?"

Was there a correct answer? Slowly Ethan nodded.

"Yes well, that was clearly a lie. And Nisha hates it when people lie to her or members of her house. You would not believe how much trouble that little lie has caused. Or what Nisha is planning because of it. But please don't ask her about it. I'm sure it will be better for everyone to find out afterward rather than beforehand."

"Oh?" *Was it a lie? But why would his uncle lie? Then again why would he ever tell him the truth?*

"Oh yes. Would you like me to tell you what I know for a fact or would you like to hear the Legend of the Fey?"

Taking another sip of the liquid Ethan said with a yawn, "Which ever you prefer to tell."

"Ah very good. Let's start with your family history. We will start with your mother's side of the family. Her name was Lady Faerydae, forgive me but I do not know her sir name. However, I do know that she was somehow related to the royal house of Feyen thou those ties are a carefully guarded secret. From what I have been able to find she was related to the last queen by bloodlines but was not related closely enough to be considered royal. Anyhow, she was still a lady of the court.

When Nisha's father and mother moved to Darke, she came with them. In exchange was given several stores and sweet shops to create the income that she was accustomed to. Since the fire, all the stores in Darke were to be given to you, however, because of your age at the time your uncle took control of them. From what I can tell he employed whomever, he saw fit and kept all the income for himself." David sat back a bit and made sure he had Ethan's undivided attention before adding, "Nisha is not pleased with any of that by the way. And I doubt once Queen Celeste finds out she will be less than pleased with how you were raised."

"No, that…can't…" Another fragment of memory. *He was in a store. Music played softly in the back.* He couldn't make out anything else. Had his mother taken him to her stores with her? If what David was telling him it might have been possible.

"Oh, but it is. You see your uncle was tossed out of Feyen for something. I'm not privy to those records. Upon leaving, he weaseled his way into your mother's house. Within the week, an uprising happened and was squashed within moments. That night the fire happened. Now I have no proof but I suspect your uncle has something to do with it. If not, he knows who did and why. Either way, Nisha has decided to oversee his execution personally."

Yes, now that made sense. Sort of. "Prince Ciron. I think he might know. For the past few years, he's been feeding…" Ethan rubbed his neck where the prince usually bit down.

"You were blood bound to Nisha shortly after her birth. He was hoping if he fed on your blood he could fool her long enough to marry her and convince her to kill you eliminating any trace of the binding. He didn't count on the fact that even if you were bled dry Nisha would know you were hers. There's something about royal blood that seems to bind itself to the very cells of a body so the binding cannot be undone not even in death. I would appreciate it if you didn't mention that to Nisha… or well … anyone for that matter. I would hate to think about what she or Lilly would do with the information. No, I know what they would do. One of the ladies would bind the snake to themselves then the other would try to kill him to see if they could break the binding."

They wouldn't…if they couldn't break the binding why did… "He tried to kill me several times… do you think…"

Patting Ethan's leg, David smiled. "We will sort that out after the coronation. Now would you like to know about your father?"

Sitting up just a bit Ethan asked, "Please?"

"I do not know much about him other than he was once a guard in the Feyen court then became Captain of the guard here. In addition, he served as the first chair on the council here in Darke. I think but I'm not too sure but his name was something like Gale… Galton or something close to that. Any records from before he came to Darke are kept under careful lock and key. The Fey can be very prickly when it comes to sharing information with anyone. And any records that had been here were destroyed in the fire."

"But you're Fey."

"True. But I'm not trusted with such documents. At least not right now. Someday Maybe… but right now?" David shrugged. "Everything in Feyen happens when it happens. Outsiders are rarely alive long enough to find answers to long-asked questions. More so if those questions might yield an actual answer."

He had been listening carefully to David. Listening to every word. And he knew two things first David wasn't just a Fey. He couldn't be- his language skills were closer to Draken or a low-born citizen of Darke than a Fey who had lived speaking properly. More so… Fey never just told you something without getting something in return. And secondly, He could just see the outline of two curved horns. Just make out the scales around his eyes. Unfortunately, he didn't get to ask anything because the door to the other room opened and both Lilly and Nisha stood in the doorway.

"Damn it David I told you not to wake him." Well, not exactly but she had implied it.

Such language from the princess of Lite. But he was not going to mention it. Oh, no he was not. "David didn't wake me."

"Uh ha. I'm sure. But since I have no proof right now I will spare him the lecture on why I wanted you to still be sleeping."

That didn't sound like much of a threat. Not when Nisha was trying hard not to laugh or when David didn't seem at all fazed. "Do you have any more of the red liquid stuff?"

"Red liquid… Red…" Lilly turned on David who was trying to slip out the door being noticed, "Damn it to hell, David, you should not be giving him liquor in his condition. I swear you make a worse healer's assistant then Nisha." Grabbing a pillow that had been laying on the bed, she used a gust of wind to toss it at David hitting his back. "I'm so mad at you right now that I should have your brothers pounce you the very second they arrive." She took a deep breath. "Nish, will you please find something for him to do before he gets himself into even more trouble?"

"Of course, after all, I would like to see the royal apartments before Aunt Celeste arrives." Nisha smiled so sweetly before making a request that would have been a warning to anyone who already knew about how the Fey settled this land. "Lilly before Ethan gets some much-needed sleep will you please tell him about the Legend of the Fey. It makes a wonderful bedtime story."

"I suppose that I have time to recite the Legend of the first Fey."

Lilly waited until both Nisha and David were out the door before sighing, "David had no right giving you liquor right now. Not with the tonics and teas that I have already given you. But you do have some color back so I guess there was no harm this time."

"He said it would help with the stiffness in my joints."

"Of course he did. Drakens rarely see healers; instead they drink themselves into a stupor or, at least, drink till whatever bruise or ache they have is blissfully numb."

"Ah." *Now that made sense.*

"You don't look too surprised."

Ethan closed his eyes. "I saw the horns. Makes sense that he is Draken."

"You saw… no, don't say anymore. I will blame that on Nisha since you are linked with her. Now, how about I tell you the legend?"

That was the second person who had said that he was linked with Nisha. Hopefully, someone would tell him what that meant. "Why is it important?"

"Well, because every child is told some version of the legend. It is up to interpretation but it's a delightful story to fall asleep to." *And telling you might allow me to find an answer to avoid war.* Not that she could tell him that.

"Alright." Slowly he pulled the warm cover over his shoulder and resigned himself to hear the story.

Chapter 32: Nisha

David slowly pressed the burnt dark wood door open. His long tail flicking with warning the poisoned tooth that he normally hid within the tuft of his tail just barely poking out. "Careful Nish. It smells as though the fire as not been out for that long."

She knew that, for she could smell the freshly burnt wood just as keenly as David.

For a moment she just stood in the doorway. For just that moment everything was pristine and new. Then...

Nisha narrowed her eyes. Just another illusion.

As she took her first full step into what had been her mother's dinning area the spell or enchantment broke. And for the first time she saw fully what had been hidden.

Dishes still laid on the table. Remnants of the last meal her mother had eaten still covering the plates. Long ago insects had devoured what had been left in the way of food. Then the spiders had dinned on the them. The webs now empty of life. Some now torn and blowing softly with the fresh air currents.

On the ground four crystal goblets laid.

"Nish?"

"This room was never touched by fire. Smoke? It appears to have been. And the soot? Too fresh to be from that night."

Using his tail, David grabbed the goblet from the floor. "Smells like poison but not one that I know off hand."

Not care about what she sat in or on, Nisha made herself comfortable on the edge of the long table. "So, I am assuming that my parents were poisoned with something that neither were immune to. But that was after the fire was started in order to draw them here."

"What are you thinking? That Edrich weaseled his way into your mother's service. Started the uprising then subdued the Queen of Darke and all of those that were bound to her?"

"No. Of course not."

"Good"

"Edrich is much too stupid to pull that off. However…" She eased down from her perch and took in the room. "A firewalker has been in here recently. And that does raise more than a few questions."

Pushing another door open David hissed, "Bastards."

"David?" Concern lit her voice before the cold rage seeped into her marrow, "What did… oh…"

There just feet away from her sat the cradle that she should have been raised in. Smashed then burned so only the frame remained. The skeleton of a woman laid on the floor. Her arm out reached. Had she been trying to escape or trying to reach the cradle?

In a soft whisper Nisha called, "Gwydion?"

"My queen?"

David spun to the voice and stopped himself from issuing a challenge. Stopped himself from doing anything that this man may decide that he a Draken would be a delightful snack.

"Do you know who this may be?"

For a moment he dissipated then reformed near the woman's body. "A maid. Not one of your mothers'. Her bones are too fresh to have been left from that night."

Just as she had thought. So why leave her here at all?

"I see." Pulling herself to her full height Nisha nodded once. "Please take what is there to one that can be trusted. I want to know everything that the bones remember."

David didn't understand. Gwydion did.

"As you wish my queen. It will be done at once." He paused and stared right at David. "I trust your cousin will remain with you until I return."

What was left of the nursery door turned to ash. "It would be unwise for anyone to remain with me until Queen Celeste arrives."

Leaving Nisha alone wasn't the best idea that he had ever had but there was nothing he could do that she couldn't do better. Yet...

His thoughts fled as an icy hand grabbed his jacket sleeve. Turning his head to see who had dared he understood something else… Gwydion wasn't just a Shade. He was death and right now death was staring right at him.

"Lord Gwydion?" David wasn't sure if that was the proper title but it was the best that he could think of in that moment.
"I offer you a warning. My queen has made some decisions about a few things it would be best if you were not around to witness those choices."

"I-"He looked closely to the man's eyes. Mist that they were yet… he was scared. A Shade was scared about what Nisha has already decided. By the gods… "-Thank you. I think I will stay with Lord Ethan until I am needed somewhere else."

Chapter 33: The Legend of the Fey

Lilly closed her eyes and began to recite the legend as best as she could. In a story teller's voice, she began, *Legend of the Fey:*

A long time ago, the Fey lived on a faraway star. Then one day, one found their way to our world, though back then it was ruled by what was then called humans. Creatures who looked much like the Fey in that they walked upright and shared a common body style. But they lacked any power other than words and what they made with their own hands, Intrigued, one of the Fey took a human as his soul mate. As part of their union the Fey gave the human a few drops of his blood and took an oath, they would share in what each had.

As this hadn't been done before he couldn't have known that his words would give his powers to his bride. Once it became clear that what had happened, those who had been the woman's family turned from her calling her a witch. Thus, becoming the first witch in the history of Fey.

Back on the star, the Fey watched carefully as this union evolved creating new life and bringing into creation the first child of mixed decent. This gave others ideas of their own.

Some saw the humans as weaker versions of themselves and sought out what they decided were stronger vessels. Though they did not speak words, the other creatures had their own language. And their own ideas of what an acceptable mate would be. Seeing this as nothing more than a game to become stronger as a whole The Fey started to take shapes of the other creatures. Wolves would become werewolves after mating. Fish and other aquatic creatures would become the ancestors to Bunyip, Kelpie, Kraken, Morgawr, Ogopogo, and many others.

Whereas others coupled with reptiles and other smaller creatures to begin the races of Amphisbaena, Cerastes, Lernaean Hydra. Those too would one day evolve into the races we have today.

However, there has always been just pure Fey. Those who choose not to mate with any other than their own kind. We know them as Fairies, Elves, and pixies just name a few. From them, we have a few who have coupled between them. They are more powerful than any other because their bloodlines have never been diluted. They have always been the High-born. The ones who rule. The ones who even if they are not chosen are laws unto themselves for no one except their king or queen can handle them. Even then, not all choose to be handled but merely live under the rule of the king or queen.

Coming to the more recent say four or five millennia ago the world now overrun with those of Fey descent started to break off into their own places. Those of serpent or reptile descent traveled south to warm climate. Those who preferred the dark or shady placed created what is now named Darke. The first residents of Darke created a veil over the land. No one has ever tried to understand it only acknowledge that it's there for the reason of the comfort of the citizens.

Others broke off, creating what is now Draken, Manicoria, and Lite. Of course, Lite is brighter than any other country. It has always been assumed that because the veil is over Darke that the light was forced to go somewhere else. The most reasonable choice was Lite.

Finishing what she knew, Lilly looked over to Ethan who had been much too quiet and saw him finally in deep slumber.

M.L.Ruscsak

Chapter 34: Ethan

Ethan woke to a warm iridescent light surrounding him. Nothing more than a familiar dream; one he had had several times over the years but until now the light hadn't been so bright… so nearly blinding. No every other time it had been like walking in a tunnel made of shade and the light… this light had been there just out of reach. Near the end of the long tunnel.

Today that was not the case. No today he could barely make out the shape of his dream friend. Barely see the way her midnight black hair cascaded down her back. Could almost see her wings of a fine blue mist. But couldn't see if she was annoyed or pleased with him. He didn't know her name then again, he had never asked. Shyly he tried to smile as he asked, "I don't remember it being this bright before."

The woman smiled as she fluttered near him. The light dimming as she did. "You are stronger today. It is time for you to learn my secrets."

Tilting his head Ethan frowned she had never spoken before, although she had the loveliest voice. It fell between the wind blowing softly through the trees and a bird singing to greet the morning. Then he remembered what she had said. "Secrets?" It was the only safe question… wasn't it?

She turned quickly away from him. "Come. You are strong enough to walk among my people."

Odd. She normally held him as he talked about his day. Held him as he cried from the pain his uncle had caused. And would hold him until it was time for him to wake. Getting to his feet he noticed another oddity, the finely tailored blue dress suit and a white shirt underneath that he was now wearing. Not silk but something so soft it could only be made in his dream. "You have never told me your name."

The woman paused and scowled at him before she smiled again… though this time it seemed forced. "Estare. My home is Lunaista. It is one of many of what you call stars."

Stars? The story that he was being told as he fell asleep. Yes, that was it. It had to be. Perhaps he should have been paying more attention to the story. Then again, his mind was already making a wonderful dream so did it really matter?

After walking for what seemed like forever he began speaking once more. Not about the endless tunnel. Or the creatures he could now see coming into view but of mundane things about his life as he had always done before. "I no longer belong to my uncle's house."

Estare paused and really looked at him then her smiled softened. "That is good. He is an ill-tempered creature." Taking a single step, she asked, "You are not old enough to have your own house?"

"Oh, Princess Nisha took me into her house." Again, Ethan frowned. "She says we are betrothed."

Estare gasped. "Nisha? Nisha Trovos?"

Something was wrong he could feel it, but he didn't know what. "I-I think that was her mother's surname. I think that the princess goes by Devros; which is confusing since a child is given the surname of the parent who has the greater ability." Ethan paused before he rambled on anymore. A breath later he asked, "Do you know of her?" *Not likely but it was a dream so anything was possible.*

"I think…" Estare nodded to herself, "I think I will take you to my home then we will speak." She almost took a step then hissed, "Say nothing more till we are in my home. These are dangerous times. Dangerous indeed."

    Her home wasn't just a home but a palace made of crystals and glittering dust. Colors he had only dreamed about was caught in the light reflecting off of everything. Shades of blue that were memorizing, reds that spoke to his heart, green the color of his mother's eyes. He somehow knew the color now though he had never been told it. "It is spectacular here."

    "It is the palace of Lunaista. All who have lived here have added to its grandeur. I have not… not yet. I have to decide what I could possibly add to such a place."

    The place of Lunaista? Perhaps Nisha would like to hear about his dream. Would he have the courage to tell her? No, he *would* tell her. He had to tell her. This dream seemed too important not to. "Is it safe to talk here?"

"These walls hold many secrets. One I will show you. Come, the map of the Fey is this way."

Several halls of translucent walls. Stairs of light resonating from his steps. And the ice cold feel to everything he touched. "The walls are ice?"

"Ice? I do not know the word. The walls are walls made from the earth beneath our feet." She paused at a solid door. The only solid door that they had passed. "Do your walls not come from the earth?"

Did they? "I suppose but they are not translucent."

"Then I am truly blessed not to live in your world. Without seeing everything one could hide many secrets. And those secrets could lead to a terrible war."

Okay? *What was that supposed to mean?*

Pushing lightly on the solid door she whispered, "Here is the room of maps. I will try to explain what you need to know."

Ethan nodded. His dream was getting much weirder than he ever thought a dream could be. Must be the tonics messing with his mind. Yes, it was a good bet that was why his mind was doing this tonight of all nights.

The door slowly opened and the map… wasn't just a piece of parchment on a table but was the room itself. Glowing pegs in every country. Yellow in Lite. Deep purple in Darke. Green in the Serpent Marshland. Gray in Draken. And blue in what was known as the Mystic Woods. Then glowing white pegs clustered densely in Feyen. Then some scattered in both Lite and Draken. But more so in Darke. "What is this?"

"The white is what you call Feyen. True Fey."

Ethan looked again. "The lights are dim in Darke." *Almost burnt out completely.*

"The Fey are dying. When the lights are nearly gone so will Darke."

There was Feyen in Darke? No… his hand touched his ear. The ear that had once had the delicate point similar to his friend's. "My uncle did this."

Estare shook her head. "Not alone. There are dark forces at work here. They come from the Mystic Woods. You will find answers there. Unless the lights go out. Then there will be no answers at all."

No Darke? No life? Fear ran through him… he had to do something. But what? "May I tell the princess what you have shown me?"

"You may tell Nisha. Make sure she keeps the box closed and never opens it. What it contains is more dangerous than even I."

Box? What box?

The fire was just starting to die down when his eyes flickered open. He loved his dreams but he really wished that he wasn't so tired after them. A movement of a small animal at his feet brought him out of his bog. Blinking he watched at the… creature…. cat? … turned into the man he had met last night.

"David?"

"Oh good, you remembered my name."

Chatty for a Draken. Hell, he was chatty for a Fey. "Is Nisha around?"

David winced. "She is meeting with Queen Celeste and with the council. Personally, I wouldn't bother her right now… but if you really need her…" He let the rest trail off.

"I think…" Ethan tried to sit up just a bit and was very glad that nothing seemed to hurt right now. " …I can wait. Do you know what I need to do… for today at least." Huh?

David looked relieved. "Nisha has a tailor waiting for you not far from here. Apparently, he is the finest in the realm."

Finest in the realm? "Lord Taliare?"

"I think that is the name. Nish wasn't very impressed with his outfit so I doubt he is very good at his profession." *Or that he was meant to live through the encounter.*

"If he is being paid generously he is very talented. However, if you pay his standard fare the garments rarely last a full day."

"Ethan, darling, the princess told him if your coronation wardrobe does not meet her expectations I get to eat him. Do you really think he would choose to die a very slow death?"

Oh well, put it like that? "I think he will be less pleased with being threatened but will not complain too loudly."

Sitting back just a hair David narrowed his eyes. "You do not seem surprised that I would eat someone."

"You're Draken. Or at least, part Draken. I assume eating an enemy is standard fair."

David gave a warm smile and winked. "True. Very true. Though it usually takes most time to understand this."

"Obviously, they didn't grow up in Darke."

David gave Ethan an odd look, then smiled. "No, I suppose they did not."

M.L.Ruscsak

Chapter 23:
Nisha

A minute after dawn Nisha was in the main hall awaiting the arrival of her aunt. The royal apartment was perfectly pristine for a place that should have been ruined by the fire. Oh, at first glance it had been. Another damn spell this one so finally made it took her more than a full minute to break it, and that was after figuring out that it was there, to begin with. David had been just as surprised with the discovery. Well before he started to piece together a few things. None of them good. And none of them added up to her parents being killed eighteen years ago.

Why would someone go through all the trouble of burning down most of the city and …?

No, she would never find the answers this way. Perhaps she should go pay a visit to Prince Ciron. Or maybe go back upstairs and explore every inch of the apartment by herself, but neither appealed to her right now. No, right now she wanted to do something. Something that would be worthy of her anger and frustration. Something that would scare the preverbal shit out of every living thing in all of Darke and possibly the entire realm.

No, she would wait to scare the realm but today she *needed* to scare the citizens of Darke. She needed all of them to understand that she wasn't just the heir… she was something more. Something the dead called a creator.

So, she stood at the bottom of the grand staircase and waited until the double black stone doors opened and her Aunt took her first full step into her palace. "Did Uncle Blake come with you?"

Queen Celeste took a step back as if she had been slapped. Regaining her composure, she very calmly said, "You know he did. He is currently speaking to the guards out front to see why *skeletons* are guarding the entrance instead of citizens of your realm."

Nisha waved it off. "Since, they *are* citizens of my realm, who am I to argue where they choose to guard?"

Closing her eyes Celeste smiled. *"So, it's going to be one of those days,"* she whispered to herself. "I thought you would still be asleep at this hour." After all, in eighteen years she had never known her niece to be awake before midday.

Crossing her arms Nisha tapped her foot impatiently. "This is more important than sleep."

That couldn't be good. Not when Nisha was never awaking before noon. And certainly not when she was already pissed off and agitated before morning meal. "Oh?" Celeste took a small step closer to Nisha. "Perhaps we should speak in a more private setting?"

Shaking her head Nisha very calmly spoke, "Lord Edrich is no longer my proxy, you are. And because *you* are my proxy, we need to speak to the council. There is something that I need to say and you need to hear. Then you need to contact those who need to witness my coronation so it can be done tonight."

She had raised this child since birth. Had given her all the love that she could. And had more arguments with Nisha then she had ever had with her own daughter. But never had she heard that blend of anger, rage, and something that could only be called death in a voice… in Nisha's voice. "Because you are old enough to rule, I will yield to your request on the condition that you will not harm those you wish to speak to."

"I promise not to kill anyone who does not deserve it. David has already confirmed who needs to be ate or shredded and who would suit being tossed into the Endless Sea for the citizens there."

Oh, my. It was one thing for Nisha to contemplate killing someone it was quite another for David, who is a Draken, to suggest who would make a satisfying meal and for who. "In that case,

I will retrieve your uncle so that he can be present for the conference."

"Aunty, really, wouldn't Uncle rather be suited to contact the other royal houses? After all, I doubt he will find this meeting at all interesting."

"True, but if blood is going to be shed, I would rather him standing witness." Not to mention he would have a better idea on why blood was being shed and how to stop it. *Maybe* know how to stop it.

Taking her aunt's arm Nisha smiled. "Very well, I will yield to your request." Pausing until she had an accurate feel of her aunt's temperament, she added, "This is why you are choosing to let Lilly rule Lite now instead of waiting."

"Yes, dear. Dealing with you as my equal is not something I would be very effective at. However, your cousin is more than willing. And for that I am truly thankful."

Nisha made her way to where the council would be gathered. Even though she had never been here… to this room… she knew what it would look like. A large octagonal room with two sides longer than the rest. The room itself would have no windows save that of the glass dome that served as the ceiling. The only furniture would be the long table in the center of the room four high back chairs on two sides. Once for each member of the council minus the two who had been banished last night. Then two seats… golden thrones… placed at either end of the table for those of the royal house to be seated. No others would be welcome in that room…

…Well, except Blake. As Queen Celeste's husband and first chair of her court, he had the authority to go just about anywhere he pleased. And that included standing behind her in this meeting.

Standing at the double doors Nisha waited for them to open. A heart beat then two and they opened as Blake announced her arrival. "Gentlemen, please welcome Crown Princess Nisha Devros. " He offered her his arm to escort her to her place at the end of the table… the opposite of her aunt. "Now that everyone has gathered, let's proceed."

Gingerly taking her seat Queen Celeste smiled. "Gentlemen, please be seated." She smiled at each until they had done what was requested. "As none of you served under my dear sister consider this your notice if you wish to remain a part of my niece's council then you should start to act like it. I have been here less than a quarter day and do not like what has become of once a great country. A country that my mother took extraordinary pride in. And a country I once helped my mother rule before ruling my own country of Lite. So, let me assure you I am perfectly aware of what the laws were before and during my dear sister's reign. And I know what they have become since."

Angry faces from the six men at the table but none spoke the words that would surely get them killed.

"Now my niece has asked for an audience with you to discuss what I can assume is a matter of upmost importance. I have granted that audience to save myself from dealing with whatever the matter is that she has already come across." Celeste paused and smiled at Nisha. "My dear, would you be so kind as to enlighten us?"

Nodding to her aunt, Nisha rose from her seat then slammed the palms of her hands to the table letting soft thunder fill the room as storm clouds filled everything except the table and the space just a hint above. "Make no mistake gentlemen, this is no illusion. The clouds are very much real as is the lightning contained in them."

"B-b-but it's impossible." One of the men stammered.

"She didn't have that ability... she can't ..." Another choked out.

She ignored her captives for the moment, but she did notice the worry in her aunt's eyes and the guarded expression of her uncle. "Since I do like to be fair, I will give you each the chance to live. By the time the last bell tolls for the mid-day hour, every slave or those who *you* call dog are to be in the clearing west of the palace walls."

"All?" A collective gasp filled the room.

She wasn't sure who said it but that didn't matter... not yet. "I did not stutter. By mid-day, I will have my audience of my choosing or by nightfall, there will be no place for you to run that I will not find. Not in Darke nor in any other country.

" Pushing back from the table she disappeared into the gray clouds.

A clap of thunder or perhaps that was the doors slamming closed behind her. Then the clouds dissolved into the men at the table marking each.

A platform had been hastily made following the little announcement of who the princess had wished to see. Barrels upon barrels of water had been brought. One for each row of expected guest. A single dipper for each barrel.

Yet none knew what would be transpiring. None worried that the princess of Darke had the power to do anything, but all wondered how she had persuaded the council to allow this meeting to start with.

And all worried what would happen to Darke once she was crowned.

Nisha barely took her seat on the platform before a rather stout man stood at the base of the steps that she had just walked up a moment before. His robes, though old, marked him as a High-born. His pointed ears were Fey of some kind but it was the look of relief that made her take notice. "You may approach."

"You have your mother's looks, but your father's deposition."

"Oh?" She narrowed her eyes into tiny slits watching this unknown Fey but also keeping herself aware of what was going on before her stage. Aware of the slaves being forced to sit in rows before her. Aware of those who had the title of dog being more than forced to line up… standing… not sitting like those who were slaves.

In a moment, she would deal with them right now she had the unknown man to deal with.

The man slowly came up the handful of steps then knelt before her. "My name is Garwig. I was once your mother's second chair and Captain of her guards."

Unlikely. But she would need to ask her aunt about his claim. "It was said all my mother's advisers perished that night."

Very quietly Garwig hissed, "Not all that has been said is the truth." Watching Nisha raise a single eyebrow in question, he very respectfully said, "I was visiting … um… friends in Draken with your mother's blessing. When news of the fire reached me, I was urged to stay put." Making a decision, he added, "Your aunt and uncle are very wise and keep their own council."

"Yes, they urge me to do the same. And I do." Nisha smiled then rose from her seat. "I would like to speak to you longer but now is not the time. Please join me after the coronation when we can find a place more suitable for more private conversation."

"I would be honored, Princess."

As the last bell tolled Nisha stood then used the wind to enhance her voice. "Please give each of those here a drink of the water provided.

One full dipper will suffice for the moment." She turned her head to see the alarm on Garwig's face. Knowing that he was worried that she was about to poison all those who drank the water. Giving him a wink, and a friendly smile, she turned back to the crowd and allowed herself to feel. If he was truly a part of her mother's court he would know what that wink had meant… however, if he was lying… well, she had an answer for that too.

Closing her eyes, she didn't need to watch what was happening before her. She knew when another person took a drink of the water. Water laced with her blood. She felt their power, their longing to be more than what they were allowed to be. Felt the pain from fresh wounds. Felt the pains of hunger and starvation. Knew within minutes who should have glorious wings and who should have pointed ears. A few minutes more and there was a tug… almost familiar to her. Ethan? No, not Ethan. He was being fitted for the coronation. Ah… but the power from that tug was intoxicating.

Leaping off of the stage she used the mist to create her wings. Wings that usually weren't shown too many. Racing over the heads of those who were now bound to her she flew faster and faster till nearly to the last row then she stopped fluttering just mere inches from his head.

Not Ethan, but clearly family. She could see it in his face… in the way despite being in pain and starved… he held himself. Confident and ready for trouble.

"What is your name?"

The man looked up at her. For a brief, second, he looked confused then he smiled as he closed his eyes. "You can only be the daughter of my queen."

"Clearly or the binding wouldn't have worked, so tell me your name."

Slowly he went to one knee understanding that no one would dare touch him now. "Galeron. First chair of Queen Adrianna's counsel. And a friend to your father. "

Ah… so he didn't die as she had been told. So, if he was here… where were her own parents? No, now was not the time to ask. Not taking her eyes off of Galeron, she raised her voice once more. "All those here are now blood bound to me. Any harm comes those who are mine, I will know. All those here are to be escorted to the Spire and properly treated as the High-Born that they are. All, except for this one." She locked eyes with Galeron. "He is to be taken to the Castle of Night." She turned her head allowing herself to see the skeletons waiting off in the distance. "Loyal sentries please help him to the castle. Princess Lilly will tend to him personally."

The crowd that had gathered had done so thinking that the princess would rid them of the blight of their country. The slaves and dogs that took so much of their resources… their food, and so much space that they used for their filth-ridden sleeping areas. Now they stood gaping in fear. The princess who had come to them boasting only minor abilities, should not have been able to bind one of these horrid slaves…

…yet she had bound all of them to her.

She had bound adults who had been her mother's favorites. Ones that couldn't be killed even now. Bound children who were worth more as food than the sacks of flesh that had been kept alive. No, she should not have been able to do this. Fear washed through the crowd as they realized the truth that now stood before them. The truth that none had wanted to acknowledge…

The princess wasn't just more powerful than both of her parents combined, but she had the favor of those who lived in the Under Kingdom. That was evident when the skeletons marched out from under the shrubs where they had hidden themselves and were now escorting the slaves to the Spire. Four carrying the last of the former Queen's Council into the castle.

No, they didn't move until the little princess was out of sight but they all agreed that she must be stopped at all cost.

Chapter 36:
Ethan

He felt ridiculous. His feet were stuffed into fluffy overly padded house shoes; shoes that Lilly had insisted he wore since his feet were nowhere near as healed as she deemed appropriate for walking. Shoes that made his feet feel like he was trying to wade through knee-deep pond muck while wearing blocks of cement tied to his feet. Of course, the thick blanket that covered his new plush house robe and newly made sleep suit didn't help matters much either. "At least, no one will see me like this," Ethan said as he let out a sigh.

David stopped mid step and smiled. "Ethan, really would you rather wear what you are currently or have the tailor see you in the bedroom?"

"I would rather not have to wear the blankets that suited on the bed better." It was a grumble and after waking from his latest dream he decided to grumble loudly until someone started to make a lick of sense. Of course, his plan could also blow up in his face but judging by David's smile he didn't think so.

Placing his long narrow finger on Ethan's chest, David smiled. "Are you willing to tell Lilly that?"

"Well no." Ethan paused and took a deep breath. "Look I'm tired. My world… *my life…* has been flipped upside down and torn apart in the span of a single day. That and I'm getting married and I'm barely nineteen years old. I just met my bride who is to be the Queen of Darke. *The Queen.* And the tonics or what, not that Lilly keeps giving me are starting to make my skin prickle. Not to mention I think, Nisha is up to no good since both you and Lilly are trying hard to keep me away from her."

"Yes well. Nisha promises not to spring anything further on you for at least a decade. So, if she holds her word you're safe for today."

"I beg your pardon?" *When did a decade turn into a day?*

David shrugged then began to return to his slow pace down the hall. "Oh well, that's Nisha. She will really *try* to keep her word but you have to remember she is a Queen. And as queen, she cannot control every little thing that happens. Nish can try, make threats and scare the shit out of those who would oppose her. But she can't control them." David paused as he reached out his hand to a red painted door. "Well, she *could,* but only if they were blood bound to her. And I really don't think she would bind every living person to her if she didn't need to." He paused really thinking about what he had just said and reconsidered. "Then again, with Nisha doing whatever that has caused both the Queen of Lite and the Captain of her guards to be held up some place, not with Nisha… I could almost bet that she is doing to do something to scare the citizens of Darke." A friendly pat on Ethan's shoulder then Davis sighed. "Best not to ask her about it. I highly doubt whatever it is would let her keep her promise to you."

Ethan didn't move trying to take in most of David's rambling. He was remarkably chatty for a Draken, but David did make some good points. Deciding to close his eyes for just a brief second and sift through everything that he had just learned, Ethan heard another deep voice coming from the room that David had been leading him to. "It's about damn time you show up. I do have a business to run."

With a shudder, Ethan opened his eyes not wanting to take another step. He really didn't want to go into that room. Didn't want Lord Taliare to touch him. Really didn't want to see him. All of that didn't matter Nisha had… *paid*… for an outfit and that outfit had to meet her standards. *Whatever those were.* Slowly he padded into the room watching David explain something so softly only the tailor would hear. "Lord Taliare."

"Is this some kind of joke? I am the best tailor in all of Darke… I do not make my finest wears for *DOGS*."

Arching his back David turned to Ethan. "Cousin, you might want to wait outside. I will be but a minute."

Cousin? No, best not to say that. Not when he could see waves crashing in David's now gray-green eyes. Eyes that had been red but moments before. No, best not to say anything right now. Instead, he smiled then backed out of the room closing the plain red door as he did.

Ethan didn't know how long he had stood there watching the door but the next thing he knew was a soft voice coming from behind him.

"Ethan?"

Lilly? Why was she here? "I was asked to wait here." His eyes never left the red door. Or the room that he had just heard a terrible gargled scream coming from just a moment before.

"Yes, I'm aware. Now I'm taking you back to bed and your outfit will be ready before you wake."

He turned slightly. "Doesn't someone need to take my measurements?"

"Oh. Well, David already has them. Best not go in that room while he has bits of cloth to play with."

What?!? "I don't understand. What happen to Lord…?"

Taking Ethan's arm, Lilly smiled. "Darling, David is a Draken. Now don't get me wrong because this is not something that David would normally do… but the idiot insulted David by insulting you. His life is forfeit."

Stumbling back Ethan glanced over his shoulder shocked by David's actions. "Because of words?!?!"

"Not just words." Lilly took a deep breath. "Look. I know this is hard to understand right now. In a year or two trust me you will never remember not being related to a Draken but, in David's case, he is also part Fey. As a Fey, he sometimes is able to pick up on thoughts. Thankfully not often but when he does…"

"The thought he picked up combined with words…" Oh yes, he could see it now. But who's thoughts had David picked up on?

"Yes well. I think he picked up two thoughts… the ass' as well as yours. You must learn not to fear everything… especially when David is right next to you. He does not respond well to fear. More so when that fear is that of someone he considers family. He would never turn on you because of that fear but he will eliminate anything or anyone who is the cause. For that matter, so would Nisha. Although she does not keep her anger hidden as well as my David."

That was the best warning anyone had ever given him, it was just too bad that Lilly hadn't told him that earlier. "I'll do my best to remember that."

"Oh, oh, Ethan don't think that you did something wrong. You must try to understand right now... right here... your fear signals trouble. Meaning David can find a meal in whatever is causing that fear. You… well, you are safe. Nish would kill him if he harmed you. And I do not wish to think about what she would do if he did more than that."

"Thank you, Pri- Lilly."

"Good. Now lets us get you tucked into bed and Nisha will speak to you shortly."

Shit, he had almost forgotten that he had asked to see her. "Thank you."

Chapter 37:
Lilly

Lilly had barely tucked Ethan into what was loosely being called his bed when she felt the castle shudder. Not more than a heartbeat later something screamed… screeched… loudly. It sounded like it had come from outside but then again it could have been the castle itself crying for help. Looking past the stone walls and toward the main door, she could almost hear the gray polished stones moan in terror. Yes, it was defiantly the castle screeching. Or at least she hoped it was the castle and not something else that was tied to this castle that was making those horrid sounds.

Closing her eyes Lilly took a deep breath. Something has pressed Nisha beyond her normal control… Or perhaps this was her idea of scaring everything and everyone into obedience…

…*It was a possibility. It also wasn't likely.* No, Nisha would never do something that could terrify Ethan. At least not until he was confident that she wouldn't harm him.

Moving as quickly as she deemed safe she navigated the labyrinth of halls until she was all too quickly standing face to face with Queen Nisha… calling the Feyen queen who stood before her anything else seemed unwise. "Your Grace." She watched as Nisha took several very controlled breaths… waited until her cousin has regained some measure of control of her rage. Waited until the lost souls of the dead were no longer visible in the gray mist that were her eyes.

"Lilly, please see that my new friend is properly taken care of. He will be needed at the coronation. Though I think it best if he isn't too near the family. At least not yet."

Okay? What new friend? No best not to ask that…at least not until Nisha wasn't still seeping with rage. "Is the room across from yours available? It would help if I didn't have to stray too far from Lord Ethan… at least not until the coronation." That wasn't entirely true but it would be more convenient not to rush from one side of the castle to the other for the next several hours. Not that she would dare say that right now. Not when she wasn't completely sure if Nisha would respond as her cousin or a pissed off Fey.

"That's fine." Nisha turned back to the way that she had come and hissed, "Skeletons make for horrible medics, but they will do anything is asked of them."

"Skeletons? You have…" Lilly paused then shook her head. "Never mind. I do not wish to know anything further about your medics. However, is there anything useful that I need to know about your friend?"

Nisha's eyes closed for several moments as dark mist like tendrils flowed around her. After several deep breaths, she once again looked at her cousin as she confirmed what she had already known. "He is a light bearer and very difficult. I knocked him out before my helpers arrived." Turning to either make a hasty retreat or to terrify someone else Nisha quickly added, "Oh, once he is comfortable I do need to speak to him. I have questions and he is most likely to have the answers."

"Of course." Lilly paused before calling after her, "Ethan needs to speak to you. He says it is very important."

Lilly counted to ten twice. She had asked for the very injured light bearer to be placed in the tub… she did not say throw him, dunk him or anything else … she had said place him. Okay… fine… maybe she should have said *gently*. Of course, this could be the skeleton's way of showing contempt… or… perhaps they didn't understand what was left unsaid? Add that to the fact that she had never seen a skeleton of any living race that had spikes for spines, razors for fingers paired with fangs. Maybe she could ask Nisha…

…On second thought…

Taking a deep breath, she slowly began to remove the bits of cloth that barely covered anything except what was between his legs. Ignoring anything that wasn't a wound she carefully washed the grim… dirt… muck and dried blood from his shoulder then cursed with heartfelt sincerity as she inspected what had been hidden underneath. "What…" A single heartbeat later and she screamed, *David!*

Instant concern came back to her, *Lilly?*

I need you. **Now**.

A moment later and David crashed through the door still wet from his own bath. "What…" He paused seeing an unknown Feyen man completely naked in the pool of murky water. "Who is that?"

Ignoring his deep growl, she snapped, "A friend of Nish's who needs my talents."

Since he couldn't argue about that, nor could he kill the man for failing to identify himself, David smiled. "In that case what do you need my help with? Since you called."

She narrowed her eyes at him. He seemed calm, but that didn't mean that he was or that he wouldn't make a meal out of this man if he saw fit. "I need to know what kind of wound I am looking at. I thought it was a bite of some sort but the more I am looking at it… I think is a burn? A bite, maybe. But not an infection."

Sliding over to her David sat on the edge of the tub to better examine the wound in question. Leaning near the man's shoulder he sniffed then very carefully let his taloned nail caress the edge of the sore to feel for what his eyes couldn't see. After several tense moments of silence, he eased back, his expression grim. "It is a burn of sorts. Has some kind of poison in it."

"Oh good, I have some ointments that might help then."

He glanced back down at his finger glad he hadn't touched anything else with his talon. "Lil, I doubt anything that you have with you will help him."

"David?"

David closed his eyes. It was easier to have this conversation if he didn't see her expressions. "This is a burn from a troll hybrid. Not one of the common types that I know but I think my father would know better. He should be here shortly." Slowly he opened his eyes and looked nervous. "Lilly if this is a breed that is… um..."

"Just say it. We'll deal with the rest later."

David nodded, "I don't think this a known breed of troll. In any case, we may have found a worthy adversary for my father to hunt." He turned his hand over to show her his nail, now brittle and turning gray.

As the last of the covers were being wrapped around her newest patient Lilly saw his tired sea blue eyes watching her with mild curiosity. "Oh, I didn't think you would be awake for some time."

The man blinked once then tried to speak, "You're...?"

Smiling brightly Lilly answered hoping she could put him at ease. Yet still cautious since Light-bearers were rarely ever at ease. "Lilly. Well, Princess Lilly of Lite. But currently, I'm the healer tasked with seeing to your comfort."

With his eyes lightly closed once more he muttered, "*Wonderful.*"

It didn't sound like he was thrilled that she was helping him so she continued to smile as she said, "Yes, well, I am fully qualified. In fact, I surpass the skills of most any Feyen Healer."

Keeping his eyes closed, he took a deep breath as he mumbled under his breath hoping that she would just leave. Hoping that he annoyed her just enough to find an adult to tend to him. "You speak too much for being related to Addy."

"*Addy?*" She had heard that name before. Oh, yes... it dawned on her "Oh, aunt Adrianna? Since I never met her, I wouldn't know." Pausing she took more an authoritative tone, "Now would you like to eat or tell me about the creature that bit you?"

"Troll."

I know that much. "I see. Troll mixed with what? Since I know several species and I have never encountered a bite such as this." Nor venom that could monetarily harm a Draken. Then again it could have harmed David because he was only part Draken. Either way his father would need to be the one to find this creature.

"Troll bred with serpent. They control the lower mines. Or should I say they own the lower mines and tend to eat anything that enters."

Patting his hand reassuringly, Lilly whispered, "Now see, that wasn't hard. But the mines are not owned by trolls. The mines have always been owned by the royal house. In any case, it will be taken care of shortly."

Opening his eyes once more he looked at her trying to get her to meet his gaze. "Do you know who I am?"

"No, But Nisha wasn't in a mood to be asked very many questions or explain much of anything other than you had to be..." The moment she really looked his face she sat back. Same softly chiseled face. Then just around the eyes "... Oh, you're Ethan's father. That explains so much..." Pausing Lilly thoughtfully added, "Oh; I don't think it wise to tell Nish about the trolls. I will tell the Drakens instead. They will be much more reasonable than Nisha. "

Struggling to sit up, Galeron gasped, "*Ethan?* You know my son?"

"Oh of course. We met this morning… or… rather late last night. He and Nisha will be married tonight. So, it is rather fortunate that you were found today. "

Then everything is not lost. "I would like to sleep now." It was the only acceptable thing that he could say that should get the little darling to leave.

"Of course. If you need anything just ask I won't be far away."

Chapter 38:
Ethan

It wasn't the soft touch of his face that woke him but the heavy feral feel to the room. It was the feeling of the air swirling around him. Carefully he let his eyes open to see Nisha watching him. This morning he had found comfort in her gaze… but right now there was nothing comforting… nothing human in those dark feral eyes. Swallowing hard he tried to speak. "Princess?"

"What happen to calling me Nisha?"

Her voice was, at least, two shades darker than it had been when she had spoken at the party last night… and still filled with annoyance. "I wasn't sure if that would be welcome right now?"

She turned her head away from him and took a deep breath. "I'm pissed off, but not at you. I need my anger for a bit longer but you have my word you are safe."

That was the second person in a few hours to say that and neither time had he believed it. Still, he asked, "Is there something I can help with?"

"As long as you do what Lilly suggest then you are doing all that you need." She paused, "Lilly said you needed to speak to me. Something about it being important."

"I- I…" Ethan closed his eyes, trying to put what he needed into words. "What you think about dreams?"

Nisha pursed her lips and shrugged not really understanding where this conversation was heading. And how could she when he didn't know himself? "Dreams? Well, are we talking about dreams, visions or premonitions? The three, although related, vary a lot."

Slowly he said, "I- I don't know..." *There was a difference?* Of course, there was. She hadn't lied to him yet so he had to trust what she was say was truth.

"Then tell me about the dream and I will try to figure out which it is. Do not worry Lilly and I do this often for each other. You wouldn't believe how often one of us has a dream that needs someone else to interpret it."

He was surprised that the two cousins would share so much with each other. Then again, they had grown up with each other almost as sisters, so was it really so strange that they would lean on each other so much? "Really?"

"Of course. We are both seers but it is hard to determine a dream from a vision or a warning." She pressed her lips together realizing what she had just told him.

She didn't mean to tell me that. Still, he said nothing about her abilities since she wasn't ready to trust him with the knowledge of how gifted she really was. Sitting up slightly he cleared his throat and began, "Every night for several years I've had the same dream. A lovely woman. Fairy I think. We are in an endless gray tunnel. Darkness at one end and bright light at the other. "Ethan paused then quickly added, " I have never seen her while I've been awake."

"Do not worry Ethan. I do not fault you for dreams nor anything else. Besides it could just be your mind reaching out to find someone you could speak to without fear. Or for that matter someone to speak to at all."

For a long time, he was silent before he whispered, "I never thought of that."

Patting his hand reassuringly Nisha smiled. "Of course not. Your upbringing has been less than ideal. Now please continue."

He nodded once. "Last night was different. I woke in a tunnel but it was blindingly bright. The light dimmed as she drew closer and for the first time, I could see that what she was wearing… I have no name for the fabric." Stopping he let his eyes closed so that he could remember all the details. "We walked among her people though I was instructed not to speak. After walking for what felt like forever we reached what she called her castle."

"The castle of where?" Her tone was nowhere near asking but rather bordered a question yet nearing a tone that said she was worried about something.

"Loon… Luna… No, it was Lunaista. Yes, that was it Lunaista a star city."

"Lunaista." She grabbed his arm, this time in earnest. "What else do not leave anything out."

Yes, there was trouble he could hear that in her voice now. "The castle was made of translucent walls except for one room. She called it the room of maps. There were colored lights in each country. I knew where the countries were just by looking at it but I've never seen a map before." Now he opened his eyes seeing if she understood. Her eyes told him that she did. "Anyhow she said the Fey in Darke are dying. And that the answers are in the Mystic Woods. You need to go there to find them before the last light goes out or there will be no answers."

Nisha sat back and let out a soft whoosh of air, "Oh that's good. Yes, I think that's good then."

How could any of that be good? "Good?"

She sat for a long moment letting her heart settle in her chest before answering, "I have your words you will not repeat what I am about to tell you?"

That could not be good. Not with the worry in her voice or something more than worry in her eyes. No this was not good at all. "You have my word."

"The Fey, all of the Fey in Darke have been forced into slavery or called dogs. Their ears cropped much like yours and their wings removed. Last night when you were telling me it started to make sense but I waited until Lilly arrived to confirm what I suspected. Today… at noon, all of the slaves or dogs were brought outside the west walls. I bound all of them to me. All but one, are currently on their way to the Spire for proper treatment. I would have had them brought inside but I do not trust those who dwell here. Nor do I have the staff that can tend to that many injured Fey at one time."

He didn't care about her sending the Fey to the Spire. Didn't mind one of them being left here to be seen by Lilly. He *did* mind that she bound all of them to her. No… No, she couldn't have. Most royals could only blood bind a few dozen citizens to them not several scores… And certainly not thousands. Yet… "You blood bound… all of them?" Ethan squeaked.

"Many had been previously bound to my mother. Others like you were young children when the fire happened. It made perfect sense to bind them so they could grow into their abilities instead of being rushed into them. Besides, it's better to have a strong Fey bond to the queen than to risk one trying to overpower the royal family."

Is that what happened eighteen years ago? Someone that should have been bound to your mother wasn't and rebelled because of it. Or did they rebel because they didn't think she thought that they had been worthy of being bound to her? Not that he could ask that, but he *could* ask, "And the one that is here."

"They need a gifted healer *now* rather than *later*. Lilly has been asked to look in on him till we arrive at the Spire sometime tonight."

To injured to move. That was what she was telling him. Still, he needed to clarify another suspicion. "So… it wasn't a dream? It was something else?"

She nodded once. "Tomorrow will be soon enough to explain that to you. For today know that your friend's fears were just and have been taken care of at least for the day. It will take me a bit to put everything to rights but I have found some that might be willing to help me. Others may be content to return to Feyen. Either way, they will be safe."

He watched her stand from the bed now content to leave. "You think I will see her again?" *Is it alright if I do?*

She gave him an odd look before answering, "Ethan, I do not know how or why that friend came to you but that is a worry for another day. However, I am willing to count on her as a trusted friend and know that she will reach out to you whenever she pleases." Nisha paused and smiled before kissing his cheek. "Now rest. We still have a few hours before the coronation and I do not want you looking peaked when you meet the other royals of the family."

Ethan slipped the royal blue jacket on that had been left him. He wasn't sure of what the material was but it was softer than anything he had ever felt before, not only that the light weight made it easy to forget about the sores on his back that were still too painful to touch. As he buttoned the sleeve he caressed the fabric once again. Not satin but some kind of fur… and made just for him.

David leaned on the door frame a sliver of something white being held with his teeth as he smiled. "Oh good, I thought the color might be right to bring out the color of your eyes. Though I could have added a bit more gold to the lapel."

Smiling at David and choosing to ignore the sliver that he could now see might very well be a piece of bone, he bubbled over. "I can hardly believe this is for me. I have never felt anything so soft before, nor had anything that had been anywhere near this quality."

Pushing off of the door frame David very slowly came over to him to examine his work. "Yes well, I found the material in the tailor's bags. I asked Nisha if she thought the material would suit after I colored it. It was a horrible muck brown color before. Not suited for a wedding. Well not suited for anything really… But it did take well to holding different colors. After her approval of this color, she asked someone what the material might be. Since no one knows for sure she thinks it must be a rare breed of animal." He shrugged. "I offered to find one for her if I should ever go on a hunt when I visit."

Animal? "In that case, there are some small breeds that live close to both the borders of the mystic woods and the marsh. They don't tend to travel this far north nor west. And several other creatures can only be found near the forbidden wastelands. Not in them of course but near the border."

"Ah. Then I should find a reason to go that far south. Usually, I find the weather too damp for my liking but I can make an exception." Tossing the sliver of bone in the hearth, David continued, "Are you ready to head to your wedding, or do you need some time to get used to the idea of being married?"

"A moment please?" With David's nod, Ethan whispered, "Lilly told me about the tailor."

For a moment, David stood there not sure how to read his soon to be cousin then finally decided on a direct path. "Oh? Don't worry Ethan, you had every reason to be fearful of that atrocity. I do not wish to think about what could have happened if I had left you to go alone… Not that you would have really been alone. Nish confirmed that after she calmed down from her meeting… But… it is no matter, he can't bother anyone anymore. Really, he can't even bother her in the Under Kingdom. Food never makes it there."

No use asking anything about the Under Kingdom… no use asking about what David considered food. No use asking anything at all since he was sure he did not want an answer to anything he might be able to ask. Closing his eyes, he smiled. "Thank you."

David shrugged more relaxed. "No big deal. Nish said I could make a meal out of any living citizen. Unfortunately, I did not recognize his race so that I could avoid it in the future."

Making himself comfortable on Ari… A fury according to the house maid. Whatever a fury was… Ethan asked, "Oh?"

Taking the other spelled chair, one that thankfully hadn't been another creature at one time, David jokingly said, "Too many bones for my taste and way too much fat. Not a good mixture. And you would not believe what I had to do in order to get the filth out from under my talons."

"And here I was worried the about the taste."

Leaning back in his chair David laughed. "See you will fit well among the Drakens of the family." Allowing the chair to lift from the floor he continued, "Come and I will introduce you to my family." A brief pause then, "Oh, one more thing… do not encourage my father. He is of the opinion that one should do battle before they get married. He is not pleased that you are not allowed to partake in that bit of fun… more so since he brought a troll for you to kill."

A troll… to kill? How would he ever be able to kill a troll? The answer… he couldn't. "I don't think that would sit well with either Lilly nor Nisha if I tried."

"Ethan, it wouldn't set well with my mother if he so much as mentioned it. Trust me neither Lilly nor Nisha would never get a word in with my mother so close by." David leaned closer to whisper, "We won't tell my mother about the troll. She thinks it is for his before dinner snack."

For several minutes neither spoke as Ethan took in the sights of tapestries depicting the first Fey that came to this land. Ones of life in a star city itself. Others he didn't know what they were supposed to be of but they were breathtaking to gaze upon. Finally, he asked, "Do you know who will be attending? Or where we are going?"

"Yes, and yes. First, you should know everyone who is attending is family or related in some way. Such as my father and mother. My mother being Nisha's aunt on her father's side. Then you have my eldest sister and an older brother who is the crown prince, but only because my dear sister refuses to rule anything other than her wardrobe. "

"I take it she has a lot of …um… things?"

"Three wardrobe closets and she still can't find anything to wear. Living with Lilly, I think it must be something completely female since she had an entire room filled with things and never has that something special to wear."

"That's…"

"Impossible? She's female. Nisha does the same thing which is why she can't touch the closets. It gets her maid all ruffled. Now far as who else will be there…" David began to count on his taloned fingers. "…Queen Celeste of Lite will be proceeding over the coronation since there is currently no council."

No council? No, that just couldn't be true. Well, not entirely true at least. But it was possible they resigned after Nisha removed the two from Darke last night. "Not to interrupt but what happen to the one that has been ruling since the fire?"

"Ethan, do not ask that question… ever… Queen Celeste is already beside herself because of *whatever* has already happened today. And I am not asking Nisha anything that I am sure I do not want an answer to."

"Nisha?" Should he mention that Lilly had thought she was going to scare every citizen of Darke? Looking at David he decided against it.

Slowly David nodded. Changing the subject back to the original he cleared his throat. "Blake, that is Lilly's father, will be there. I think that is it but with Nisha, it's hard to tell. After all, she may have invited the entire Under Kingdom for all we know. Not that I'm supposed to know that she has friends there."

Why… or how… would she be able to invite those who are dead. Another question he would not ask since the answer… the possible answer was terrifying. "Would she?"

"Nish? Depends on if Freya was able to talk her out of it or not."

"Oh." Freya? Another name he should learn since she sounded like someone who could help him curve Nisha's judgment of some things. "I was told once that there would be parades and balls. A grand affair for the ages."

"Oh, don't get me wrong. There will be balls and a parade… as well as many people coming and going then you will ever see in one place… but that will be once we reach the Spire. Freya, That's Nisha's personal guard I'm sure you have already met her but have no idea who she really is. Well, she does not think that this Castle can be properly guarded for such festivities. Nisha agrees. So, they are having everyone, who wishes to congratulate the new queen to do so at the Spire."

"Freya? The Fey that stalks the halls?"

"That's her."

A thoughtful pause. "So the ceremony will take…"

"Less than twenty minutes including the wedding." David paused as the chairs landed softly outside a pair of smoke gray doors. "Don't think much about it or you'll work yourself into cold feet." Listening to the chatter beyond the doors he frowned "What is Queen Alista doing here?"

"Queen Alista?" *Was this another name he should be learning?*

"The… um… Queen of Feyen. She never travels outside her own country… ever. I did not think she would come here for the wedding. But rather have Nisha come to her in Feyen at a later time."

Chapter 39:
Celeste

Celeste fussily tied then retied the black lace bows than had been added to the back of each of the handful of chairs. After only having hours to plan this event that should have thousands standing in attendance it was only a handful of people and none of them were from Darke. Letting out a frustrated scream she shook her head and tried not to cry.

It was too dangerous to have the festivities here but Nisha wanted the crowning done on the balcony. Nisha nor Freya trusted those who worked here at the castle yet she was inviting strangers that had little to no use in the room to be here to watch her become queen.

…It made no sense. None. Then again Nisha never made much sense. She was so much like how her grandmother had been. So much so it was downright scary.

Hearing a door slowly creak open she turned sharply to the sound already preparing for an attack. Then she saw the woman who she had known for these past eighteen years. "Freya, you startled me."

Saying nothing she glided over to where Celeste was standing. Stopping closer to the middle of the room she frowned. "You do not yet have the table for the crowns set."

She glared at the fey who should speak to her with more respect… yet she had never spoken to her with more than civil tone. "I am not taking off my crown until it is almost time."

Freya took a single step closer to her and raised her voice. "You sound like a child. Need I remind you this is not about you but about the ceremony. In fact, this day is more important than any crowning has ever been."

Not to be out down she raised her voice louder than what Freya had used… "And need I remind you I am the only one who can preside over this ceremony."

It was then Blake gave the open door a token tap before entering completely, "My dear, there is a guest you need to speak to."

She watched him slide his hand through his blond hair nervously. Watched as her husband who rarely showed any signs of nerves looked more worried than she had ever seen them since they were wed. "Something wrong?"

"Depends on who you ask."

Answer but not an answer. "Freya, will you stay?"

"As I am already here I see no reason to leave only to return."

How did Nisha deal with her every day? The answer Freya liked Nisha, she was her queen by choice not by simply living in a country that Nisha ruled over. Not that any of that ever mattered to Freya. Oh no, she would speak to anyone however she saw fit and that had included the Feyen Queen. "Thank you. Blake, please show…"

"I do not have time for this." Black mist swelled the hall leading into the room till an older woman with raven colored hair stood before her. The same violet eyes that she remembered growing up gazing into. The same command pretense that had always overshadowed her own.

"Mother."

"Daughter." Queen Vasilissa glanced over her daughter's shoulder to the other Fey, "Freya."

"Your Grace." Fray gave a small nod of respect… still not showing proper respect for a queen.

"Tsk. I am not here as a Queen nor have I been one for more than two hundred years nor do I plan on leaving this damn forsaken place one."

"Mother! Be nice this is a joyful day." *Or at least it should be a joyful day.* In any case, she was not going to let anything dampen her niece's special day. Not even her own mother.

Vasilissa glared at her daughter anger brightening her eyes to an almost fluorescent hue. "Happy? You call this happy? A few members of a single family huddled in a secret room to watch a queen that should be the most powerful take her rightful place among the most gifted since the first Fey came to this world. And you call this farce *happy?!?!*"

"Queen Vasilissa you forget your place."

Vasilissa hissed with annoyance. "Not now, Freya-"

Shadows fluttered in along the walls where no real shadow could have been. "Do not make me remove you from this realm. You will not damper the joy of Nisha on this day."

"You wouldn't…" Shaking her head and reigned in her temper. "Of course, you would. I am not your Queen nor any friend of yours. You wouldn't hesitate to remove me."

Her mother backed down? Impossible yet she had just watched her do just that. "You came from the Under Kingdom. Why?"

"To watch my granddaughters be crowned. Why else?"

Celeste looked away as she whispered, "It is possible only one will be."

Taking Celeste face in her wrinkled hands Vasilissa smiled. "If you believe that, you are a fool. Can Nisha rule both Lite and Darke? Without question. After all, she is *my* granddaughter. But does she wish to rule more than she needs to? My girl, look around you Nisha has more to take care of here than anyone ever could imagine. In fact, if I would have thought it was this bad I would have ruled as her proxy to fix some of this long before allowing her to step foot in this kingdom."

"You were already part of the Under Kingdom."

"By my choice not because I was or am a citizen there. I was looking for your sister or any of the Fey."

"And did you find any answers?"

It was then Lilly rushed into the room, "Oh Grand'Mere I wasn't aware that you had arrived?"

"I only just. Now rushing around wearing a filth ridden smock is no way for a princess to dress."

Lilly looked down at her smock and underlying dress and smiled, "Which is why I'm here. Mother I could use your help getting one of Nisha's friends ready. He is very difficult to tend to and in little condition to even be in attendance."

Letting out a sigh, Celeste asked, "And I suppose, telling your cousin that he can't join us is out of the question?"

Lilly brought her finger to her lip and tapped appearing to be considering telling her cousin, "Well we could tell her but I doubt it would sway her opinion. She was very adamant about this guest being here."

"Very well. Mother, can you please see to the rest of the preparations?"

"Go. I will do what should have already been done. And leave your crown. This is about the ceremony, not your foolish pride, my daughter."

Nearly to the hallway that would lead then to the guest suites, Lilly let out a pained laugh, "Grand'Mere is in a rare mood today."

"You knew she was coming?"

"Mother, I do not ask Nisha things. She only mentioned that several of her citizens expressed interest in seeing her crowned Queen. I dare not ask who. Not that Grand'Mere really is a citizen of the Under Kingdom, but still."

If her beloved daughter knew about her grandmother not being dead then what else was she choosing not to tell her about? The thought chilled her. "So, the balcony is for…"

"The scores of citizens that are no longer fully alive. Nisha proclaimed that none shall enter the castle wearing a glamor spell. Well, she couldn't have them in Darke not wearing one and she will not sacrifice them to a fate worse than death because they wanted to see her crowned…" Lilly took a deep breath. "…It was the only solution that everyone would be happy. Besides nothing is going to enter that castle without the dead knowing about it. Think about it… it is an extra precaution in case Freya is right about the castle not being safe."

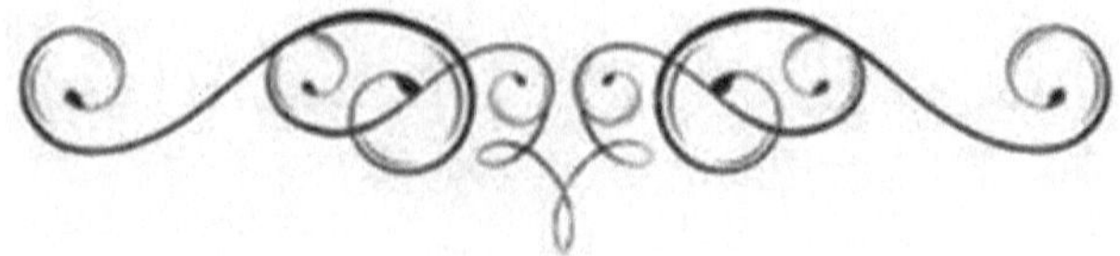

Scores of… no best not to ask… trying to keep her mind from Nisha's latest escapade Celeste pushed open the plain black door that was holding the person that her daughter needed help with. Taking a single step into the room she froze seeing a fully-grown man in a light sleep with nothing more than a thin sheet covering him.

Taking a slow deep breath, she glided over to him and gasped even with his skin hanging loosely from his body she would know him anywhere. "Gale?"

His eyes didn't open but he let out a pained whisper, "Addy?" When she didn't respond he opened his eyes seeing his mistake. Same voice but the wrong sister. "After all this time, I still cannot tell you apart by voice alone."

Knowing enough that he would never apologize unless it was absolutely necessary, Celeste said nothing. Not that he need to apologize, at least not about confusing her voice with that of her twin. Gingerly sitting near his middle, she decided on a blunt response rather than a soothing one. "You look horrible."

Closing his eyes once more Galeron let a smile twitch his chapped lips. "I feel worse, I'm sure."

Kissing the forehead of a man she once thought of as a brother she smiled. "Well let's get you feeling a tad better before your son's wedding."

Trying to sit up and knowing better to argue with her Galeron asked, "Why did Nisha do what she did today? Even her mother was not that careless."

"You mean? Declassify those who were not considered citizens?"

Fear ran across his face. "You didn't hear." Laying back and really wishing he was not the one to have this conversation he added. "Celeste, you are my friend so please do not take this the wrong way, but I understand why she did that. In fact, I am thankful. But what I was referring to was why she blood bound every Fey or part Fey that is currently in Darke? Not that we have not been preparing for this day."

"*She did what!?!?!* That… that's insane. No, more than insane, that's…"

Understanding lit his eyes. "She didn't mention it to you?"

"No, she didn't mention it to me." Looking to the door and to the daughter who had been much too quiet for much too long Celeste snapped, "Did you know about this?"

Edging into the room Lilly tried to look demure. "Well, not exactly. But I would rather eat stone then ask Nisha anything that was really none of my business. I mean really, why would I want an answer to anything that I could just as simply pretend not to know about... Besides, when Nish told me about... well, Lord Galeron and his condition... she was beyond pissed. You *did* hear the castle moan didn't you?"

"I thought it was the wind." was said at the same time as "The castle moaned? When Myrddin was pissed the gargoyles would scream."

When both ladies paled Galeron laid back and let out a pained laugh. "You both are mice. There is no way she can be worse than both of her parents combined."

Celeste glared down at him. "Would you like to bet on that?"

Chapter 40: David

Looking worried David began to stand up from his chair. Noticing Ethan doing the same he shook his head. "No Ethan, stay seated."

"But…"

Squeezing the bridge of his nose and truly wishing he was not the one to explain this to Ethan, he sighed as he began to say, "You're a part of Nisha's house now. That gives you certain rights."

Ethan narrowed his eyes in question, "Rights?"

"Hmm. You only stand when Nisha enters a room. Do so for others only if *you* feel inclined to do so. Nisha is very difficult and doesn't follow normal courtesies. I suspect that you will find her way of doing things much easier than doing them correctly. For today, stay seated until the doors reveal Nisha. No one will think twice about it. If they do, they will tell her about it. Or complain to each other when she is not around to debate it."

Making himself once more comfortable in Ari's embrace, he asked, "Do you think anyone will? Tell Nisha I mean."

With a huff, David hissed, "Hell no. No one in that room discusses anything with Nisha unless necessary. And complaining because you are following her example is not a necessary conversation."

"Because of her temper?"

"No. Because of what the possible answers may be. Trust me. Speak if you feel like it but stay seated. Lilly will have my hide if you are up moving around too much. And Nisha will have more than my hide if you look unwell for the ceremony."

Wait? What? "So… I shouldn't be walking yet I was walking this morning?"

"Confusing, isn't it? Just go with it." Looking at Ari, David frowned. "Well, this simply won't do to meet the Queen of Feyen." Pointing his long taloned finger at the fury, it's color went from a purple faded gray to a deep green. "No. That color doesn't suit the occasion." After several more tries and he was finally satisfied with a royal blue with gold trim. A color that nearly matched Ethan's suit. Then hints of black to outline Ari's eyes it was a precaution really so everyone would know this wasn't just a chair but a fury. "There that should do it."

Ethan looked down. David hadn't just changed the color but the material as well. Ari had been... made?... out of some kind of thick material that looked smooth but felt rough to the touch. However now... soft velvet covered every inch of the fury. And the content purring... Ah... Ari must approve the change as well. "How did you do that?"

"Oh well... my mum is Feyen and very powerful in her own right. She taught each of us certain spells and incantations. Only those that fit our personalities. For me, it's anything to do with cloth. Now are you ready? I do so want to find out why the Queen is here before Nisha."

With a nod, Ethan asked, "Do you think she'll react badly?"

Turning his back to Ethan, David hung his head. "I think today is going to filled with more entertainment than is needed."

Opening the tall golden doors, David paused seeing not only Queen Alista but Larna as well. Although she was seated near the back of the room staring out into space … she was still there… and still very much a threat. It was unwise to turn his back to an enemy but there was nothing Larna could do… at least not with the shadows fluttering near her. Turning to look over his shoulder, he made sure Ethan was following then carefully took the few required steps over to where Queen Alista was very quietly discussing something with… "Queen *Vasilissa*?"

"Who?" Ethan looked up now, worried since David had gasped. And Drakens never gasped… never showed fear or worry… and certainly would never do so in front of a royal family.

David never took his eye off of the two queens. "Oh, this can't be good."

Now more than worried Ethan started to stand. "David?

"No, stay seated. Something is wrong. Queen Vasilissa has been… um… dead for nearly fifteen years." Though looking at her she didn't look at all dead. No, she looked very much alive and well. Catching his breath David took a more princely posture and placed his hand on Ari's back. "Stay calm and act uninterested." It was the best advice that he could give for the moment. Now only if he could follow it himself.

"You mean to say nothing and hear everything. Yeah, I got it."

Great just great, he just managed to insult the one person who he didn't want to… especially since speaking to Lilly and finding out that he was an untrained Fey who powers and abilities were yet unknown. "Queen Alista, Queen Vasilissa, a pleasure to see you. May I introduce Lord Ethan Leuthar, the groom."

Alista turned to see who had dared to approach her without being told to do so. Her large sea-foam green eyes narrowed as she looked not at David but the boy who was sitting on a fury. "Leuthar? There is a family in Feyen with that name. Two now sit on my council of elders."

Trying to smile David softly said, "His mother was Lady Faerydae, your grace."

Her dim golden wings snapped open then shut with frustrations. "I see. Then you, Prince Davkren, should have instructed the boy on how to properly receive a visiting Queen."

Ethan leaned forward a bit in his chair. "If there is a problem with how you were received you should speak to Princess Nisha." *What the hell did I just do? I know better than to insult a high-born.*

"Yes, I see you are of the Leuthar bloodline. Now leave me. *Vasilissa* and I have much to discuss before the ceremony."

Taking a small bow David used his finger to guide Ari away from the two queens. As he left he could hear Vasilissa snapping, "You forget your place, Alista."

Nearing the balcony Ethan whispered, "What was that all about?"

"I don't know, but she's said to be a very grumpy Fey. Now would you like to see the crowns, or take your position on the balcony?"

"Whichever is safer for the moment."

"Then we will start with the table that holds the crown, then head outside. And hope we don't find any surprises out there."

Worry and suspicion filled Ethan's voice. "What kind of surprises?"

"Oh, don't sound so worried. It's Nisha so a surprise from her could be anything from a silver dragon soaring through the skies and scaring just about everyone…"

Ethan gasped. "Dragons don't exist… do they?" Winged horses, sure. Dead horses that carried the living to the tunnel of the dead … he couldn't prove it but he was willing to bet on their existence. but Dragons?

"Well… we have never been able to prove that if it was an illusion or real. And Nisha refuses to say either way."

"I don't think I want to know."

"See, you're catching on already. Now …" David stopped mid step and gasped. "This isn't right."

"What?" Ethan peaked around David's side to see a gold table with three crowns and two scepters. One crown made of gold with some kind of clear gem in each of it points. The matching scepter laying off to the left of it. Then a circlet of silver with no embellishments to say that it was crown at all. Finally, a crown made of black polished stone. Red gems glittering near the points. It's scepter laying to the right a dragon wrapped around the hilt a raven claw holding a single black gem. "I know the crown of Darke, but the others… why are they here?"

David gasped trying to find words for what he was seeing. "I don't know. The gold one is from Lite. It was supposed to be Lilly's but…"

"But you think Nisha…" He left the rest hang in the air as the double doors crashed opened and a tall stout man with large bovine horns stood in the doorway dragging a Wendigo by its foot. "Edrich."

David smiled at least one thing was taken care in proper order. It was enough for him to regain his composure. "Ah good the beast has been found. I should have told you sooner, my father is an excellent huntsman." Turning from the crown and the worry about what will happen in a few minutes he smiled. "I should introduce you before the festivities. He tends to get cranky if not told things beforehand."

Following David over to where his father stood, Ethan took a deep breath. Not because who he was about to meet but because of who was being dragged into the room.

"Father..." David glanced down at the filth that was unconscious on the floor. " ...I see you found Lord Edrich."

"Lord? He is scum. Not even fit for food. Even the trolls will not eat this one." His taloned fingers tightened around the leg snapping bones cleanly in two. "Bah. Worthless bag of bones. Not even muscles for a snack."

"Craykren, Behave yourself." A tall slim woman with coal black hair and ruby wings came up behind the Darken and slapped his arm hard enough for him to turn to her. "You will not eat that filth in my presence."

"I will not eat it at all. It is not worthy of food. The trolls do not want it either." He banged the head of Edrich against the wall more from frustration than from trying to break open the skull.

David blinked. Never... not once has he ever heard his father deny his prey an honorable death. Ever. His mother must be as surprised since her eyes were nearly twice their normal size. "Perhaps, one of the guards can remove him from this room until you decide what will be done with him."

"Yes. Very good. Filth is not welcome to the ceremony. Perhaps fatten it up. The hide may be useful."

Blake who had been standing on the balcony overlooking the crowds edged closer to the Draken King, "Cray? Perhaps one of my guards can take him now? We wouldn't want to upset the ladies."

Craykren thrust the limp body toward his friend. "He is slippery. Slit his throat if he tries to escape."

Looking at the limp piece of flesh he didn't think the ass could escape. At least not this time. Not with his legs broken, nor with his skull bleeding. But then again, he had eluded everyone else who had been looking for him.

"No." Not a voice in the room but one just outside. Quickly Celeste flew into the room. "No, his crimes are too many to a simple death. Freya, please see that he remains in the dungeon until Nisha can properly take care of him."

"Of course. Conspiring to kill the royal family is a heinous crime. I wonder what others he has committed."

Celeste nodded once and watched the Feyen warrior take possession of the beast, then turned her attention back to her guest. "King Craykren may I introduce Lord Ethan. Nisha's betrothed."

Sniffing the air, he nodded once. "You are injured. We will not battle today."

"Craykren, I swear if you make so much as one disturbance during my niece's special day I will turn you into a pixie… *again*."

David turned sharply so not to let his dad see him smile at the threat. After all, seeing his father turned into a brightly colored pixie wearing a skirt and only about the sixth of one of his long talons… it was hard enough not to laugh. It was also a warning since his father had remained that way for nearly a week the last time. He had not been happy *at all* about that.

Chapter 41: Myrddin

Myrddin's head rolled to the side as he slowly started to become aware of his surroundings. As his skin started to recognize the pain in his back, he jerked his arm in response… the iron chains that bound him to the cave ceiling rattled and banged together. Keeping his eyes shut he let his mind wonder for a brief moment…

…For too many years he had been bound here. According to his captors he had been stripped from all of his abilities and dark power. If they only knew the truth… If they only knew that he could escape at any moment … that he could destroy them with nothing more than a thought and with doing so nothing of them would remain… not a drop of blood nor sliver of bone. If they only knew he could have prevented all of this. Every ounce of pain he had forced himself to endure for all these years. Every attempt on his life. Every threat that they had told him. He could have destroyed them all years ago… but there were reasons that he hadn't…

…Nisha…

…If he had, his daughter… his only reason for being would have never grown into her full strength. Into all of the abilities that she should have by now. The gifts she would need to save not only her home but his as well. She would never have learned all the lessons that she needed to. She would have never known love. Never have learned when to trust those around her or when to ignore them completely. No, as much as it pained him he needed to remain here.

And alive.

Alive. Something his captors learned rather quickly that they could not make him. It didn't matter if they starved him nor set him on fire. Didn't matter if they filled his lungs with water nor if they tried to suffocate him. It didn't matter. Not even cutting his body into tiny pieces hadn't killed him. And that was a surprise to even himself and not an experience that he wanted to go through again. However, staying alive and unable to die had come with the price of maddening pain that even when there were no visible wounds he could feel the ones that were long healed. Then the hallucinations that were becoming all too frequent were starting to make him question his conviction about seeing this through. Made him rethink his sacrifice for those he loved.

"You sssshould let yoursssself die, Dark Prince."

Dark Prince, a name his captor had given him some time ago. Long before the uprising. Long before Nisha had been born. A time when the snake had tried to pose as a friend. Yet even then he refused to give the bastard the satisfaction knowing his true identity. A truth that even Adrianna, his wife didn't know. Couldn't know. "Apep." Yawning, he tried to sound uninterested as he said, "Have you come up with something new to try to kill me or come to bore me with your feeble attempts?"

Stepping closer to his prisoner Apep smiled as much as his tight lizard-like skin would let him. "My sssson will ssssoon wed your precious girl. Then you will watch her die."

"Your lies bore me snake."

Placing his four-fingered claw over his heart Apep laughed. "Me? Lie? I have no ussssse for liesssss."

Closing his midnight blue eyes, Myrddin smiled as he chose to see the ongoings in the Castle of Night. "We shall see who is lying and who will rule the Fey." Opening his eyes once more he leaned forward as much as the chains would let him and whispered, "And we will see who watches your children scream as they die."

For just a moment flames danced just behind his eyes.

Stepping backward Apep fell over his long green robe. "You have no power here. You can't."

"You think not. Then how am I still alive, snake? How?" Nothing more was said until he was once alone in his cell… then he laughed until his heart ached at not watching his darling daughter grow into the beautiful woman that she had become.

Alone shrouded in darkness Myrddin let the invisibility spell fall from around his wedding band. Until now it had been the last spell he had cast… feeling the cold metal against his skin he allowed himself to feel not just the band itself but beyond it. Dae had weaved her spell remarkable well for what her skill had been all those years ago. But that was not why he smiled… he smiled because his beloved Addy was wearing hers.

She was alive. Despite his inability to locate her… despite the snake going on and on about her demise, he had known that she was alive and now he had the proof that his heart needed. A moment longer and tears fell from his eyes. She wasn't just wearing the ring… she was looking for him. Their hearts already beating in time with one another's. Would she understand why his felt so weak?

No. He had never shared with her the spell that he used. Nor told her what he had done the night Nisha had been born. So, for now, she would need to be content that he was alive and take solace in knowing he would find her.

Although it might in all reality be she who found him first.

Taking a deep breath, he slowly let it out. It was time. So many would want his blood when this was through but that couldn't matter, not now. Not in this moment. He allowed himself a single heart beat to reconsider calling out for help. A heart beat more to debate what he would and would not say. A breath more and he hoped with all of his heart… with all of his being… that he was not making a mistake. He needed her help to end this but even he did not know if she would end this nightmare and save both of their lives. No, she could very well leave him there and seal the fate of both of their homes and their lives.

"Estare." He knew she was listening. The darkness was all she needed to hear even as far away as she really was he knew she could hear the words of any true Fey. After what seemed like hours, he called out once more, this time not hiding the rage and frustration in his voice, "**Damn it, dear sister, answer me!** " A moment longer and he added a bit more bite and authority to his rough voice but didn't sway in his conviction of calling out to her. **"Answer me!"**

Finally, bright iridescent light surrounded him, melting the rust covered irons that had held him for too many years. As the light pressed outward lighting the room, black fire burned, blocking the exit and any chance of someone racing in to interrupt their meeting. Knowing that there was nothing he could do until she chose to make herself known, he took a seat on the blood-soaked ground and waited until…

"You… *ungrateful… backstabbing… bastard.* What right do you have to dare summon me?"

He didn't see her, which really was terrifying since he could feel her every word vibrating off of his bones and ringing in his head. Sitting back so he would appear to be unfazed he rolled his eyes. "Hello to you too, dear sister. Shall we speak openly or do you wish to scold me for leaving Lunaista?"

Stepping through the wall of light, she pressed her glittering wings together and her narrow face blazed in fury as she growled, "You didn't just leave Lunaista, you *stole* our baby sister when you *fled*."

"I saved both of your lives. Or haven't you figured it out by now." He couldn't help it centuries of never speaking of this… never returning to confront either his mother or younger sister… he would be damned if he allowed her to speak to him so coldly. "No, I can see in your eyes that you didn't."

"Damn you. Mother and father killed themselves over your disgrace."

"They killed themselves as a sacrifice to appease the other star cities." Getting to his feet he stood towering before her. "Haven't you received a trinket box with nothing more than a few pieces of flesh laid inside?"

"Yes, but…"

Letting a burst of raw power flow from his hand he exploded the back wall of the cave then came to stand before her once more. "Damn it, Estare, open your eyes. It was pieces of the other children who could have ruled. The spare offspring of the royal Fey. A gift so the others would know that they were no threat."

Stumbling back, she pressed herself against the stone wall. "No… That…"

Taking in her fear… he continued in a voice that no one would dare question, not even his wife, his queen, "Do you really think I would allow myself to become King to *anything* if it meant killing you? *Killing our baby sister*? Then being forced to cut both of you up to send pieces of you *to them*? No, be mad at me if you will. Be blind if you must, but I will not apologize for doing what was right."

She watched him turn and being to pace, then in a soft whisper responded near tears. "You could have told me sooner."

Myrddin shook his head. "It was forbidden. As were so many other things that you have since made public."

"You know?!"

"Come now, we both know even among the other stars and royal Fey there is no one who is half as powerful as I am."

She turned her back to him trying to hide what it was that she was feeling. In a soft voice that she seldom used, she said, "So you want your crown back." Not so much a question but a hopeful statement.

"Hell, no I don't want that crown. But *I do* need your help."

Estare took a deep breath, "Go on dear brother. What, pray tell, do you need my help with? Since you are all so powerful."

He didn't fall for banter, but instead tried to keep his voice level, "Your niece, have you reached out to her?" He hoped but he also doubted that she had. Not when she believed that he had abandoned her to the cold dead place that she called home.

"No, but by accident I reached out to her betrothed." Which had puzzled her the first time… now?

"Ethan? Good. Faerydae, that is his mother, is Magmas' daughter. He sent her here to save her from the sacrifice. Do not doubt to hide those blood lines or his own ability."

"Magmas? But he… He's ruler of all of the star cities."

"Yes, I know. Sounds impossible he would have a shred of compassion in him. Never the less… It's his bloodline that rules what is called Feyen. However, that is not of common knowledge, at least not here."

"Oh wow. I knew that our people were the protectors of the Fey here on the solid earth but not about the other."

"We don't have time for this. After this is over then we shall speak about what needs to be done to save our home. Right now, I need to save my daughter's."

"Very well. We will discuss the others later. Tell me what needs to be done."

Creeping over to the wall of black fire, he peered out. "If I cross the fire my wife will be killed before I reach her. You need to tell Nisha that she is being held near the mouth of the healing river."

"Is that not where one of the pillars was said to be? The landing site for the fey who choose to come here?"

"Yes, the Eostre once lived there. In fact, they were the official greeters for those who came to this land." He paused feeling his anger grow once more. "And that is why they were slaughtered. Someone wanted the power that they bleed away from those who traveled there. I suspect it was the same bastards who now hold my wife captive."

Estare turned to the mouth of the cave. "No, the chicken lizard is much too young. Perhaps a distant relative may be responsible."

"Possible." He took her cold hands into his, "Will you help?"

"For as powerful as you are. And for knowing things that others cannot possibly know… how do you think I would not help my niece even if she is *your* offspring?"

Giving a soft kiss to her forehead he whispered, "Thank you. Now go my little phoenix."

Stepping away from him she nodded and slowly began to transform into the shape that so few could hold. And fewer knew could still be formed.

Chapter 42:
Nisha

Nisha stood looking at herself in a tall silver full-length mirror that she was floating before her. A few moments before she had been deciding on how to wear her hair and picking out the few pieces of jewelry that she was going to wear…

…But that had been before.

A moment ago, she had felt something. That something had been enough for her to take caution and look for whatever it had been. Turning to see the whole room she knew what she was feeling - Something or someone was watching her. Who or whomever they were far away. Not in Darke… no… even the border of the Mystic woods felt closer than the person felt. So, they were no threat. Lest not today. However, following the feeling, she knew that they felt relieved to see her. It felt as they had been hoping she would be doing exactly what she was… getting ready for her wedding. Which made no sense - none at all? If someone wanted to see her wed they just had to come to the castle and watch. Unless something was preventing them from doing so. "Tomorrow will be soon enough to find you." She said to her reflection but hoped whoever it was would take it as a warning.

Sighing once more she took in her reflection and tried hard not to think. She had always been good at hiding most of what she felt. Loneliness was masked by a sassy tartness. Worry masked with over bubbly enthusiasm. Love? Affection? She had always cared for her aunt and cousins both David and Lilly but feared if she loved them they too would be taken from her… so she had never said the word. But today?

Would she have the courage to allow herself to fall in love with Ethan? Would he ever return that affection if she did? Lilly made it look so easy with David. From the first time they saw each other, she had wanted no one else… But Ethan? Even bound to one another he seemed more likely to follow any order than to give affection. Then again, he may just need time to adjust to not being a slave.

But that too was a worry for another day… Today …

Today she was giving in to a few moments to wish her mother were here to tell her what she could do to make the dress appropriate for a wedding. She was giving in to the moment of regret of not having her parent who she knew loved her with everything they had had. Sniffling she looked back at her dress. Not really a wedding dress but the finest one that she owned and all she could come up with to make it look more appropriate were a fine black mist intertwining with the cobwebby gray dress that faded into a thin veil that covered her legs. Her mother would know how to make it completely breathtaking after all if she could design a dress for her coming of age ceremony just hours after giving birth surely, she could design a wedding dress.

It should have been possible. It should have been.

Yet… it wasn't.

Sniffling once more she held her tears at bay. As she let her raven colored hair cascade down her back she pulled a single strand over her shoulder then placed her little bone earring in the lobe of her ear allowing herself to trace the delicate point. Her aunt didn't have the pointed ears, neither did Lilly so were they inherited from her father? She didn't know. There was not a single picture, hologram nor painting of him. At least, none that she had found in any castle that she had ever been in. Including this one. Then again, her aunt Alyisope didn't have ears like hers either. But they could have simply skipped her. Touching her ears once more she sniffled, it was the only thing she had of her father.

Not giving into the tears she stomped her foot in frustration. He should be here to escort her to her betrothed. Perhaps in a way he was. He had given her Ethan. He had chosen him from any other.

Closing her eyes, she put her parents to the back of her mind. What good could becoming weepy do her today? No, she needed to be confident. She needed to be the Queen of the Under Kingdom and the crown Princess of Darke. She needed to be fearless and breathtaking. She needed to appear fierce.

She needed her wings. The wings that were also from her parents.

Not her wings that she created every so often. The ones made of mist and whispers. No, she needed her wings. Wings that her aunt thought of as fake decoration. The ones that terrified Lilly. Lilly would forgive her, after all, today was about appearances and not appeasing her relatives. Keeping her eyes shut tightly she arched her back as her wings formed to her back. A moment to get over the tearing pain that had always come when either removing or forming her wings then she took a final deep breath to see them.

Beautiful. Breathtaking. And deadly. They were perfect.

They didn't have the shape of fairy wings, but rather resembled those that belonged to the great dragons. Curving over her head they nearly linked with one another with their silver talons. Her eyes looked at them making sure that they hadn't become damaged somehow then breathed in relief as she saw how they stopped just a breath before the floor. For a moment, she pondered them.

By some happenstance, they were made not made of skin nor flesh. Not made with feathers nor membrane, not even scales. No, she wasn't sure what they were made from but she knew they were clear. Save that of the gray, blue and black wisps of color and the silver outline. No, they were an oddity. Stronger than stone, unlike fairy wings that were so frightfully delicate. Yet they appeared to look more delicate than even the tiniest butterfly. Yes, they were perfect and after today, she wouldn't need to keep them hidden.

Her blood red lips curled into a smile. So, few had seen her wings. Even among her family only her aunt and Lilly had seen them, and only Lilly knew they were real. It didn't matter after all she was not wearing them for her guests, she was wearing the one thing that she had from both her parents. The single gift they had given her and hid from everyone until she had been old enough to hide it herself.

A knock on the door kept her from thinking anything further. "It's open." She didn't mean to snap but she needed to so not to cry.

"Nis--" Lilly stopped and peered around the room. Mounds of dresses, tunics, hair decoration all scattered about. "Oh, you are in so much trouble."

Turning to her cousin she smiled so sweetly. "I doubt it. After all, Mari made most of the mess herself."

"Marigold? Did this?" Lilly took a step back in disbelief, "Surely... Not." Then she noticed the wings. "Nisha?"

"I know they make you uncomfortable but as queen of Darke I need them. My parents understood that."

Closing the door so no one could hear Lilly lowered her voice. "You know they make you look like the first Fey."

Softly she whispered, "I know." After all, she had seen the tapestries in both the Spire and Castle Sun-tear. And had seen more than that in her dreams. The dreams that she still hadn't brought herself to tell her cousin about.

Pull herself upright Lilly took a slow deep breath as she said, "Well, they are yours so who am I to judge the wings of another royal?"

Nisha smiled, erasing the last bit of her sadness. "That's why I like you, Lil, you see me for me and yet don't fear me."

Lilly returned the smile. "Fear you. Oh, you terrify me on a regular basis, but we are bound to each other so I know you cannot harm me."

Linking her arm with her cousin she asked, "You haven't told anyone about that have you?"

"Nisha… really why would I ever tell a single soul that when we were five we drank each other's blood and swore never to harm one another? Do I look like I want to hear a lecture on blood binding?" Not to mention the other binding when they were thirteen. No there was reason to ever tell anyone about either.

Both girls laughed for a moment before Nisha straightened up. "We should go. The dead are getting restless."

Slowly walking down, the long hallway, Lilly leaned into Nisha. "Ethan's father is seated in the back row. He has a clear view of his son."

Stopping short Nisha swore, "I'm sorry, I should have told you who needed to be healed. I was just... so... confused... pissed... I don't know. But I should have told you."

"I'm glad you didn't. Frankly, I'm not sure if I could have believed you if you had. I mean really... we were told he was gone... dead. So, for him to be here now and alive? No, I wouldn't have believed you until I saw him with my own two eyes."

Blowing a breath out once more, Nisha asked, "Is he comfortable?"

"As much as possible. He needs to eat but that will be taken care of soon. And sleep... lots of sleep. Then I need to find something to help heal some of the wounds that I found. Even mum doesn't know how to treat them."

Great. No, she wouldn't damper the mood instead she would take joy that he was there to witness this occasion. "We're going to the Spire for the reception. Freya wants to go through the entire castle without needing to watch after me."

"And here I thought the shades could do that in just a few moments."

The color drained from Nisha's face. "Lilly, don't ask them. Far too many have a thirst for blood. I want to know who can be trusted and who needs to not be here... *before*... I let them hunt."

The fact that Nisha was worried about her shades... oh yes, they were more dangerous than everyone had thought. "Yes, that sounds like a very good idea then. For a few minutes, more neither spoke till... "Queen Sedna arrived a few moments ago."

"Oh good, I was hoping she would be able to come. She doesn't need an orb of water to sit in does she?"

Lilly just nodded, "I thought you had invited her. Mum didn't believe me." Then remembering the question, she added, "Oh, she's fine. Apparently, sirens can walk on solid ground for several hours and sometimes days. And if that makes sense please tell me. Because I am really horrible with those who dwell in the sea."

"Sedna's mom was a siren, her father as you already know was a water dweller. His exact race I don't know. I do know he couldn't leave the water and was very pleased that his daughter could. Or so I've been told."

"So being part siren she can walk the land."

"Yes." Nisha shrugged, "Though, her coming on land for a day to explore is not the same as coming for a special occasion."

"Ah, so the coral crown and glittering dress made of fish scales are for show."

"Darling you have no idea. The last time I visited her, she was debating what color coral would go with her hair… and that was all that she was wearing."

"Please tell me the coral covered her."

Giving her cousin a sideways looks she shook her head then sighed. "We set rules for when we visit. Such as she will be dressed in something I recognize as clothing or I simply will not stay."

Chapter 31: Ethan

Ethan took a deep breath and slowly let it out. He didn't know if it was his own instincts or if Nisha was telling him she was close… but he could feel her. Almost smell her. Almost feel her caressing his skin…

"Ethan?"

Looking up at David he watched him nod to the door. Closing his eyes, he slowly stood. "Is Nisha sure about this?" *Not the place but marrying him.*

Facing Ethan, David placed his hands on his new cousin's shoulders. Both to steady him but also hold his full attention. "You are the only gift her parents ever gave her. Trust me even if you were a hairy drooling troll slug she would marry you."

Troll slug? Was there such a thing? Didn't matter it had caused him to smile which was probably David's intention to start with. "Thank you."

"Boys."

David hung his head at Celeste's stern warning. "We'll behave… *mom*."

Her eyes just narrowed a bit more but before she could say anything the doors opened as Lilly fluttered into the room. Her feet lightly skimming the floor as her crushed red dress formed around her. "Daughter."

"Nish is on her way. Um… someone needed her attention to deal with something? I didn't wait to see or hear she needed to know before entering."

Keeping his eyes on the little drama Ethan forced himself to keep a straight face when the Queen of Lite muttered, "Someone alive I hope."

Lilly just looked at her mother and smiled choosing not to say anything further about the person who was talking with its queen, "Should I go find her?" A tap on the door and she saw her father standing there. His royal blue suit perfectly pressed and adorned with so many medals and ribbons that his jacket was nearly filled. "Never mind I guess…" She stopped suddenly and shook her head. "David some assistance please Nisha is having a slight problem."

David brushed past him and gave just a tiny single nod to sit. "Your grace?" *That was an acceptable term, wasn't it?*

"Ethan, darling you're family. Aunt Celeste will do just fine. "

He let himself absorb the words. Not just aunt but family. "Is there a reason Lilly and David just floated the one guest out to the Hallway?"

"Probably. With luck, I will never know the reason." Seeing her husband coming to her with a look of fierce determination on his face she knew that would not be the case. "Blake?"

"Does he know?" He glared down to Ethan who was once again sitting in the chair.

"Not yet."

"Do I know what?" Ethan squeaked out.

Blake locked eyes with Celeste then both nodded in agreement, "Nisha can explain it." Then seeing fear creep into Ethan's eyes Blake went down on one knee so Ethan wouldn't have to look up at him, "You have my word that what is going on will not harm you. Just confuse you. In all honesty, it confuses me but it is a good thing. You have my word."

"And Nisha is…"

"What I can tell you is that the man who was escorted out was a close friend of her father's. She wants him to escort her here instead of me." It should have hurt his pride but it didn't. Not when he was overwhelmed that someone had lived through that night. Not when he had missed his friend and was relieved to be able to see him once again. And Not when it gave him hope that everything that Nisha was already beginning to unravel would turn out for the best.

Too simple. Yet light bearers didn't lie. Couldn't lie… at least according to what was told about them. "That doesn't sound too bad."

A breath more and both Lilly and David reentered the room. When his eyes met her's, Lilly smiled brightly at him, "We may begin now. Oh, and Grand'Mere please refrain from scolding Nisha, I'm not sure she could deal with one more thing today. Her temper is already frayed beyond even her tolerance."

The moment Nisha and her unnamed escort were in the doorway he stood. From where he was standing, he couldn't see her clearly. Not till she was nearly half way to him then…

…A vision of beauty that Estare couldn't even complete with.

And he was marrying her. He would be by her side for all time. How had he been so lucky to be chosen to be her husband?

He didn't need an answer. Really didn't want one. No, all he wanted was to remember every moment of this wedding. He needed to always remember the gray cobwebs intertwining with midnight black mist. A thin gold necklace and its red pendant hanging just above the heart-shaped neckline. But it was her wings that were so much more than breathtaking but he had no word to adequately describe them.

A snippet of a memory tugged at him. He had seen wings like this in Lunaista. Not Estare but there had been paintings of others who had had them. Later he could explore that memory… today he was only going to think about those in this room. No, he would only think about what his life would mean now that he was marrying the most unique and audacious person that he had ever met.

Then he saw the man who had been taken out of the room just moments before. Narrowing his eyes, he decided that he was much too thin to be just thin but… No, he couldn't think right now. Or at least, not to think of the reasons he was so thin, or why he appeared to be sick. No, he definitely couldn't think about that. But he would concentrate on Nisha, his soon to be wife and queen. After the festivities were done then he could worry about everything else.

Watching Nisha as she took her last step out to the balcony he squinted his eyes not understanding the tiny nod to the man until he kissed her cheek and took a seat. Still, he pondered that little friendly kiss until Nisha asked, "Aunt Celeste?"

"We'll speak after." Then the queen of Lite stood as tall as she could and let the wind enhancing her voice, "Dear citizens and family, thank you for assembling for this glories day. As the Queen, of Lite it is my honor to bestow the crown of Darke to its rightful queen."

The roar of the crowd who stood in the courtyard took him by surprise, but Nisha was patting his hand soothingly so he would remain calm. Then Nisha turned to him her mystical wings flaring out just a hair.

"Ethan?"

He could no more look away from her then he could take his own life. Her voice was washing over him. She was doing something to him. She had to be since he couldn't see those who had come to witness this day. No, he could only see her and a wall of solid black mist. "My queen?"

She touched his face attentively and smiled. *She has such a lovely smile.* He thought just before he heard her say, "Nisha will do just fine."

Ethan nodded then turned his head to kiss her fingers. He didn't know why he had but it felt right. The smile on her face confirmed he made the right decision. "I don't know the words to be said."

"Do you trust me?"

Did he? Could He? He only nodded. "No one can see us, can they?"

Her smile changed from a happy smile to conspiring one, "Lilly can. Everyone else? They see something. Hear something. Each will see and hear what they wish."

He took a deep breath and looked deep into her eyes. Deep chasms. Hints of fire and smoke. Ice spiking. Then he saw something. Death. He could see it in her eyes. The lost souls that didn't make it to the Under Kingdom. The souls that no longer had bodies to hold on to… all of them waiting to be unleashed. "Nisha?"

Her finger pressed against his lips. "Do you promise to share all that we create together?"

He licked her lips when her finger withdrew. "I do."

"Then as this day forth I will share all that I am with you. You are my equal in the truest meaning of the word." A small knife appeared in her hand. The point pricking the tip of a single finger. Blue life blood swelled up just before she placed a single drop on his bottom lip. "With this, we are bound. In life and death what is yours is mine. What is mine is yours. I affirm this bond." Then she took the blade and pricked his finger taking the single drop of blood to her lips.

For just a moment his vision swayed and he was sure he could see things beyond the room… beyond the castle. A score of people trying to break in. Something he couldn't see keeping them out. A shield of some kind? "Nisha?"

"I know Ethan. I see them too. There is nothing in this realm I cannot. *If* I so choose to." She pressed her lips to his. Then stepped back ending whatever spell she had created.

Celeste looked dazed. "Um… Excuse me I seem to be at a loss for words."

"Perhaps we should complete the crowning?" Nisha smiled in a way that made a question into a command.

A shake of her head then Celeste recovered. "Of course." Floating the long gold table over to the balcony Celeste stood proudly. "Usually, only one crown is presented… however on this historic day, Crown Princess Nisha Devros please choose your legacy."

Two crowns for two countries and the simple circlet of the Fey. A crown that had been made for the first Queen of the Fey. Nisha let her hand hover over the table. Let the whips of Darke tendrils caress each of the crowns letting the power speak to her. "Lilly come here."

Ethan saw Lilly give both Nisha and her mother a confused look but took the few steps over to the table. "Nisha?"

Very carefully Nisha picked up the golden crown then turned, "By the power granted to me as Queen of the Under Kingdom I crown you Queen of Lite."

This wasn't what was supposed to happen. It wasn't. The collective gasp from the room told him that much. The fact that the room… a room that had been candle lit was now was filled with a brightness that only the sun could match. Made whatever was happening much, much more terrifying. Still, he could say nothing.

The brightness slowly faded and Lilly the new Queen of Lite nodded to her mother who was looking more apprehensive then she should have if this had been planned. Carefully Lilly caressed the crown of Darke then placed it upon the silver circlet. " By the power granted to me as the Queen of Lite, I crown you the sole queen of both Darke and Feyen."

Just before the crown touched Nisha's heard a terrible scream erupted from the woman who had been seated in the back. "*Nooooo!!!! It's mine!!! MINE!!!*"

Chapter 44: Nisha

Slowly Nisha turned to the sound of the screaming woman. Her eyes blazing with a dark fire. "So, the puppet can speak after all." She took a few steps closer to the woman, her dragon wings uncoiling just enough where spikes could be seen around the edges. "Funny, according to my father's spell you should have no control of your tongue unless you gained a heart. But not *your* heart since that is still locked away."

Larna tried to lunge for the crown that now sat on Nisha's head… barely made it to her feet when hands made from mist grabbed her pulling her to the ground. "It's mine! MINE!!! You can't have it. I won't allow it!"

Everyone who had been seated in the small room quickly got to their feet… and just as quickly pressed themselves against the walls. Including King Craykren, who couldn't trust that even he would live through an altercation if Nisha's temper slipped. Or for that matter if the mist that was now holding Larna was truly the deadly race that were only known as Shades.

Reaching out her hand, Nisha caressed the fallen queen's face with nothing more than the tips of her long red nails. "Yes, I see you do have a heart. Pity it does not belong to you. Nor did you receive it honestly." She turned her eyes now locking on Ethan who like everyone else was trying not to move. "My husband, would you like to know how it is that I know her heart is not hers… in fact, it's not even from a Fey."

How could she know? Only one way to find out. Ethan nodded once but refrained from speaking.

"Very well." Suddenly a scepter made of bone appeared in Nisha's grasp. A heartbeat later as did the scepter of Darke. Creating a bright purple light, the two scepters forged themselves into a long staff. A black stone dragon now wrapped around pieces of bone. The raven claw now holding not only the Stone of Night but a clear red stone with swirling mist contained inside. That stone could only be the long-forgotten Seer's Stone. "I call for what had been hidden to be seen." A silver box with intricate inlays appeared before her.

"Nisha!" Ethan screamed out. "Don't open the box." He stumbled a few feet before he could no longer move. Something was preventing him…

… Not something… Nisha.

For a heartbeat, she locked eyes with him. "None shall touch the contents but me. You have my word, Ethan." A thin veil of white light surrounded her as she slipped the lid open. Inside was not just the heart that her father had taken but another as well. Tentatively she touched the larger of the two. Images flowed to her. Not those of the murderer but those of her father. Images of her birth. Then images from much, much later.

She would find the answers to the questions those images had shown her but not now. No not, right now but after she dealt with Larna. Locking her eyes with the Feyen queen she grabbed the heart. She had been given a letter addressed to her just moments before entering the room for her coronation. It had been from her father sealed until her eighteenth year. Now she understood why he had taken the heart. Too bad she couldn't share the images.

"Long ago my father took your heart and all those who witnessed it were bound not to speak of that day. I release them from that binding." Her fingers squeezed the still beating heart just enough so not to lose her grip. "My dear Gwydion please stand before me."

Black mist swirled before her slowly transforming in the shape of a man. Carefully he knelt before her. "My queen?"

"I know some of the lore of your people. Is it true that the heart of an enemy is a rare delicacy?"

He looked up at her, his eyes no longer orbs of mist but liquid fire. "It is."

"Then please accept the heart of an enemy who would do the same to all the Feyen lands that a traitor did to yours."

Gwydion nodded once. "You are most gracious, my queen." Slowly he stood taking the heart from her, "With this heart, I release her soul to wander for all eternity." Bringing it to his mouth he bit down once, letting her black mist-like blood drip to the floor.

Nisha watched as the body of Larna crumpled to the ground. Her soul already trapped within the stone of her scepter. The heart that she had stolen dying with her. The heart of Lord Edrich. Taking a moment to breathe before she became sick she turned to her guests, her eyes never showing anything but confidence. Later she could ponder how Larna had conned Edrich out of his heart. And much, much later she would decide if it had been Larna or Edrich who had destroyed all that her family had worked to build. But right now, she had other things that took priority.

In a clear voice one that only a queen should use she spoke, "Honored guests, the castle is no longer safe for you to return to your carriages. I have other means for you to reach the Spire."

The butt of the staff tapped the stone floor three times. "Gate of the Dead, I command you to open."

Bodies of the dead formed the doorway itself. The door nothing more than a red mist. "If everyone would be so kind to walk through. You have my word no harm shall come to you."

Lilly was the last one in the room, other than Nisha. "Nish, what's going on?"

She turned to her cousin, her eyes filled with tears. "My father is alive."

"Really? Oh, Nisha…" She wrapped her arms around her cousin. "This is wonderful news."

"No, it's not. Lil, he's in so much pain. I can feel it." Embracing her cousin, she let the tears fall until she could catch her breath. "Come, we have to get everyone to the Spire, then we have work to do."

Slowly Lilly pulled away wiping the last of Nisha's tears. She couldn't ask about Myrddin but she could ask, "Can we really go to the Spire this way?"

"The doorway only leads to the world in between the living and the dead. Nothing can harm those who enter. And just this once those who travel through this gate will remain living. I really don't want the entire family in my realm, not for several more centuries. It's already bad enough to have Grand'Mere there and she's not even dead."

"Then let us go, and by this time tomorrow, we will know where your father is and who is holding him."

Nisha grabbed her arm hard enough to bruise. "Lilly, I know who. I need to find the where. And then I need to figure out why."

Seeing the souls of the dead screaming in Nisha's eyes, she had no doubt of what her cousin was saying. And no doubt that whatever fate awaited them death would only be the beginning.

Nisha paced a large empty room at the Spire. Her family was all huddling together in what should have been the reception. They were all scared, cold and worried. The fact that she could feel their unease should have worried her… should have but didn't. No, she had much more pressing things to worry about.

One being how to explain where she needed to go and why. Secondly… her father. How was she ever going to explain that he had torn out his own heart in order to save himself? No one does that. No one should have had the ability to do that.

Then again maybe he… her father… should be the one to explain that much. Yes, right after she made sure he was bound to her so no one could harm him after he explained himself. Yes, that sounded like a much better idea.

A soft tap on the door made her freeze mid-step. "In."

Ethan poked his head into the room, "Can I enter?"

Taking a deep breath, she used a light gust of wind to pull open the gray panel door, "Ethan, you do not need to ask permission."

"You haven't seen your eyes." He gasped, clearly not meaning to say that. "I mean…"

"It's quite alright, I know my eyes are not human when my temper flares." Another deep breath. "I'm calm now."

He slowly took a small step into the room. "Your wings are breathtaking."

She smiled shyly. "No one has ever said so before. They don't frighten you?"

Coming over to her, he carefully touched the outline of the wings. "Why should they. They're you. Powerful. Strong. Unique. And completely breathtaking. But I've already said that." He paused. "I'm rambling."

Yes, you are but I don't mind. Joy lifted her heart. "Did Lilly say you can be up walking about?"

A shrug. "She didn't say that I couldn't. Then again she has other things to keep her busy for the moment."

Taking his hand, she pulled gently, "Come on, we better find you a bed before Lilly remembers that you still need her care."

Shaking his head, he refused to move. "I'm fine, Nisha. Better than I ever have been. Really."

Placing her hand on his face she let tendrils of mist flow around him, then sighed. "No Ethan, you're not. How you are feeling right now is from the excitement. I fear what will happen when your body remembers it is still healing."

"But…"

"No, you are getting tucked into a bed and Lilly is going to do what only she can. Then in the morning, I will have some answers. You have my word."

The Spire was said to house the largest library in all of Feyen lands so she should be able to find a map. Or at least, something that she could use to locate her father. Should didn't mean that she would. Glancing up at the columns and rows of books, parchments and other things that her ancestors had chosen to use to record everything from spells and incantations to weather and history… she doubted she would be able to find what she needed before morning. Doubted she would be able to find what she needed before next year.

The light breeze voice coming from the hallway caught Nisha's attention. "Oh dear, if you're in here then there has to be trouble. You hate reading… *anything*."

Looking over her shoulder, she tried to smile at her cousin while holding up a rather dirty book in one hand and a rolled parchment in the other. "Help?"

Lilly took a single step into the room and quietly closed the door behind her, "Before I help, we need to discuss what happen before coming here?"

Of course, they did. Nisha took a deep breath. "How is everyone? I thought they would calm down if I stayed somewhere else."

"The Drakens are fine. It was a good show of power and they are proud that you are family. Queen Sedna has gone back to her kingdom. Apparently, she doesn't want to know why she needed to enter the Under Kingdom. *Grand Mere,* well she is calm or mostly calm. You know her, she is currently blaming mum for you opening that gate instead of dealing with whatever was trying to gain access to the castle."

"Trolls. Legions of them. Ogres who were helping the trolls. A few Menehune, which makes no sense since they live in the Marsh Lands and in the warmer areas of Draken. Then there were some Taraque. Taraque, one of the legendary creatures made by the first Fey and said to be extinct yet they were… are in Darke. Think about it, Lilly, they were working together to gain access to the castle. Someone or something must be controlling them. And I need to find out what. I fear what will happen if I do not."

Swallowing hard Lilly waited for several moments before trying to say anything. "Oh wow, well…" Seeing her cousin on the verge of hysterics, Lilly fumbled with her words. She didn't dare ask Nisha about who she thought might be controlling the beast. At least not right now. So, she chose to use a bit of offset humor and hope she didn't make matters worse. "At least, it wasn't a Drague."

"Oh, don't be silly Drague don't really exist. Or at least, haven't since…" She paused and reconsidered everything she had learned since yesterday, then nodded in agreement. "…Then again you could be right. Yes, you very well could be." Taking another deep breath, Nisha asked, "How is Aunt Celeste?"

"Oh, mum is beside herself. She had my coronation planned right down to the feast and the balls. She is *not* happy that you chose to crown me today. Nor is she happy about your wings."

Insulted, Nisha arched her back her black tendrils of dark mist seeped out to every corner of the room as her temper began to flair. "They are my wings. My *true* wings, if she approves of them or not, it's not up to *her*. If *my* mother… her very own sister… wanted them not on my body they wouldn't be *attached* to my body."

Placing her hands in a surrendering posture, Lilly took a step back. "Whoa, Nish. I doubt mum knows they are your true wings. Since you keep them hidden and wear the mist ones more often. Once you show her they are not decoration you know she will be intrigued with them. Just as Ethan is." Which was something that her cousin should have done ages ago, but until Nisha was calmed down she, like everyone else, was not going to say a word about what she thought that Nisha should have done well before now.

Taking a deep breath Nisha turned away from her cousin and closed her eyes as she tried to regain her composure. "I hide them because they're different. I wanted Ethan to see them. He likes them so I won't be hiding them too often. Not anymore."

She needed to turn her cousin's mood turn quickly, for she didn't care for the way Nisha was flipping from anger to weepy, so she offered, "So what do you need help with?"

Wiping her eyes Nisha sniffled as her breath hitched just once. Her emotions too raw for her own liking. Too unpredictable. In any case, she still had work that needed to be done. "I need a map. One that shows all of the Feyen lands. And the Mystic Woods. Hell, I would love to find one of the Under Kingdom but I know that does not exist."

"All?"

"Yes, Lilly *all*. I think Myrddin is in the Mystic Woods, but I could be wrong."

A large round wooden table appeared in the center of the room. "Before I call in the maps, may I ask why you would think he was in the woods?"

Calling in the silver box, Nisha sat it on the table, then ever so carefully opened the lid revealing the large beating heart. The heart of her father.

Edging over to the table Lilly peered into the box. "A heart? With blue blood, still within its veins?"

She nodded once. "It belongs to my father. He's alive, Lilly. *Alive.* And I need to find him. And I cannot wait much longer. Nor would I want to. Something is terribly wrong. I can feel it like tiny points of lightning dancing under my skin. I felt it the moment I was crowned the Queen of both Darke and Feyen."

Lilly turned back to the door making sure it was closed… as well as locked. "There may be another way."

"Lil?"

Whispering since she didn't want anyone knowing they had this particular gift, Lilly said, "We have the power, Nish. You know we do."

"Yes but… it's dangerous beyond all stupidity."

"Nisha Devros, we have both Dream-Walked before. And don't you dare tell me that you're scared. I know better."

Looking around the room Nisha smiled. "I would need to be protected. I would be cut off from all of my abilities while I'm somewhere else."

"I know." Lilly raised her hands encapsulating the room in a golden light. "I locked this room. None may enter without my consent. Or my knowledge."

"Are you sure?" Not that she doubted that Lilly locked the room but sure she could help her find her father.

A simple single nod was her answer.

"Fine, but you forgot something." Raising her hands above her head she quickly flung them down to the ground. A low rumble tore through the room. "I Nisha Devros, Queen of the Under Kingdom forbade any to enter living or dead." The library shook violently as purple swirls intertwined in the light that Lilly had created. "Better. Much better"

Rolling her eyes Lilly smiled. "Oh yes, we can't have dead disturbing you."

"It will also keep the shades out. You wouldn't believe how nosy they are. Especially when I'm doing something that I don't tell them about beforehand."

"Nish, I do not want to know." Hopping up so she could sit on the table she asked, "Do you have the candles?"

Thirteen purple candles appeared around the room. Then a single golden candelabra. A single white candle in its center. Red to the left and black to the right. "I will wake when the white candle blows itself out. I should have twelve hours. But it could be less depending on how far away he is. And how weak."

"I'll keep watch. And Nish..." Nisha raised a single eyebrow. "When you find him, be nice. I'm sure he wouldn't like being scolded until he is home. Then we can take turns. You, me and Mum. I suppose David's mum and dad as well providing his mum is also hidden away somewhere. But the three of us will definitely be first." Lilly paused and pursed her lips together before adding, "I suppose Grand Mere would also like to scold him."

"Oh, don't worry I plan on waiting until I can truly touch him before I scold him. After all, scolding is so much better when wringing a person's neck."

"Yes, I suppose you're right."

Breathing in the scents of sandalwood and jasmine she closed her eyes. Sage would carry her soul to the astral plane. Sea salt would keep her bound to the living. Myrddin. The only person she wanted to pull to her. She knew his name but nothing else. No that wasn't true… she was his daughter, a bond as thick as blood… she would find him. She had to.

Slowly a bright iridescent light surrounded her. Bight purples and blues. Hues of greens and yellows. All intertwining swirling together making an astonishing mosaic all around her. Yet no other person.

Closing her eyes while in this dream world, she called out once more. *Myrddin.*

There a tug. He was fighting her. She could feel it. Digging her feet into the ground she willed herself to pull harder. *Myrddin.* One more tug on a line that only she could see then the mosaic changed around her. No longer bright vibrant colors but Deep purples. Midnight blues. The greens changed to nearly black as the yellow to grays. Slowly a figure formed before her. Black robes of a high-born, gold on the cuffs and down the front. Royalty. True royalty. One that she could bet was not from this realm. Slowly his hands and face formed. Lastly his wings … mirrored from her own but black as night and not nearly translucent. "Myrddin?"

Slowly his soulless eyes focused on her. Then a slow reluctant smile. "Daughter." He took a single step toward her. "You must work on your dream walking, but this will do for what we need to discuss."

His voice was deeper than she had imagined. And he was taller that what she had thought he would be. Nearly two full feet taller than herself. Looking she was sure that he was more than a head taller than her aunt. Yes, definitely not of this realm. No Fey royal or otherwise had been this tall since the first Fey fell from the stars. This was something that only those of the Under Kingdome still knew. And something she would never discuss outside the Castle of the Dead. Taking a single breath Nisha quickly said, "Larna is dead."

"Ah. So, you found my box." Then his eyes narrowed his eyes. "And opened it despite being told not to?"

She nodded once. "It led me here." Cautiously she asked, "You knew what was going to happen that night didn't you?"

He turned from her. "I will answer your question but not here. Not now. There is little time."

They had all the time that they needed now that he was helping her instead of fighting her. "For?" Nisha slowly asked.

"Do you know the story of the Eostre?"

"Some. Gwydion and I have haven't had time to discuss his people in detail. At least not yet."

"Gwydion?"

"The last king of the Eostre. Do you know him?"

He knew she would be powerful but never imagined that she would be able to befriend an Eostre. Then again, it could be using her for its own purposes. "Nisha, listen very carefully. What you know as the truth is not the whole of it. The Eostre are not dead. At least not all of them. Before the war, several went to a summit. They wanted more than just being the caretakers of the Fallen Fey. The Fey... the true Fey were debating it in the star cities. While there at the summit with the royals of the star cities, there was a terrible crime committed. All of the Eostre who were… here… on this earth… they died. The ones who were at the summit declared war on all those they claimed were responsible. All of the Feyen of both this earth and of the star cities. They came back to their homelands and destroyed the pillars… the landing places for the Fey who needed to flee.

After. When boundaries were set the Eostre who were left claimed the Mystic Woods. The whole Mystic Woods and its power for their own, as the woods had always been their home, and it would remain. The sites where those who came from the star colonies rested and became comfortable with this land, they were mostly destroyed preventing most from making their way here. Most, but not all."

"Wait… What? Are you saying…"

"Just listen, little one, you need to know the whole of it." When she nodded he continued, "Somewhere in the Mystic Woods I am being held. Or at least, I think I am. Then again, I could be near the ruins of the Great War. Either way, if you come to me first your mother will die. If I escape, she will die. If *you* enter the woods, *you* could be killed."

Wonderful, just what she needed; another puzzle. This one needed to be solved in order to save her family. "You know where my mother is?"

"In the Mystic Woods. It… the woods are a strange place they take away learned abilities but enhance natural ones. I think she would be near one of the ruins of the pillars. The powers that control the woods are strongest there. Strongest at the mouth of the healing river."

Nisha turned from him. "Alright, so to find mother I'm in for a fight. What else?"

"My box. It cannot enter the woods. Those there will take it. It's too powerful and I fear it will destroy not only this realm but the stars as well. Not the contents, but the box itself. Even if you vanish it somewhere to be called to you… those who live in the woods will be able to snatch it from you."

"I can't leave it at the Spire. I don't think there are any there that can protect it."

No, the Spire wouldn't be safe enough. At least, she understood that. "Ask your aunt. She may have a solution."

"Aunt Celeste? Oh, I can't, she's already rattled. And I haven't even told her that I found you."

"No, my dear. Estare. Summon her. Not Dream-Walk but summon her. She'll answer. Don't expect her to be nice. In fact, brace for a fight when you do. She is not one to be summoned. Really not one to be summoned in dreams such as these. Know this she is powerful but not as much as you. But she has more years of experience in her abilities than you do. Expect her to use every ounce of those skills against you."

The mist started to change. Their time together was almost over.

"When I find you, I want explanations… not riddles or more question. I want answers to every question that I can come up with."

"When we return to the Castle of Night you will have every answer you desire. So will your mother."

Chapter 45:
Ethan

Ethan waited until he was sure Nisha had left not only the room but also the hallways near the room as well before. Pulling the bed covers off, he decided to explore the large room where she had left him... No, not a room but *rooms… an entire suite…* he corrected himself. The bedroom had been colored in a deep purple that nearly looked black but with white-gray dressers for contrast. The bed, on the other hand, had been made of gray and black marble with wisps of other colors periodically found within the columns.

He puzzled over this since nothing matched. So, either this suite was pieced together with the belongings that no one wanted anymore or Nisha had very strange taste in decor. Both were a possibility. Slowly opening a door that didn't go to the hall, he found a sitting room that he could fit the entire downstairs of Edrich's… *of his home…* in. Off positioned in the far corner there was a stone lion that was made into a waterfall. No, not a lion, he decided upon closer look, but a Merlion or a Chimera. Either way, the sculpture was magnificent. Then he watched as the water sparkled in gold's and blue's landing in a pool of crystal. Taking a step closer, he felt the liquid as it poured out he could see clearly now that this was not water. Not really. Sure, it was clear and liquid but much too silky to be just ordinary water. It had to be.

A tap on the door made him jump. Thinking he had been caught doing something forbidden his shoulders slouched as he turned to whoever had entered. To his surprise, it was a young girl in a gray servant's garb holding a large tray. "Um… Can I help you?"

The girl smiled slowly. "Lady Nisha and Lady Lilly thought it would be better if you dine alone. It appears the adults are too rumpled to be dealt with this evening. Even Prince Davkren has requested to dine alone this evening. Which for him is very peculiar."

Rumpled? From what he had observed, the former queens were somewhere between shocked and scared, yet still bordering pissed. Not the yelling pissed that Lilly had said they would be but the kind where someone would pay for it with their blood. "Dining alone sounds reasonable."

Setting the tray on a low table the maid smiled again. "The staff wasn't sure what you like so we put a bit of everything on the plates." She made a face. "Except what the Drakens eats. No one eats that stuff except them." Sticking out her tongue, she continued, "Yuck. I despise being the one to take them their meals. The blood gets everywhere." Giving herself a moment to compose herself and not gag, she continued, "Anyways if you find something you like let us know and more will be brought up."

Lifting the first lid off the dish, his eyes widened. A mound of food. Everything carefully labeled. "I can have more… of anything?" This was more food than he normally ate in a year. And he could have anything he wanted at any time. His mouth already watered with the smells he was picking up on.

"Lady Nisha said you are much too thin. In addition, Lady Lilly said you are still very weak. Both Ladies want you properly fed. If I may add, you should start with the last plate it has some very delicious desserts on it. They are sure to help you put the weight on."

Looking down at his night shirt that was beyond comfortably baggy and the night pants that he had tied a bit of cloth around so they wouldn't fall, Ethan asked, "Would you disagree with them?"

"Oh, I would never disagree with Nisha, but Lilly? It is good to keep her on her toes."

Since she seemed willing to chat, he asked, "Why not Nisha? It would appear we're married but I only just met her."

"Oh well, Nisha has very fluid ideas and when challenged the person disagreeing usually ends up agreeing just so she will stop explaining her point." She patted his hand. "I'm sure you'll find it more reasonable to say thinks like I understand your point but… then explain *your* point. It is disagreeing, but she may listen to you. Then again, she could tell you that the grass is purple even though it's clearly green and then she'll tell you why it's purple. Unless she changes it to the color to prove her point."

Ethan stumbled back a step. "She would do that? Change the color of something to prove she's right?" How she could do that was beyond him, after all, there was no Fey with that ability. Or at the very least not one that he had ever heard of. In any case, it was good to know not to argue his point very often.

"*If* she would… darling she has. The pixies were not very happy with David since he was the one who challenged her. Now I should go and you need to eat."

He nodded once with respect but also regret that he might have gotten her in trouble. "Oh, I'm sorry for taking up your time."

"Don't be. The staff that works at the Spire has been raised around the royals. We all speak freely and do whatever brings us the most joy. It's our jobs. Mine is seeing that guests including royals have all that they need. I suspect what you need is someone to talk to. Of course, that includes food. Lots and lots of food. But we will start with the plates that I have already brought. It will give you an idea what you enjoy and what you don't."

Now he looked at her and didn't see a young girl but a fairy. Pointed ears. Crystal green eyes. Only her wings were not visible. "You're a fairy?"

"A sprite. A fairy of the house. Please don't confuse me with a house elf."

Not knowing how to respond he simply said, "I'm sorry but I don't know the difference. My education in the Feyen races seems to be lacking."

"Oh dear. Well, I must simply educate you. But not tonight. Tonight, you eat, and when the Spire is cleared out of those who are very prickly I will educate you in all that you need. For tonight, however, I can tell you both sprites and elves may do some of the same things but elves are very rude where sprites are bubbly."

"Thank you… Um…"

"Eolande. It means Violet Flower." Seeing he didn't understand she turned into a small flower.

A violet. Then turned back. "Lesson one: Fey are named for what they can turn into."

"So, Lilly can…"

"Oh no. Miss Lilly is much too powerful to be just a flower. She is the sun. Bright and golden. You do not ask her to turn into her other form. It's very distressing. Even for a queen of Lite. And Ethan, please do not ask Nisha to show you hers. Ever."

Cautiously he asked, "Why?"

"Nisha is the daughter of the night. She does not have one form she can turn into … well… anything fable or not, real or her own making. *Anything* that was once said went bump in the night."

"So, the dragon…"

Eolande once again came near him then lowered her soft cheerful voice to just above a whisper, "You will not tell the others that the dragon was Nisha. It is forbidden to discuss it."

"I understand. Thank you for telling me." Still, seeing a dragon sounded interesting. Maybe he could find a way to ask without asking. Yes, he would have to think on that. Then again, was the dragon big enough to ride? Would he have the courage to ask his wife for the experience?

Maybe after she was calmer. Yes, he would definitely have to ask if for nothing else than his own curiosity.

Ethan took a bite of the sweet confection that Eolande had foolishly put into front of him. One bite and he wanted more… just the right amount of sweetness and moisture that it melted in his mouth. Closing his eyes, he savored the taste. Reaching for yet another of the little cream covered balls he noticed Lilly standing in the doorway watching him. Swallowing the last bit that was in his mouth he smiled holding the plate out for her. "Would you like some?"

She shook her head but returned the smile. "It must be a boy thing. Put a tray of sweets before you and you forget to eat the real food first."

"Real…" He turned, seeing a covered dish that he hadn't already peeked under. "Oh. I haven't gotten to that one yet."

"Uh ha. Well, you can come back to it shortly. Nisha needs to see you."

He shrugged. "Can I bring this?"

"Darling, do I look like I would dare separate you from your sweets? Although you may want to slow down. I really don't feel like making sure your stomach doesn't start to sour because of it. Although I'm sure David has already decided not to heed that warning."

How would his stomach sour? That didn't make sense. Then again, how would she know about David or what he was eating if she was standing before him? Not something he could ask right now. "Where is Nisha?"

"In the library. Come on. We will go see her then you can get lost in all the wonderful books. You do like books, don't you? Nish thought you might."

His eyes widened. "*Books?* I can read them?"

"Oh, for the love of Lite. Of course, you can read them. Actually, I encourage that you do so since Nisha refuses to pick any of them up." She took his arm and pulled him until he started moving in the direction that she needed him to go.

After turning down several corridors and coming the center of the Spire, Lilly had stopped a few feet before the plain wood door. She had said Nisha needed him so perhaps Lilly wasn't invited to this meeting? Possible, so why did his skin prickled in warning?

Pushing the door open he saw her long dragon wings fluttering restlessly as she looked at something on the round table. "Nisha?"

"Oh, good Lilly found you." She turned slightly. "Did you have a chance to eat?"

"I ate something." He couldn't remember the name of the sweet. Later he would have to find out what it has been.

He watched her nod once before she sighed. "I need your help."

"My… help?" His shoulders tensed up. The last time someone asked for his help he was beaten until he couldn't walk then starved for over a week.

"Oh, no, Ethan, it's not bad, I promise. But Estare knows you and I need to speak to her. It's very important."

Relaxing some, he tried to smile. "She finds me when I sleep. I don't know how to contact her."

She moved to stand before him so he wouldn't need to come further into the room. "It's alright because I do. I just need your help in doing so… I understand if you can't…"

Hearing the nervousness in her voice he took a step closer to her. "What can I do?"

"Just hold my hands."

That he could do. In fact, he felt grounded whenever he touched her. "I can do that."

Her hands felt like two little blocks of ice in his hands. Closing his eyes, he allowed his own instincts to take over. Then he heard Nisha begin to speak.

"Queen Estare, I summon thee. Come forth before me."

When nothing happened, he felt something. Power? Electricity? He couldn't be sure. Opening his eyes both he and Nisha were surrounded by black flames. Yet the flames didn't burn. Then Nisha looked at him her eyes nothing but two black orbs. No, that wasn't right. Gazing closer, he could see thousands of stars. Thousands of tiny lights. Colors and patterns, he could only be imagining. Then he felt her tense.

"Queen Estare, I know you hear me. I command you to show yourself."

Oh, that couldn't be good. He knew Estare well enough to know she was not a person to command anything from. Knew enough that she would not respond well to those commands. He should warn her but before he could say anything…

Before he could say anything, Nisha's voice roared through the room, ***"NOW!!!"***

The room shook violently. Books that had been nestled on their shelves flew around the room crashing into each other before falling to the floor. A fire erupted in the hearth burning uncontrollably. Cautiously he tried to make her stop. "Nisha, perhaps…" His words stopped as the glass in the windows shattered. Windows that had once opened to indoor courtyards now laid at their feet.

An archway made from the broken glass formed and iridescent blue light swirled within it. "Who dares summon me?!?" Not really a question but a command. Then she stepped out from the mist her long black hair blowing with a breeziness that was both beautiful and terrifying. Her wings still hidden in the doorway.

Nisha let go of his hands and turned to the woman who was now standing before her. Her shoulders squared. "I did."

Estare looked around the room and scowled. "You're but a child. How dare you? Do you even know who I am? What I am?"

The crystal archway exploded in fury, "I am the Queen of both Feyen and Darke. As well as the Queen of the Under Kingdom do not underestimate me... Aunt."

Aunt? Ah, shit. This was bad. So very, very bad. Estare knew all of his secrets. Nisha was his wife and his queen. "Ladies?" Both ignored him and looked ready to attack each other.

Estare stepped back first. "You spoke to my traitor brother. He is the one who told you to summon me. And you foolishly listened." She crooned.

Taken back Nisha very cautiously asked, "What do you mean traitor? And why should I not trust him?"

Waving off the question Estare turned now taking in the room, "So this is the hole he chose to live in rather than rule Lunaista. How odd. But he was always the odd one. Even among the Fey."

Taking another step back, Nisha looked confused, even worried. "He was a royal before marrying my mother? But how?" That explained so much to her. Enough for Ethan to know that she just let one the questions that she had had just been answered.

"Of course, child, he was a royal. The most gifted of all of the star kingdoms. Truthfully, he could have conquered all of them if he so wanted to. Not that he thought of that as a solution." Narrowing her eyes, a cruel smile formed on her face. "In fact, so could you rule over the star kingdoms as the absolute ruler. Even now he does not have the power that you do." Slowly she began to prowl the room, her fingers caressing the shelves where books once laid. "Why am I here?" Slowly she turned to Ethan. "Ethan could find me if he had chosen to and must less dramatically, I might add."

Taking a seat on the table while Estare prowled the book covered floor, Nisha softly said, "I need your help."

"Oh. And what kind of help does the *oh-so-powerful* queen need?"

Ethan took a step back. He didn't know if Nisha was aware or not but Estare was getting ready to attack. Pity he didn't know how he knew this.

A bored look fell upon Nisha's face. "If you attack me, you will be dead. Now should we speak civilly or see who rules whose homeland when this is over?"

She knew. Nisha knew. He was amazed, however, the look on Estare's face said she was horrified.

With a huff, Estare pulled herself to her full height. "Why am I here, niece?"

Calling the silver box that once held Larna's heart, Nisha held it out. "Do you know what this is?"

This time it was Estare that was taking a few steps back in horror. Ethan watched as she nearly tripped over the books that now laid about the floor. She had known that Nisha had a box but had assumed that it had been the contents that were far more powerful that it would be beyond stupid to open it… however, she had not known that it was the box itself that contained the power… until now. "How did you get that? It is forbidden to leave the stars. It's much too dangerous to leave them." *Why had her brother stolen that box? The box of the first kind of any of the star cities? The box that siphoned all of the power of the dead. Why had her brother chosen to steal that box? If he were to steal any of them, why could it not be just a simple tribute box? The answer was simple… he knew something.*

Somehow, he had heard the thoughts of Estare, but how?

Judging by Nisha's puzzled look it was not the response she was expecting. "My father left this for me here at the Spire. It once held the heart of a… let us say… the corrupt queen who wished to enslave all the Feyen lands. However, currently, it holds my father's heart and his power." Taking a step closer to Estare she continued, "He told me you could help me find where both he and my mother are located at in Mystic Woods."

Catching herself Estare smiled. "That is a tribute box. Until recently I thought it was a way for the star kingdoms to share their power with one another. In truth, they send…" She stopped decided not to go into detail. It would do no good to explain how the power was shared. "The box cannot enter the Mystic Woods, neither can I keep it safe in my home. There are many that would seek out that power."

With understanding, Nisha nodded once. "What do you suggest?"

Slowly Estare got to her feet, making sure not to touch the silver box. Thinking about everything, thinking about all that she knew… not only about her homeland but of what she had been taught about this land, she asked, "Have you explored all of the Under Kingdom?"

Odd. "Not yet. Why?"

The books were once again in motion this time when they fell they had made a map. Or at least, an outline of a map with borders. "This is the whole of the under kingdom as it was made. It is possible that it is now larger."

"Alright?" Nisha vanished the silver box then pointed to a spot on the center that looked like a sealed box. "What is this?"

"The eye. Only the queen can enter and not be destroyed. All the power of those who no longer have bodies … is stored there. It's the safest place for that box."

"Why didn't my father tell me that?"

"Because he wouldn't have known. It is a secret that is passed from one ruler to the next after the tributes are made. In my case, I found out in scripture rather than by mouth."

It didn't make sense but, in a way, Nisha knew she was telling the truth. "Alright, So I have to put the box there then find my family."

"No dear. Once the box is there, you will have two days, three at most to return the heart to your father. Or he will be beyond even your grasp."

For a long moment, Nisha just stood there before she wailed, "Two days? How am I ever going to find both my parents in two days?"

A breezy cough from the doorway had the three of them turning.

"Gwydion?"

"I maybe some assistance." He took a step into the room and tried to smile. "I believe your mother is in what once was my home. Recently a little mouse asked for help from the ancestors. I heard her. It is very distressing that a mouse should speak. More so that I have not been able to locate it since."

Alright, that would take care of one parent. "And my father?"

This time, Estare spoke. "In a cave. I might be able to find it and mark it. But your father was very clear your mother is to be saved first."

"Agreed." Going over to the door Ethan watched as Nisha poked her head into the hall. "You can come in now."

M.L.Ruscsak

Chapter 46: Nisha

With Ethan's head resting in her lap Nisha stared out of the window as the Pegasus flew over the border of Lite and Darke. Their weaving pattern was taking up time but was ensuring nothing was following them. Not that very many things could but she appreciated the extra precaution.

"When are we landing?"

She glanced down at Ethan who looked calm until she saw his fingers grasping the hem of her blouse. "As soon as we reach the outer edge of the Wastelands. It won't be long now. I already feel the difference in the wind currents." Her fingers lightly caressed his head. Hopefully the motion was soothing for him.

"Oh good. I don't think I like being in the air."

Galeron lifted his head from the seat across from them. Still too weak and sore to do much more than lay still. "You'll get use to it eventually." *Of course, flying with your own wings was much better than flying in a box carried by flying horses.* Not that he would say that... not to his boy and not to the queen who he still didn't understand. Couldn't understand and probably never would.

Feeling Ethan tense under her hand and knowing that he wasn't comfortable with the man who was laying across from him, she decides to try to telling Ethan who he was and why he had to come with them instead of with Lilly and David. "You haven't asked anything about our guest."

Slowly he raised up and sat. His eyes narrowing for a heartbeat before saying, "I'm not in the habit of asking questions I don't want answers to."

Coughing so not to laugh Galeron mumbled, "You sound like your mother. She rarely asked questions either. Of course, that didn't stop her from criticizing just about everything unless she had thought of it herself."

Ethan's eyes narrowed a little more, "How would you know my mother?" His voice a stiff growl thinking the man was lying.

Looking at Nisha, Galeron's face showed nothing than just a hint of anger when he snarled, "You didn't tell him?"

Nisha shrugged. "It wasn't my place to tell him. Besides *you, Galeron,* didn't ask me to. And I would never reveal a secret of someone unless that secret put someone I cared about in danger. Then again if it put someone in danger it would be dead and no longer a secret at all."

Now Galeron sat up ignoring the fact that he was still weak, He ignored the way his body shook with the effort. "You…" Several words slipped his lips… none of them flattering to the Queen who she was nor the daughter of his dear friend. "Your father wasn't… isn't… this difficult. Neither was your mother."

Shrugging Nisha smiled. "I'll take your word for it. From my understanding, he was much worse."

Looking back and forth between Nisha and the Feyen man Ethan hissed, "What am I not being told?"

Laying back down Galeron matched Ethan's hiss. "Ask your wife. The little vixen needs to learn when not to keep secrets. And when not to be a thorn in the side of someone who might eventually help her."

Batting her long eyelashes, Nisha turned into a red fox then sat all too calmly swaying her tail. Her paw resting on Ethan's lap annoying both of the men who she was riding with.

Sitting up Ethan grumbled, "I doubt I can get an answer from her while she's no longer a true shape."

"Bah. Parlor tricks. If she was a true shape shifter she would choose a more intimating form."

Turning back Nisha grinned. "Actually, there's simply not enough room to shift into a dragon, but perhaps later I will take you for a ride in my talons. *Or would you enjoy that?*"

Galeron dismissing her threat, he dryly said, "Dragons don't exist."

"Who's to say they don't? Just because *you* have never seen one does not mean they don't. Should I show you Lord Galeron?"

The carriage dipped. Lying back down so his stomach wouldn't come to his throat, Ethan sighed. "Oh, good, I think we're landing. And I don't think he would find riding in talons enjoyable." He paused then menacingly said, "You should take him some time."

Nisha got out of the carriage and placed her hand on her hip. "Well I guess 'Wasteland' means desert of black sand that even the dry wind can't blow."

Galeron yawned, poking his head out of the covered window. "Actually the sand was once white. During the Great War so many died their blood soaked into the ground, forever changing the sand to black. Or at least that is what I've heard."

Looking back at the sand Nisha was astonished. "Oh wow. I'll have to ask Gwydion to see if he was here before the war. I would love to know what it looked like before."

"Who is Gwydion?"

This time, Ethan answered from inside the carriage, "He's the shade who follows Nisha. Or at least, I think he's a shade. Only seen him a few times."

"Oh good, you two can ponder that while I take care of something, then I'll meet you near the mouth of the Healing River."

"You want us to go there by ourselves?" Galeron stammered.

A door to the Under Kingdom opened. "Of course not. Gwydion is going with you. Since he's from there he can make sure nothing tries to *eat* you." Nisha shook her head, "Out of all the things why would you think I would send you someplace without a proper escort? I swear, for having been on my mother's council, I thought you would know better. I see I will have to see that you are properly educated once this is all over and things settle down a bit."

Watching Nisha disappear through the door, Ethan snapped, "Would you like to tell me what she's talking about? Or who in the name of Darke you are?"

Nisha looked around at the walls of bones. She had never been in this part of her kingdom before. Never knew something like this labyrinth existed. Lightly touching the wall, she wondered what races the bones had come from. *Were they some of the first? Where they those of the star people? Fey? True Fey? Or had they been created by accident when the fey took the others as mates? Then killed because they served no real reason for being.*

This was so exciting! Later she would have to come back and see every inch of this place… Right now, she had something important to do.

Slowly she found a door that she hoped that she needed after opening several that only led to room created with bits of flesh and rotted muscles. Seeing this too was not the room that she had been looking for, she turned down several more corridors until she found another door. Actually, the only real door that she had come across. The only door that had not been made of bones but rather a dark wood of some kind.

Nervously she placed her hand on the crystal handle. Her aunt said something powerful would be just inside. What that something would be… Estare didn't know. A little nervous she took a deep breath. She was the queen and only the queen could enter. That didn't mean she *should* enter. But there was no place safer to hide the box and it wouldn't take two days to retrieve it. As a matter of fact, she was going to bring her father here to stand outside this door when she gave him back his heart.

Another breath then she pushed the door open. Not yet taking a step into the room she looked in awe as the most beautiful creature that she had ever seen look right at her. Hard to tell what it was or had been but the face was that of a Fey with glorious wings half the size of her own but exactly the same. On second glance, they were not the same. Hers were solid black, not translucent at all. "Um. Hello?"

The creature transformed into a Feyen woman only the face and wings remained the same. "Only the queen may enter these halls."

She smiled oh so sweetly. "I know."

Then the woman smiled. Not a friendly smile but one that was cruel and menacing, "There is no Queen of the Under Kingdom."

Taking one step into the room Nisha smiled. "You must be mistaken for I have ruled for nearly ten years."

Leaping at Nisha, the woman screamed, "YOU! You think you can dethrone me? I am the greatest Queen that ever was!"

Seeing the former queen unable to touch her, Nisha yawned. "You bore me. If you were so great then you wouldn't be locked up in a room created from the bones of those who were blood bound to you." She didn't know where that idea had come from but the look on the former queen's face told her she was correct.

Transforming into a specter, she flew around the room frantically. "This cannot be! Why can't I touch you? You reek of life, not of death. How can this be?" The woman flew around the room several times. At each pass trying yet again to touch the little Queen.

Finally, Nisha outstretched her wings filling most of the room. "ENOUGH! You are a citizen of the Under Kingdom. You are no longer the queen. Yield."

"I yield to no one!"

Making her voice as loud as she could, she said once more, "I said YIELD!" Her hand outstretched and a tendril of untrained power wrapped around the woman's… The specter's… bare leg pulling her to the ground. Using her own fingernail, she poked her finger and allowed a single drop of blue blood to swell up. The tendril held the woman's head squeezing her pale cheeks till her lips were forced open. The drop of blood fell onto her lips. She didn't want to do this but she didn't have time to think of something else.

"With my blood, I bind you. You and all that were yours are now mine. You will yield."

Power filled her more than she had ever felt. With it the knowledge of the first Fey. *This was the first Fey. The first to fall. No, not fall… she dove to the solid earth.* The stories had been wrong. It wasn't a man who came and fell in love, but it was a woman determined not to wed a man who only wanted her power. The power of the dead. The power to bring what should be dead back to life. The power to create as well as destroy. The power to conquer all that she wished. And the power to create new life out of nothing but air.

"What have you done? You will destroy my creations." The woman wailed.

Releasing the woman from her tendrils Nisha took a step back. "I do not take joy in destroying anything. And if *you* would have yielded I wouldn't have bound you. However, now that you are I understand why you surround yourself with the bones of those who were loyal to you..." She paused then asked, "They are your army? They are protecting you so you could not be found. Protecting you since because of your power you are unable to die and you fear that even now the royals of the star cities will come for you."

Folding into herself, the woman whispered, "Yes."

Carefully Nisha came and sat before her… this lost queen of the fey. The first queen of Feyen. "I need their strength to protect something that I hold dear I will return for it soon."

Stunned into an unusual silence she finally said, "Anything living only lives two days. Three if it is strong. Even now my powers are too strong to keep things alive much longer. At least while I dwell here."

"I understand. I should only be gone one." Nisha tilted her head, "What is your name? Usually, I know the names of all that are bound to me but I can't find yours."

"Primitiva."

Nisha nodded once. "Then Primitiva, I leave in your care this box." The silver box of her father's materialized in her hands. "The lid will only open to me."

"It is a tribute box. These are not from theses grounds but from the cities of stars. They are very powerful. *You* should not have such a box… not here. Not outside the Star kingdoms."

Nodding once more Nisha said as she turned toward the door. "One day I would like to know more. But not today, I must go now. I do not have much time to set things right."

Clutching the box in her hands Primitive sniffled. "Queens are not to be bound to another."

"True, but you should have yielded. The binding cannot be undone." She was sorry for doing that to a strong queen but she had left her little choice.

Nisha created a doorway to lead to the very spot where the carriage should be waiting. Wasn't too surprised to see it just coming into view. Knowing she had a minute or two she looked at the water. Not clear like she expected not even a blue-green color of the Endless Sea. No this was a light purple like a fine mist. Touching it she could feel power absorb into her skin vanishing the small prick that she had made.

"Huh. Very interesting." Calling in her little bag of healing supplies she pulled out several empty vials and filled them before vanishing it once more just as the carriage landed. She noticed Gwydion before the carriage door even opened. "Are they alright?"

"You're… consort… is ruffled. He is not very good with having those who were dead to him showing up now."

"Yes… well, there was no effective way to tell him that everything he had been told was a lie. But I did try to prepare him."

Gliding over to her Gwydion bowed just a hair. "My queen, nothing can prepare a boy to meet his father who he has no memory of. One that he had thought of as dead. But I'm sure both men will get over today in order to build a future that both deserve. More so if you can find the ones that you seek. In my opinion, woman tend to be the peacekeepers between their male family members."

True. Or, with both being Feyen men they could spend a century or two not speaking. *Which was entirely possible*. Not that she would debate that right now. Maybe later. Or maybe she would let her mother debate it for her. Yes, that would be much better. After all, she had heard stories of how her mother loved to debate things. More so if the person being debated with was both male and Feyen in blood. "Will you ask them both to come here?"

Staring at the river, Gwydion asked, "You plan on using the healing waters?"

Bristling, she asked, "I do. Is that a problem?"

Gwydion tilted his head. His dark eyes narrowing into tiny slits, "Do you not possess the power to heal?"

"I…" Did she? After all, she was linked to Lilly as Lilly was linked to her. No, wait their link wasn't a true binding only another way to ensure neither could harm the other while her binding with Primitiva? "…I can try. Gwydion may I ask a question?"

He looked her puzzled, "My queen?"

"If you had the chance to live again would you take it?"

His face looked sad for but a minute. A bit regretful even. "Even you, my queen, does not have such power. Only one has ever and she will not use it even now. She has been asked."

"When this is over, I will speak to Primitiva. As you said, too many died that were innocent."

If he had been solid he would have stumbled back... being made entirely of mist he dispersed before reshaping. "You *saw* her?! How did you pass the guards?! They feed on everything that has flesh. Living or not."

Going over to the carriage, she smiled. "Am I or am I not the Queen?" Opening the door, she took a good look at both men who if they were out in the open would be squaring off to fight or some such nonsense. "I'm sure we do not have time for what the two of you have in mind."

Galeron hissed while pointing weakly at Ethan. "You should have told him."

"Why, when you are much better at explaining all the things that I truly do not have time for, *if* we are to rescue my mother and not kill my father in the process." Seeing an arc of lightning in his eyes she continued, "Now, would you like to be fully healed for this venture or stay as you are now and explain to whoever we find why you refused to be healed by a queen who you are now bound to?"

Ethan sat back against the seat, understanding the threat. "I would love to see the true color of my skin again. How about it, light-bearer? Or do you think she does not have the ability to do so."

Turning slightly to her husband she very quietly scolded, "Ethan, be nice. Neither of you has had a good two decades."

"My first two years were fine. Or so I can assume."

Puzzled, she looked at him. "I thought you were born within a year of my birth?"

Pressing himself into his own seat Galeron snorted, "He was. The second year he was being created. I take it was a good year for you but you put your mother in a frenzy. I'm glad I only had to live through that once."

Good, they were playing nicely so she could do what was needed without them fighting her. Closing her eyes, she tried to see what she needed. Allowing herself to feel all around her she could almost see in her mind both Ethan's and Galeron's bodies. Could almost make out a third though it had no substance. Bones came first the color of ivory. White and strong harder than they should be. Tiny strings… nerves… gray with information being passed. Blood vessels blue in Ethan but nearly purple in his father. Ah yes, now she understood the third body as the blood vessels formed, black as night in Gwydion. Very interesting now that she could see the spines and the long reptilian tail that was starting to form. Muscles red with lines of sinew. Milky cream flesh to cover… Not her dear friend, no, he was a mixture of grays and green. Browns and blacks. Each armored scale blending into the one next no two colors the same next to another. His teeth all three rows sharp as needles. His claws sharper still. But his face… what a handsome regal face any man would be proud of.

She opened her eyes just as the blue light faded from inside the carriage and she saw not only those of her family completely healed but saw Gwydion sitting frozen staring right at her. Fear and apprehension resonating in his dark misty red eyes. "Your people have always been able to transform into the mist, but I think it is time to be more?"

It took him a moment to remember to breathe… Another moment to understand what he was seeing with his own eyes. "How?" His voice a pained whisper. Gwydion held out his hands before him before shifting them into the smoother ones that his wife had once preferred. His eyes filling with tears that shouldn't be there. "This is impossible. Only a creator has this power."

"It is not important. Those of your people who wish to regain what was taken I will grant them life. *After* we rescue my mother."

Gwydion blinked then swallowed hard remembering his mission. Later he might have the nerve to ask more about what his queen had just given back to him. "She is housed in the great city of my people. Those who rule now are not friends. They feed on her power keeping her weak. I know a way in but…" He looked at his hands and sharp claws not yet remembering how he had once opened a door. "It has been some time since I opened the door myself." Then he blinked again... not knowing how he knew with certainty what he had just told her.

"Please tell your people that any who try to stop me, they can to do with what they will."

"I..."

"Gwydion, they are still bound to you. The binding you made in life didn't stop in death and is stronger now. I made sure of it. You have the power to speak to them with nothing more than a thought. Much the same way you have been communicating for years."

Turning to the light-bearer, Gwydion asked, "Did you know she could do this? I didn't know she could do this. And I have been with her since a little after birth."

Swallowing hard because the race of the man who now sat next to him had been rumored to kill anything friend or foe and never was scared of anything... now not only looked scared but sounded horrified. Galeron hesitantly said, "No. But after today, I'm looking forward to seeing what else she is gifted in. And pray her mother can train her properly."

Nisha looked up at the large dome. It looked to her like it had been made from the midnight sky, including the stars that danced in the moonlight. "What was this place?"

"A place where the first could come and drain some of their power before venturing off to find their place."

Nisha stammered, "Drain their…"

"Most were too powerful to live here and not be drained to a safe point. The first decided on this safeguard. It kept the balance in check for several centuries." Gwydion nodded toward a large bush that was now growing wild. "I hate seeing my home this way. This used to be a wondrous garden the fountains glistening with water from the rivers. It's a horrid place now overgrown and uncared for. And look the fountains are nothing more than rubble."

Placing her hand on his shoulder understandingly, Nisha said, "Gwydion, you will make it beautiful again. But the door please."

"Yes." He paused. "Only natural abilities work inside the dome."

"Understood."

Sliding against the wall behind the bush he found the door. "It is here but… Forgive me... it has been too long since I have had a use for such a thing."

She touched his shoulder again. "Let me." Then to Ethan, "Are you ready?"

Ethan nodded once. "I always wanted to be the hero. Looks like today I get to do that."

People were talking inside. One a serpent judging by drawn out S's. The other she couldn't be sure. Carefully Nisha tried to listen to what was being said. Too muffled to hear actual words but the tone… yes, the serpent was not happy about something. In a voice barely a whisper she asked, "Gwydion, can you see or hear?"

For a moment he listened then smiled, "The little serpent is distressed. His son didn't finish his mission on marrying you. The other is pissed that the prince was so weak. They want you, my queen. They want the power they think *you* will let them control." He nearly laughed at how foolish they sounded thinking she… his queen… would ever let anyone control her.

Oh well, obviously they didn't know who or what they were asking for. Taking a queenlier posture, she smiled as she said, "Then I shall receive them properly."

Ethan made a move to grab her arm but it turned to mist before his hand could touch her. "Nisha?"

"My mother named me well. Trust me." Her head high and shoulders back she stepped into the large empty room and clapped slowly. "Bravo, King Apep. You managed to form an alliance with those who will bring death to all."

"You. You sssshould not be here."

"Ah yes. Well, what did you expect? That I would marry a snake instead of my betrothed?

Come now, your brain is not that small, or is it?" She paused, seeing a man that had similar looks to Gwydion but less defined. Less threatening. Yet still an Eostre. "And you. Being a descendant of the Eostre you should *really* know better. After all, it was your ancestors who caused the great war. Or have you been conspiring to finish the work that they had started?"

The man took an unsure and guarded step toward her. One more step when she didn't move and he was on her but when he tried to attack he merely passed through her body. "What is this?"

"Oh, don't you know? All Eostre are bound to me. Try to grab me all you wish. Unless I will it, you will not even remotely come close to me. However..." Black tendrils flowed from around her the tips burning with fire. A single whipping motion and both men were wrapped in burning vines. "...I can hurt you." Letting the tendrils tighten around them. "Now, where is my mother?"

"You-- you bitch." Another voice. A third race she didn't know its kind. Couldn't tell if it were male or not. But this one flew on wings that any bat would be proud of. It's tail ... well, she knew a dragon with one that was more impressive.

"So, you want to play? Alright... I'm game." She looked over her shoulder and yelled, "Find my mother; I'll deal with them!" She waited until they had slipped into a hallway before transforming.

Before letting her true form… her favorite form… take shape.

M.L.Ruscsak

Chapter 47: Primitiva

Primitiva paced the confines of her throne room. Her fingers tracing the bones of her beloved Shesha. He had been her first creation. Her greatest protector. And her loyal friend. But there had been others. Her first…

Soon they would need to be awaken. They would need to come back to the realm of the living. Now that the child had been born. Now that she had the power of all of those who had died. And had the power of those who were still alive.

It had been many star cycles since she has spoken in words to another fey. Many more since she had been pressed into using any of her true abilities. Now… She didn't have a choice.

Nisha had bound her. Her abilities were now the child's for the taking.

Primitiva returned to the throne of bones. Solace finally coming over her. Soon all of the lies that were told would come to light. All of the suffer would soon be over. The Rule of Magmas, the ruler of Pallas would soon be at an end.

But at what cost?

He had already taken her love and her child. Would he take her champions as well? No… No, the child of her long-ago vision would never allow for him to gain their powers.

So, for now she must trust this Fey. A fey that she knew only as the Darkness.

Chapter 48:
Ethan

The building shook and the ceiling started crumbling around them. Horrible shrill screams came from the room they just left. "Gwydion, where would they keep Nisha's mother?" Ethan screamed over the sound of stone crashing to the ground.

"The… There is only one place. Come, it's up ahead. The door is a rock."

A rock. Of course. They were in a stone building that was crumbling so why not a rock? It had been years since he had used his powers. Longer still since he needed a shield. His eyes closed for just a minute as a golden light encased them. Galeron gasped with an effort to hold the shield, "We must hurry. The shield will not last long. My body may be healed but my strength is still weak."

Racing down the corridor and trying not to trip on the debris they came to a wall. Ethan's eyes scanned the wall for some signs of an opening, "Where's the rock?"

Gwydion pounded on the wall. "The room is beyond here. I can feel the power." He pounded on it once more. "They walled it up. They do not wish for the room to be found."

Ethan tightened his fingers into a fist. He had one task. One. Save Nisha's mother. The was no way he was going to fail. *NONE.* His fist slammed into the wall with every bit of temper he had flowing into the punch. The wall shattered with a great explosion.

Galeron stumbled back. Then dryly said, "Yes, you are your mother's son." Then he saw not only his queen but his wife. Both trapped behind some kind of clear dome. The black stones of the building falling on top of it. Tiny cracks were starting to spider from the top. If it shattered both women would be killed. Anger coursed through him, giving him the strength to do what needed to be done. Lightning arched around the room causing both his son and Gwydion to step back. It couldn't hurt the Eostre but he didn't have time to explain. Faerydae was trying to tell him something… He couldn't hear her. Didn't want to hear her. Forcing himself to dig to the very depth of his power he was engulfed in light… in molten gold… His steps forever melting the stones beneath his feet into liquid magma. His hands just touched the dome as it too melted in globs to the ground leaving a doorway just big enough for the two women to pass through.

"Gale. Enough, we must go."

His face turned to the sound. Not his wife, no, worse. *Addy.* A deep breath and the power eased. "Nisha is back that way." His fingers found Faerydae's hand. "I told you I would always find you."

"Yes, husband, you did. Though it took you long enough."

Going back the way, they came they crammed into the doorway just in time to see a dragon breaking through the top of the building. Her head snapped to the sky as something fell between its jaws.

The area that had been the main room filled with a blackness that no moonless night could compete with. The darkness engulfing them as explosions, crashes and the sounds of people screaming in both terror and death came from all directions. Then came a terrible, dreadful silence.

When the blackness settled to the ground Nisha stood before them. The only thing left of the once grand building was just enough of the hallway that covered their little group and an outline of the circle. Nothing else… nothing… not even a pebble remained.

All three men went down on one knee unsure if this queen would even recognize them while still seeping with anger. Slowly Nisha's head tilted before she smiled. "I told you, Galeron, dragons do exist. Or would you like to debate it some more?"

Adrianna took a small unsure step forward. Her hand covering her mouth as tears ran down her face. "Nisha?"

Nisha blinked once not really comfortable with seeing her mother cry. "Sorry it took so long to find you but father was very vague on the details." Then she realized what she had done. "Oh, oh Gwydion I'm so sorry. Should I rebuild it?"

Rebuild it? He almost considered it but reconsidered. "No, my queen. This building had no purpose. At least no longer. The Fey no longer fall from the stars. Nor would they dare."

"Daughter, your father?" Worry filled Adrianna's voice.

"Oh, Lilly and David are there waiting for some sign that you are safe. Gwydion would you mind telling your people? I really do need to release him before nightfall if at all possible."

He nodded once. "Of course, my queen." Then his body turned into a mist as he was carried away on the wind.

Chapter 49: Lilly and David

David yawned as he picked his teeth with a bone of whatever creature had been guarding the entrance. "Maybe I can ask Nisha to find out what this was."

Lilly blinked. "David, my love. If you wanted to know what it was perhaps you should have left some of it for identification."

"I did." Holding up the sliver of bone. "It was too tasty to waste."

Lilly rolled her eyes as she said, "How wonderful for you. Now that you have a tummy full, do you have any idea how to pass a wall of black flames? I've only encountered them once… and Nisha was in no mood to be bothered then. So, I dared not try to pass."

Turning to the opening of the cave, David shrugged. "Since we are not to pass before the Nisha sends word. I'm not going to try. Besides…" He placed his hand up to the flame. "I can pass without injury."

Placing her hand on her hip, Lilly narrowed her eyes. "You think you can carry Myrddin out of the cave by yourself?"

"Unless he weighs more than a full-grown troll I don't see why not." David paused and gave a rueful smile. "You do know Drakens can carry things many times our own weight?"

"Of course, I do. However, you, my love, are part fey and have yet to test exactly how much that you can carry. But I understand your need to prove how strong you think you are."

Before David could come up with a proper response, a gust of wind blew across the ruins of the Great War. Slowly black mist began to form and a man stood before them.

Startled Lilly blinked unsure of what she was seeing was truly real. Hoping that she was correct about who was now standing before her she cautiously asked, "Gwydion? It seems you have flesh now?"

He turned to Lilly. "The queen is generous." Then to David. "You may enter now." Gwydion turned just enough to look over the cliff. "How odd to be standing here once more."

Lilly linked her arm with Gwydion. "How so?"

He looked down at her arm and fought hard not to snap it from her body for touching him. Then in a low hiss that would have scared anyone but apparently his queen's cousin he said, "Many have died for touching me."

"If you try I'm sure you will live long enough for your queen to make you regret it."

That low hiss that would have scared anyone else, but seeing it didn't even faze her, he answered her question. "This was the last battle of the Great War. I died here while my people died in our homeland. My brother betrayed me. The crater there beyond these cliffs is where all who were here that day died. Both sides. Those with Fey blood and those without."

"There were homes here at one time. Some paintings remain telling of a village made of ice that never melted."

Gwydion nodded. "One day I will tell you about the war. Not today. I must return to the Queen. She does not know where her sire is. Even now her sense of where people are, is a bit lacking. It is a skill that I will need to help her hone."

M.L.Ruscsak

Chapter 50: Nisha

Waiting patiently Nisha watched as Ethan attentively spoke to his mother. Looking over to her own she smiled. "He remembers her."

"As he should. Until that night, she never let him out her sight. Not for one minute. Not when she slept nor any other time that I can remember. She was always too worried she would wake and he would not be there."

Turning to her mother she asked, "Do you remember what happened? How you came here."

Adrianna squared her shoulders. "I would like to discuss that when your father is near. He has much to explain." She turned away. "You are far more powerful than I imagined. That too I will discuss with your father. I believe he has been keeping things from me for far too long."

"So, *is* father? I mean more powerful then he said he was? But we can discuss that when he's close by. I'm sure you will want to wring his neck by time the conversation is over. I know that I do."

"Aye, there have been times I wished to wring his neck for a great deal of things over these years. One for leaving me alone with Dae."

Slowly Gwydion appeared before her. "Your sire is in the ruins of the great war. A day's ride by Pegasus."

Nisha nodded. "Ethan?"

He turned to her the moment his name was spoken. "Nisha?"

"Please take our parents to the Spire. I need to retrieve the rest of the family. Alone."

"Daughter."

Even if she hadn't been raised by the woman she recognized a warning tone. "Either I can go alone and meet you at the Spire with my father. Or, you can go with me in time to watch him die. The choice is yours as you would know him better then I."

Closing her eyes Adrianna pulled herself together not hesitating in making her decision. "Travel safely daughter. I will prepare a room for your return. I am certain your father would like to rest upon his return."

Her staff materialized within her hand not a breath later. As the end touched the ground, her doorway to the Under Kingdom appeared. "Of course. Gwydion, please escort them? And have any of your people who wish to join you meet you at the Spire. I will return by the morning."

A slight bow as he replied, "As you wish my Queen."

Lilly jumped back as a doorway suddenly appeared not on the ground, but feet in the air just above the canyon going into Darke. When Nisha appeared. "You do realize you are in mid-air?"

Nisha smiled. "My dear cousin, ground or air is the same to me. It makes little difference where the doorway opens." Carefully she jumped down from the doorway to the ground before the cave. "Is David still inside?"

"He said he could carry Uncle Myrddin out. That was some time ago."

Looking at the sky turning from day into night Nisha nodded. "Please wait in the carriage. David will be out shortly to take you back to the Spire."

Worried Lilly narrowed her eyes at her cousin. "Nisha?"

"I do not have time to explain. I promise once I return you can ask anything you wish and I will try not to confuse you with the answers. But as today has been full of unexpected surprises I make no promises."

With a smile, Lilly said, almost in a mumble, "I will hold you to that."

For several minutes Nisha didn't pass the black flames until she knew Lilly was safely in the carriage. Once inside she called out, "David?"

"Nish… I don't know what to do. I can't…" David looked back down at the man who was crumpled on the ground in so much pain just breathing was causing tears.

Seeing the condition of her father, she nodded. Primitiva said he wouldn't last long, however she failed to mention the pain he would feel as he was torn apart cell by cell. "Please take Lilly back to the Spire. Say nothing about my father. Nor his condition. Not to her, nor to anyone else. I do not wish to alarm the family."

David looked back down at the man. "But?"

Her eyes changed just for a second… changed so he could see the souls of the dead screaming over endless chasms. "Go. Do not make me ask a second time."

A small bow and he slipped back out of the door. He did not fear his cousin but rather feared what the Queen of the Under Kingdom would do if pressed any further.

Kneeling down beside her father she whispered, "You are lucky mother didn't decide to join me."

"She is safe?" His voice not as deep at it had been in the dream realm. No, right now he had little voice at all.

"Of course. Now… are you going to help me move you or are you going to make me do all the work myself?"

The pain wouldn't kill him… not as long as the heart… his heart… Was someplace safe. Using every bit of strength, he had he managed to get to his feet. "I do not think I could walk far." The fire he had burning was draining him in a way that it had never done before. In a way, that even now it shouldn't have. Then again, something else was causing the pain.

Placing her arm around him she hissed, "Two steps through my doorway then two more to the Spire. Can you manage that?"

His mind was too clouded to really care what she was saying. "Two steps."

When he opened his eyes from completing the first two steps he was no longer in the cave but in a corridor made of bone. "Daughter?" It wasn't possible …yet… No, he could not be seeing what was before him. He couldn't nor would he believe it until the very moment that he had to.

"Oh, it's perfectly safe for you to be here. Here rest against this wall." She helped him to the ground. "I shall return in but a minute. Just rest until I return." Opening the door, she saw Primitiva still clutching the silver box. "I told you I would return shortly."

"Here. Take this wretched thing." She thrust the box into Nisha's hands. "That should have never left the city of stars. It is much too dangerous to be here."

"City of stars?" The star cities?

Primitiva waved it off as though she had explained this several times before, "Pallas, also known as the city of stars. It is the largest of the Star Cities. It houses all of the tribute boxes. Both used and unused after the tribute has been seen. Or at least the ones that hold the stronger of the Fey's powers."

Interesting. "I will come back then we can talk more about this."

"Bah. Talking is for inferior creatures."

"That may be but I enjoy it." Nisha turned. "Since you have no desire to leave this place I will return when I'm able to discuss this with you in length." Then she was out the door. As the door slammed behind the force caused the rattling several of the bones that were nestled into the surrounding walls. It was then she looked at her father and vanished the box. "I think we will give you your heart when you look more whole."

"Your mother is going to kill me for letting myself look like this."

Helping him to his feet, Nisha smiled more to herself then to him. "No papa, she won't, but she will make sure you stay in bed for the next decade."

His eyes lightly closed. "I don't think I would like that. Too much that still needs done."

With a deep sigh, she said, "Very well. Once we get you tucked into a bed we will see what I can fix and what will need to heal on its own."

Chapter 38: Myrddin

Myrddin barely tried to let his eyes flicker open. *Too much effort.* A single breath and he wanted to pass out. Just breathing was extremely painful and he was sure the weight of his skin was going to break his what was left of his bones. Then he felt something… Something beating in his chest. His heart? But… No, that couldn't be right. Could it?

A fragment of a memory. He could remember a young woman… Nisha … standing before him. Almost remembered her taking him somewhere… which was ridiculous because no Fey could transport themselves at will… and none… absolutely none could make portals from one place to another. It couldn't be done…

…Yet… They had traveled from the cave to a hall created with bones.

"Easy, husband. Nisha is not skilled enough to heal your body completely. At least not yet. She is working with your sister to learn what she must."

He knew that voice. "Addy?"

Peering over him so he would not need to move she forced a smile even though his eyes were still lightly shut. "Hmm. When you are healed completely we will speak on why you kept so much from me."

He drew his lips into a thin line, refusing to say anything.

Slowly she moved easing away from his side. Once again seated next to him, she started to speak keeping her voice still light not yet wanting to distress him. At least not yet. "Lilly says you need to eat to regain your strength and your sister, *Estare* is making something for you to drink. A tonic I think."

Now that got him thinking. In a surprise, he gasped. "Estare? Is here? She cannot be."

Ignoring him Addy continued, "As is your other sister. Who wants an explanation as to how she has a sister that she does not remember. And, a score of other things she says will make your ears blister by time she is finished asking her questions. Or by time you finish answering those questions in exact detail. Neither is currently pleased with you."

Shit. Oh, this was bad. Worse if the two sisters talked. "Any chance I can sleep?" *Or be rendered unconscious.* Yes, that would be even better. Wonderful even.

A voice from the door. "Not until you drink this, my dear brother."

Estare. Damn it. She should not be here. In a bridge between the waking and the dreaming sure… but not here. Why didn't Nisha send her back after they spoke? Hell, why didn't she take herself back… having already done so once. "Sister?"

"You look worse than I left you. Now drink." Then to Addy. "I do not know why he isn't dead. Surely he knows a spell to cheat death and look more presentable."

Leaning on the doorway, Nisha shuffled into the room, "Actually, as queen of the Under Kingdom I sometimes get to choose if someone is worthy of death." She yawned sleepily. "In this one instance I would rather him here than someplace where no one could question him. Besides, I almost understand how your physiology works. But if it matters some of his conditions are because of the effects of hiding the box where it was."

Estare turned to Nisha and narrowed her galaxy blue eyes. "You are going to be a thorn in my side."

"Hmm, well since you weren't given a chance to know me during my… what did Aunt Celeste call them… Ah yes, my scary years… I think you can get to know me now that we are equal."

Turning her back once again on Nisha, Estare hissed in her brother's ear, "This is your doing."

Drinking the cool liquid, he allowed for his eyes to fully open and take in the room. Not a place he remembered which was odd since he had been in every room of all of the castles of all of the Feyen countries. "Where are we?"

"At the Spire. It is so much more convenient than one of the castles. At least, while the entire family is here." Padding over to the bed Nisha peered down at him, "Should I try to heal you now?"

The Spire? Why would that be more convenient? Any of the castles were larger than the Spire, which was little more than a vacation home for the royal family of Lite and Darke. Not asking that question, he remembered the other thing. Nisha had said try. What did she mean try? There was no trying; you either could do it or not.

There was no in between. Sweet darkness, was he going to have to teach her how to use all the wonderful gifts that she now possessed? "Daughter I doubt you will be able to."

"Then we shall see." Calmly she closed her eyes and let herself feel. Again, she started with bone. Though his felt different … Looked different. Long and silver spurs of white. Oh, a shifter. But, not just any shifter, one that could change into anything much like herself. Interesting. Then muscle red with strands of not silver or white but black sinew. Fire-walker or Specter. Organs. Two sets of lungs. One for air the other water. Lastly the flesh. Not much to do but stretch it over the new muscles. Ivory mixed with silver. Black fingernails. Poisonous to the touch, if he so chose to use them that way. Finally, his wings. His true wings, not the ones he wore for people to see but a pair of dragon wings that nearly resembled her own. However, his were a deep black with hints of embers glowing around the edges.

Slowly she opened her eyes and smiled. "Yes, I do believe you look much better in your true form."

Looking at his fingers, Myrddin gasped, "How? This is impossible. You should not be able to break my spell."

Nisha tilted her head. "You want to look ordinary?" She shrugged. "If you wish you are more than capable of transforming. Why you would want to, is beyond me."

Patting her niece on her shoulder Estare smiled. "He does not want the Star Cities to know he is alive."

"Oh. Well, that is ridiculous as well. His powers are much too strong to be masked unless constantly surrounded by the bones of the dead. They have always known he was here. In fact, Primitiva was aware of him the moment he came to the Mystic Woods."

"Primitiva?" A collective gasp.

Rolling her eyes Nisha said, "Yes. She's still very much alive you know. Protected by me now. None may use her powers nor her abilities without my consent. And, none who ask will receive that consent. It would be much too dangerous to let someone not trained in her gifts use them without censor."

Estare landed hard on the bed. "Primitiva is said to be our ancestor. She had a child in secret before fleeing."

"Oh, that's why I was able to bind her. We were already related. How interesting. I should tell her. Should I call her great Grand'Mere? No... that doesn't sound right. I will think of something. It simply is not right to call her by her name when she is much more."

Myrddin scrubbed his face with his hands. "Perhaps we should talk about that night. Yes, I think that would-be a less distressing conversation." Anything was less distressing than talking about the Star Cities. Then again, talking about those that lived there were definitely less distressing than speaking of Primitiva or her abilities.

Addy crossed her arms. "I'm all ears."

Gingerly sitting up he took a deep breath. "We both knew about the uprising. And for the most part, it was taken care of within minutes of our arrival."

Pulling up a chair Nisha asked, "Can you tell me what happened?"

Addy turned to her daughter and softly said, "The people who lived near the castle started to set things on fire. Both natural and not. It made no sense at the time."

With a nod, Myrddin continued, "Edrich was working at the castle at the time. Had just started to a few days before. Being Dae's half-brother we gave him the work until he could find something more suitable for himself. It doesn't really matter now, but when we returned to the castle he was waiting for us in the residence babbling on about nonsense as always. When the food was brought up none of us thought much about it. Poison wouldn't kill us. So, we ate.

I'm not really sure what happen next. But... when I came to the entire council except one was in the lower mines shackled in something that kept us from using our powers or abilities. I think the shackles came from the Mystic Woods. Galeron was beside me then.

The two of us had enough strength to get out of the situation but since you, my dear wife was not near us... nor could I find you. I told him to do nothing. It was imperative that we find out where you and Dae were. He agreed and we both hid our wedding bands. The only way for us to find you should you wear the mates." He waited until she understood that he knew about Dae's spell. When she nodded he continued?

"Over the next few days... months the members of the council were taken from the mines. They were fed to the trolls. I remember their tortured screams as they were torn apart and later died." He paused trying hard to remember everything. "During one of the times it was only Gale and myself, I placed an incantation over him so he couldn't be killed. Hurt yes. But he wouldn't die. I knew that I wouldn't die, either, not after Nisha was born."

Nisha interjected, "You ripped your heart from your chest and left the box for me. Along with Larna's heart." She paused, then added, "I'm not sure if I should be impressed that you did so because you knew what was to come, or worried that you didn't consider that I could have destroyed both hearts instead of just one."

He nodded in agreement. "I knew I wouldn't see you grow into the woman that stands before me. I could have stopped it. Your mother and I together we could have, but you daughter would only be a shell of who you are. I chose to give you everything you would need. And I will not apologize to anyone for making that decision." Making sure his wife and sister understood he would fight them both over that decision.

Addy took his hand. "And nor should you. I do not agree with your method but looking at our daughter I can see the result. And I am thankful." Then she took a deeper tone, "And you will not do so again."

"My dear we only have the *one* daughter. I doubt I could keep anything from her." Actually, he knew with certainty that he could not. Knew looking into her eyes that sometime before he woke she had blood bound him to her to make sure of that. Or at the very least tried to bind him to her. As it was the binding wasn't complete but would be enough where he wouldn't be able to keep secrets from her. And also had the benefit of others not being able to manipulate him into doing something that may cause her harm. Well, her or those who were truly bound to her.

"Well good because I am barely four hundred years old and you promised me more than just one daughter. And no longer being queen, I need something to do with all my time."

Nisha smiled, "And that is my cue to leave. Um, Aunt Estare? Will you be coming with me?"

"Yes, I believe I will. I have a sister to speak to whom I missed for far too long."

Chapter 51: Queen Nisha

Only a handful of days passed before Nisha summoned not only her parents but her entire family to join her in a large receiving room with only a single large table and several chairs held with it in. Her place was at the head of the table while Ethan sat quietly at the foot looking unsure as to his reason for being there.

As their family filed in Nisha smiled at each of them. Smiled at her parents who had been caught several times in deep discussions about things that her father had knowing left out long before they had wed.

Smiled at all three of her aunts. Two she had known at birth and one that she had only just met.

But it wasn't them who she locked eyes with. Oh no, it was Ethan's mother who she spoke to first. "Lady Faerydae, as I have already spoken to my father about some of what he knows. It has come to my attention that he hasn't been the only child of Star City to once again leave their star and choose to reside here. I would like an explanation."

Dae looked at her queen, her friend and closed her eyes. "I know this day would someday come. But before I speak of all that I know. It would be best if the creator Primitiva would join us. As I know she has much knowledge in some of what we need to speak of."

Once Primitiva was seated at the table and looking closer to a true Feyen woman rather than some creature that she chose to resemble, Nisha once again nodded to Dae. "Now that we are all present and accounted for…"

Slowly mist formed behind her as Gwydion stood at her side. "I do hope you do not mind, my queen, but I to would like to hear this."

"Very well, but I do not wish for any others to join us."

Gwydion nodded only once and took a step back. He would still be a part of this conversation but not directly involved in whatever was to be said.

Locking her eyes not on Nisha but on Primitiva, Faerydae started her story, "Shortly before Myrddin came here, my father Lord Magmas sent me here. Not because he thought that I would seek any Fey out that may actually know the truth about how we came to this place. But rather, because as a female I am unworthy to rule Pallas in his stead.

"Having seen at least some of the history of this place I took what I could and sought out my only living relative. Queen Alista. After assuring her that I had no intention to take over her lands, she made me a lady in her court, even though by the standards here I was not more than a child."

Now she looked at Myrddin. "We knew the day would come that you would seek her or her daughter out. So, despite her demeanor at the time, she knew who you were and where you came from. We both knew once you arrived the start of the final war would begin."

Primitiva raised her hand slightly to be recognized. "Am I to trust Magnar no longer lives within any of the known Star Cities?"

"Magnar and his bride left for an uninhabited star more than three thousand years ago. Neither has been seen since."

Lilly looked confused bust politely asked, "Um, excuse me but who is Magnar? And why is he important?"

Sitting back in her seat Primitiva sighed, unsure on how to explain anything. "He and I at one time were the only living creators. The last of our race of Fey. His bride is my daughter. Before I left I asked only one thing of him, that was to keep her alive unless she became too troublesome. We both knew the day would come when things within the Star Cities would become volatile once again. We both knew a great war would brew and wake the Silent Ones. Knowing this we both decided long ago to do what we needed to ensure we would be here when it did."

Nisha raised her head. "Can anything stop the war from ever starting?"

"No, my child. What has been seen from a creator can never be changed. We may be able to keep it from happening for a day or even years but we are unable to stop it. But know this, never trust those who rule the Star Cities. None that are not blood to you. Each will say they side with you. Each will fight and even die to show their loyalty to you.

But they all have one thing in common. They all want… crave… the power of Pallas. And they will stop at nothing to get it."

"And Magmas who rules Pallas now? What about him?"

Narrowing her eyes, Primitiva let out a low thunderous hiss. "Before this is done I will see him dead."

Looking around the room Nisha nodded. "In that case, Galeron I would like for you to sit as second chair on my council and be the captain of my guards. Or, at least those who are living. Papa, please accept the position of first chair and be my liaison between Lunaista and myself."

Both men nodded understanding what was coming would be far worse than the Great War.

Continuing, Nisha looked down at the table. "Gwydion, I want you to sit as fourth chair and take over the responsibility of the warriors of the

Under Kingdom. Their skills will be needed in the days will come."

"Of course, my queen. May I suggest asking Freya to once again retake her position as captain of the elite guards?"

"Do as you see fit." The to her husband. "Ethan, you will sit as third chair on the counsel. As has been a tradition since as long as I can remember."

Primitiva looked at Nisha and narrowed her eyes. "I know of others who would benefit you on your council. They were my trusted first. All but one still lives."

"Very well. I task you at finding them so they can help me understand and prepare for will come." Getting stiffly to her feet Nisha asked, "Now since I have three Star City Fey sitting at this table would one of you please help be turn a fury into his former self?"

For just a moment Primitiva's eyes turned tear bright. "Ari? Did you find my Ari? He is safe after all this time?"

"He is. And I would bet he would love to be something more than a chair."

Epilogue

Ethan curled up around Nisha. His arm growing heavy around her middle. At least, he was starting to become content with sleeping not only in a bed but in a bed where she was. Ever so carefully she moved from beneath his arm not yet ready for sleep. Not yet ready to succumb to sleep despite the late hour.

Sliding out for the bed and grabbing her blue silk house robe, she thought about all that had happened in such a short amount of time.

For the past month, she had been trying to learn the laws of not only Darke but of Feyen as well. Trying to figure out what laws were there for a reason and what needed to be done away with. More than that she was trying to figure out how to stop a war where countless of lives would be lost.

A deep breath and she pulled a soft cover over Ethan's shoulder and smiled. At least, he was contently sleeping. Over the past month, he too had changed so much. His hair which had been only a fingers width when they had first met was now long enough for her fingers to comb through. His skin although milky pale was starting to gain little sparks of glitter sporadically throughout his body. But it was his confidence that was the greatest change. No longer was he afraid to speak… afraid of being punished for any little thing. Oh no… now he would challenge just about everything unless he had come up with it.

So much like his mother. A woman who she was also starting to respect and learn more about.

Then again, Ethan was learning that unless she had made whatever decision and didn't ask for advice his was not needed nor wanted. His father, however, as a member of her court… her second chair in fact… not only would he challenge anything, it was his job and he took perverse pleasure in it. Between the three, she had learned to curve what she wanted to do with what was possible without scaring everyone. Not that she was pleased about that.

Creeping over to her desk, she lazily flipped open yet another book of laws. *"How could one country live under so many ridiculous laws?"* She mumbled to herself as she read through the page. Half tempted to declare most of the laws archaic, she closed the book before doing something her council would need to discuss.

Not that there would much-discussing anything… not when her father was her first chair and ruled over the council… something she sometimes regretted that since he had a no-nonsense attitude over anything. And, not since he was now also helping her Aunt Estare restructure her own little kingdom that consisted only of a single city. Oh no, she was not going to press him since he was the only member of the council that was not truly bound to her… nor would she ever consider it. Partly yes. Enough for her to make sure he was not keeping things from her… but she had found out after he was healed that she could not bind someone to her who was as closely related to her. It was also the reason the binding with Lilly worked only so well.

Of course, he could have told her that before she had tried to see what the extent of his powers were. Or, had tried to learn how powerful his abilities would be. Instead, he had growled at her for trying. Then had left for her aunt's star city to keep from giving her a lecture he was sure she would just ignore.

And in truth, if he had tried she would have completely ignored him… just because she could.

"Nisha?" A tired voice called from the bed.

Coming back over to him, Nisha sat on the edge of the large bed still close enough to touch him. "You should be sleeping."

His eyes were not yet open. "I was. You're thinking too loud."

"I was…" She paused and pressed her lips together. Yet another change that Ethan had been going through; his abilities or powers were starting to show themselves. Without the training that he should have had since birth, those abilities were both frightening and intriguing. "I didn't realize I was."

"It's easier not to hear when I'm awake. But I wish for sleep now."

She bent over and kissed his temple, something he was starting to let her do without flinching. "I could come up with an enchantment so you can control it while you sleep?"

Now his eyes opened as he studied her. "I would much rather you sleep while I do."

"There is just so much to do… and…"

"Nisha, you have several centuries to get everything you want to be done… to be the way you want it. It does not need to be done tonight. And having made up conversations with your father when he is not here to discuss them properly with you… will not help anything."

He was right. She knew that but with the other Star Cities bristling over … whatever they were bristling over. Her Aunt Estare was preparing for war since she was certain it was going to break out any minute… and the Eostre were busy trying to rebuild their civilization within the Mystic Woods while still serving her… Nothing was as simple as it appeared. "I know. I think I would feel better if my father hadn't decided to return to Lunaista right now." Or feel better that he if he hadn't decided to go there rather than discuss things with her.

"Your mother is here. And you have Galeron."

"You can call him your father."

His eyes narrowed into tiny slits, "He should have sent me to live your aunt until whatever it was that your mother sensed had been taken care of."

"Ethan, the choice wasn't his. It was that of my father; which you already know."

Slowly he sat up. Black fire burning in his eyes. "I know. I still don't think he knows as much as he claims."

Placing her hand gently on his cheek, she whispered, "You can take that up with my father once he returns."

"Why, when he will turn me into a chair?"

Hard to disagree with that after finding out that he was the one who turned countless other furies. Harder still was the fact her father had already turned him, her husband, into a dresser because he was talking too much. No, not talking but asking questions. "He won't turn you into a chair. I already discussed that he's not allowed to do that to anyone in the family."

"Will he listen?"

"He will or I will send him to debate things with Primitiva." And that was something she could do. In fact, it was something that she had done once already. Neither Primitiva nor her father had been happy about the meeting. Her father less after he figured out he could not leave unless she… the queen of the Under Kingdom… so willed it. Her mother on the other had thought it was a grand idea to leave him there until he learned not to keep life changing secrets.

"She will kill him."

"No, but she would make him wish that he never laid eyes on her. For her own reasons, she finds most men beneath her. But then again since the only one she could have married before the fall was one that wanted her powers for himself… I think she has a good reason."

"I think I will stay away from her anyways." He laid back down making sure his head rested on her lap. "You should come to bed now."

"Oh?"

"Hmmm. You have a long day tomorrow if we are still going to visit the city of Manticora. And see what can put to rights and what you will need help with."

"Yes, I believe you're right. I'll need my strength in case we come across any of the water dwellers who have been attacking those who live on the land."

Ethan yawned. "Just remember they are only attacking because the land dwellers are polluting the lake."

Before she could say anything, the room was filled with a bright red light that blended into a golden beam. Then her aunt… though not solid… was standing just before the bed. "Estare?"

Her wings of light flared out. In a voice that could have been made of water, Estare said, "It has started. The war of my people. And possibly the death of yours."

M.L.Ruscsak

About the author

With her first book being nominated for both the 2017 Top Female Author Award and 2017 Summer Indie Book award, M.L.Ruscsak has continued her series with "The Fallen" and is currently working on the third book in the series.

Living in Richland county, Ohio she lives with her autistic daughter. This is her writer's oasis.

For more information please follow her at
https://www.facebook.com/OfLiteAndDarke

or

M.L.Ruscsak

Find exclusive information about the world of Lite and Darke at www.Doveanddragon.com

And Look For